The Unlife of Lisa Cooper

J·M· CELI

For Georgia.

Acknowledgments

This book was made possible by a slew of awesome people to whom I am enormously grateful. First and foremost, I have to thank my wife, Georgia, for supporting me from the get-go and being my proofreader when these episodes were in their serial version. A huge thanks goes out to my original "street team" who helped publicize *The Unlife of Lisa Cooper* in its serial format and helped me gain the following I have today: Meghan Aldridge, Katrina Cobb, Eric Crockwell, Ben Pick, and Lauren Adele Wheatley. Thank you to my parents, who have always supported me throughout the years and always made me feel I could do the things I set my mind to. To my beta readers, whether they beta'ed the first few episodes or read them all, thank you for helping me make my story the best it can be. Last, but surely not least, to the readers of my original serial series and you, the reader today who found Lisa's story and decided to check it out – thank you!

Author Notes

The Unlife of Lisa Cooper was originally published in a serial format, with one episode released per week from June 2022 through March 2023. What you are reading is the anthology of that series. Instead of chapters, there are episodes, and they are presented as they were in their original publication, albeit with some grammatical corrections.

I thought it was worth mentioning in case you noticed you were being reminded of details so soon after the details appeared in a previous episode. Originally, this was done to refresh the reader's mind on certain details since it was often a week or more for a reader to grab the next episode after reading the previous one. I wanted to keep the integrity of the original series, so I left the "reminder prose" alone.

I hope you enjoy Lisa's adventure. Thanks for Reading!

Episode 1

Nightclubbing

I'VE TRIED TO GET into modern music, I honestly have. I say that every year, and every year music seems to drift further and further from what I would call... listenable.

It's just one more thing I hate about night clubs.

The muffled bass pounding from the Imperial night club saturated the evening air from its minuscule parking lot to its adjacent streets.

I went to the front of the line and shot the bouncer a smile as I ran a hand through my hair. I know it's cheesy, but it works.

"Hey, why does *she* get to go in?" a woman protested.

I felt a pang of guilt for cutting in front of the people waiting to get in, but there were only so many hours in the night, and I didn't want to waste time standing in line. Spring had come and the nights were getting shorter.

The bouncer opened the door, and the full force of the music accosted my ears. The same six notes played over and over again to the backbeat of some drummer who seemed only to have owned a kick drum.

Techno. Benny Goodman rolled in his grave.

The Imperial was the hottest club on Tremont Street. Maybe all of Boston. A DJ stood in a circular booth in the center of a sprawling dance floor. Dozens of multi-colored lights swerved this way and that, illuminating the dancers and painting them in hues of green, blue, and red.

For those not dancing, puffy couches coupled with tiny round tables were positioned around the perimeter. Pretty girls in tiny skirts and heels couriered beverages to the patrons who only came to drink, socialize, and people watch.

A long L-shaped bar straddled the left side of the club, for the "classic crowd" who liked to sit on stools and drink. It was always filled with meat market singles, playboys, arm candies, and a plethora of hopeful wingmen.

That was the sweet spot. The hunting grounds. Anticipation burned in my chest.

My phone vibrated. I glanced at the screen and pressed my thumb to check the text.

It was from Brian Sommers. "Hello Lisa, A bunch of us are getting together. Would you like to join us? Brian."

In so many decades, Brian had yet to master the brevity of text messages.

I texted back. "Will Ivan be there?"

It only took a minute before my phone vibrated again. "No, it isn't anything formal. It's just a few of us. We may go out for a fly later. I should warn you, the event is catered"

Catered. Brian's *warning* meant he knew my disdain for it. Catered was code for the fact that they would have guests to dine on. I don't like feeding in groups and if this wasn't a formal gathering, I didn't mind missing it.

"I'll pass. I'm already at a club. Please be careful." I sent back.

The *be careful* was my hope that he wouldn't drink too much or draw too much on his power. I knew he knew what I meant. He was a good guy – a friend – and I didn't want to see him fall deeper into his curse.

"Yes, mom." came his response. That passed for acceptance.

I turned my attention back to the crowd.

There was always a mix of patrons at the bar. The "two guys chatting up two women" scenario played out at least three times from what I was able to see. Those were fun to watch. Usually, one guy was holding his own with one of the women, while his friend floundered with the other. You can see it in their body language. The laughter. A light touch on the arm. Or awkward fidgeting and eye rolling. There was a gaggle of five women who had taken over the bend at the L of the bar. One of them wore a small tiara with a white veil trailing behind it. There were a few couples too.

The trick was finding someone to separate from their group.

I moved into the club, skirting around the dance floor and avoiding the press of bodies. I made a beeline for the bar. I started to take note of what people were drinking. That was always a consideration. It was the usual fare. Men usually drank beers or whiskey, but most women drank mixed drinks or wine.

I preferred to feed off women. It's nothing sexual, but they're usually the ones drinking the most delicious sugary drinks. A daiquiri or a piña colada does wonders to the taste of blood. But women were also harder to lure in places like this. And I avoid using my charming gaze until I need to.

Men on the other hand? I was a woman all alone at a bar. That's what makes men so easy. All I had to do was stand there.

The problem I had was there were too many people. All the stools were taken, and there was no place to stand against the bar itself. The crowd surrounding it was two or three people deep.

I always had to get creative when I hunt. So, I got in character.

I surveyed the scene until I found two men sitting alone. Over the din of the thumping music, I heard one tell the other, "This place is tapped. Let's try Fitzy's."

"I don't wanna drive all the way to Fitzy's. Let's just hang here a little longer. The girls are hot."

That was my cue. I stepped up to them and pretended like I was trying to flag down the bartender. He'd never see me. That was the point.

This was the part of the hunt where I needed to get noticed.

My black skirt graced the top of my knees. Nothing too short. My blue top clung nicely to my chest, but it only gave up a hint of cleavage. I learned a long time ago if you show off too much, a lot of men get intimidated. But if you show of a little, then you are what men like to call *hot but approachable.*

This game was harder for others of my kind. Many of them looked too pale or sunken. They had to rely on their charming gaze from the get-go. Even the ones that had once been good looking before their comeliness left them. Ravaged by their curse.

I've kept my mortal looks. It has been painstaking, but it makes hunting easier when you're still a pretty young lady with fair skin, dark hair, and green eyes.

It didn't take long before I felt the eyes of the two men on me. I pretended not to notice. I still pantomimed a weak attempt to get the bartender's attention.

The guy that didn't want to drive to Fitzy's leaned toward me. "Hey, what're you having? I'll flag the bartender down."

"Oh, my God, thank you! A white zin?" I flashed my smile and matched his volume so he could hear me.

I watched the guy feverishly attempt to get the bartender's attention before finally hitting pay-dirt and asking him for the zinfandel.

"Thank you so much." I smiled.

"No problem."

"What?" He forgot to speak up. I pretended I couldn't hear. Little tricks like that help things feel more normal.

"No problem!" he repeated, louder.

I started for my purse, and he waved his hand. "No, no... it's on me."

"Thanks." I said, keeping my smile on.

"Just you tonight?" He looked over my shoulder as if looking to see if I had a friend or a date.

"Just me. My friend bailed with some dude. I was going to leave, but then I figured fuck it. I want to dance."

It was an obvious invitation, and he didn't miss a beat.

"You wanna dance? Maybe after your drink?"

I glanced at his friend. Friends can kill a hunt. Nobody likes being left alone. But he seemed fine as he swiveled his head between his friend and me.

"No, let's dance now," I replied.

"Yea? Okay!" His eyes lit up. He turned to his friend. "You okay?"

The other guy leaned toward him to answer. "Yea, bro, go ahead."

That's all it took. A couple of dances, an ignored glass of zinfandel, the obligatory "Please, dude, she's into me" conversation with the friend, and I had him walking me to my car just one hour later.

I had no car.

Bosworth Street was a short walk away and right off Tremont Street. As late as it was, the street was bound to be abandoned with a few parked cars at most. It was an overgrown alleyway. I steered the man toward the side street. I never did get his name. I never really wanted to know anyway.

"How far away did you park?" he asked.

"Not far. Just down—"

I turned to look down Bosworth Street. There was a couple arguing very loudly about whether or not the boyfriend or husband had been hitting on the Jell-O shots girl. *Dammit.*

"Just down... through... the Granary," I improvised.

Instead of leading him down Bosworth, I crossed the street and headed into the Granary Burial Grounds. He followed behind me, casting a confused glance down the other street.

The Granary Burial Grounds was a cemetery that boasted the graves of John Hancock, Sam Adams, Paul Revere, and the Franklin family. It wasn't ideal, but the center of the grounds had a tall, chubby obelisk: the Franklin Monument. It would have to do. My escort was already getting wary.

"Through the grave? What'd you walk three blocks to get to the club?"

"It's just on the other side. Sorry, it's just so late. So dark."

"Yea, of course. No problem. I can call you tomorrow, right?"

"I'd like that." I feigned a smile. Just a little longer.

The Franklin monument sat on a raised square with grass on the top and stone walls. A black plaque upon the obelisk read FRANKLIN.

'You know, Ben Franklin was born in Boston, but he moved to Philadelphia later."

He seemed proud that he knew that little piece of trivia.

I hopped up on the low wall of the stone square and stood on top of the little patch of grass.

"Are you allowed up there?"

I laughed and grabbed his hand. I pulled him up. The Grounds was a wide-open space, but the fat obelisk would provide some cover.

"Hey, you're pretty strong."

This was the part. The end of the hunt. Some vampires try the seduction thing. Flirting. Kissing. I don't kiss the people I hunt. I have no illusions that they are victims, but I try to keep things as consensual as I can, until...

I peered into his eyes and called upon the powers of my curse. My charming gaze. For my kind, the gaze is easier to use when the victim knows them a little or is enamored with them. I could have gazed him in the club, but it would have taken too much. And I don't pull on my curse too heavily. When we pull on our curse, our curse pulls back.

"Oh... wow. You're beautiful." The man smiled at me.

I took his hand and guided him against the shadowed side of the obelisk. My eyes never left his.

I saw his pupils shrink. Eyesight was always the first to dull. He was ready.

I leaned into his neck, letting my fangs elongate. His flesh was cold in the night air. His arms wrapped around me. I let my teeth sink into him.

The taste of copper hit my tongue, tinged with... *Whiskey. Jameson, maybe?*

"Wh-what are you doing?"

Blood had barely started flowing through my lips when his neck jerked away.

"What the hell are you doing!"

He pushed me back and stared at me, mouth agape. His eyes fell to my bloody fangs.

Oh, shit.

Episode 2

The Curse

HE HAD RESISTED MY charming gaze and was still lucid when I bit into his neck.

I felt sick over it. I had tried to make it as clean as possible, but either I tried to feed too soon, or his will was just too strong.

I grabbed his shoulder and pushed him into the obelisk. Guilt settled into my stomach like a brick. I had to fight through it. I couldn't risk exposure. Any of our kind guilty of that would face their final death.

"What the hell are you? Help! Help!"

I gazed into his eyes again. I was loathe to do it, but he left me no choice. Our gifts are like muscles. Exercise them and they will become stronger. Neglect them, and they will atrophy. I had neglected my gifts for decades. A sound price to pay for looking alive, but it left me weaker than most others of my kind.

I pushed myself. Tapping into a reservoir of power that would threaten to cost me my semblance of living. I had no choice.

The power I drew upon surged through me, warm and intoxicating. It filled me with euphoric tingles through every limb and extremity. It beckoned me to take more, to give in.

I wrenched myself free from its pull. The tingles were replaced with pangs in my stomach. My curse beckoned me to take more, and it punished me with ice in my veins. I resisted.

The vice on my stomach eased off.

I leveled my charming gaze upon him once more. His eyes widened. His breathing slowed.

I held him in my eyes. He had stopped protesting. He had stopped moving.

"Wow...," he said. A goofy smile played on his lips.

I leaned in and let my teeth sink into his neck a second time. He was utterly within my sway.

I drank. The costliest drink I'd had in many years.

When I took my portion, I pulled back, letting my fangs recede and licking my lips. He was still dazed. My heart sank.

"Nevermind those cuts on your neck; they'll be healed by morning."

"Oh. Huh. Uh-huh," he droned.

I wasn't lying. My ability to heal quickly was due to the power in my blood. My bite left saliva in his wound, which had the same healing effect. He'd probably wonder where I'd run off to when he came out of his haze.

I looked down at my hands. They were pale with death's pallor. "Dammit."

I hopped down from the stone platform the obelisk sat on and made my way out of the burial grounds.

A forty-minute cab ride later, and I was back to my cozy brownstone on Monument Ave. You'd think I was driving clear across the state, but Charlestown is less than halfway across the city from Tremont Street. Fucking traffic is unbelievable.

When I got inside, I made a beeline for the bathroom to check myself in the mirror.

My complexion was definitely pale. My fingers felt cold. Granted, I didn't look as pale as Tracy or some of the others who regularly draw on their curse, but I was noticeably less rosy.

"Dammit." I glared at my reflection. Had I tried to feed on the guy too soon before my charming gaze kicked in? No. More likely, the guy was just particularly willful. Either way, it didn't matter. The damage was done.

Then I remembered Brian.

Brian was going to a gathering with some of the others from our bleed. They always tried to push him, like they push me. To give in to the curse and tap enough power to survive and then balance it off. But Brian wanted to live like me and pass for mortal.

I locked eyes with myself in the mirror again. A fine mentor I turned out to be.

Brian was very susceptible to peer pressure. He liked to make others happy and be one of the gang. Before getting too hung up on my own problems, I wanted to check up on him.

I rang him, but it went to voicemail.

"Hey, it's Lisa. I guess you're out flying. I just wanted to see how the gathering went. Call me back."

Ironically, I had blown off the gathering because it was *catered*. They had willing thralls milling around the room for anyone to drink from. Those scenes can turn macabre real fast and sometimes someone gets hurt. But if I had a willing thrall tonight, I would never have had to force my charming gaze on anyone.

"Dammit."

I rang Tracy next. Tracy Marchetti wasn't my biggest fan, but I needed her help.

"Hello." Tracy's flat voice answered the phone.

"Tracy, it's Lisa. Hey... did you go that gathering tonight?" I tried making small talk. I never really knew how to banter with Tracy.

"That sausage fest? No. Why?"

"Just curious. Listen, I need a favor."

It took her a moment to respond. "I'm listening."

"I had to draw on my curse. I'm... pale."

Loud peels of laughter erupted from the phone. Typical Tracy. My stomach tightened. I wasn't going to get any sympathy from her, but I still needed her help. Despite it all, her attitude pissed me off.

"It's not funny. I'm serious. It's been a long time since I slipped up like this."

"No one says *draw on their curse*," Tracy scoffed. "You drew on your *power*. And about damn time too."

"Yea, well I want to let it atrophy."

"Jesus Christ."

"I'm serious. What if it happens again and I haven't let it subside? I don't want to end up looking like Jacques." Jacques was an extreme example. Honestly, what I meant to say was *I don't want to end up looking like you*.

"Jacques is an example of what happens when you take too much."

I nearly blurted out my ask of her. "I need to feed off your thralls, just until I can get a handle on this."

"My thralls? For how long?"

"A month?" I winced as I replied.

"A month? You're out of your fucking mind. I only have Kevin, Tommy, and Diana."

"What happened to Stephen?"

"Richard happened to Stephen. Look, I can't sustain you for a month."

"Then just some. Whatever you can spare." It came off a bit more desperate than I wanted.

"Don't you have thralls of your own?"

"No, not since Eric."

"The guy you willingly released because he wanted to get married?"

"They were in love."

I frowned. She had known Eric's story. She was just bringing it up to make a point.

"Then you should have taken her too. Eric and whatsername would have been together and you gain another thrall. Win-win."

"That's not... listen, can you help me out or not?"

"Maybe. How much?"

"I don't know. A pint?"

"Not blood, Lisa. How much money?"

"Oh... five hundred?" Five hundred dollars was nearly over twice as much as a thrall's catering service. I figured if I high-balled her, I could just get this over with.

"A feeding? Make it a thousand."

Son of a bitch.

She had me over a barrel and she knew it. I ground my teeth and bit back my words. "Fine."

"But you have to call first and come to me. I'm not sending them all the way to Charlestown."

"Sure. Thanks." I couldn't believe I had stooped to this.

"You know I'm not doing you any favors. We need our power to survive out here. If you already had it, you wouldn't have needed to *dig into your curse.*" She said that last part with a mocking tone.

"It's one compromise, then another, and then another. I can't start down that path."

"Whatever. Call and schedule when you need them. I reserve the right to refuse you if I think they've been tapped too much."

"Thanks. I know we don't always—"

She'd hung up.

"Thanks, Tommy."

I kept my mouth closed and ran my tongue over my teeth. All evidence of his blood wiped away in a smooth gesture.

Tomás, or Tommy, was handsome. His parents came from Guatemala and his dark curly hair, brown skin, and deep eyes made him just about the sweetest eye candy among Tracy's thralls.

He wiped a hand over his neck with a wry smile. "My pleasure, Miss Cooper."

"Just Lisa, Tommy. Come on."

He winked at me and leaned in, stage whisper style. 'You know, you're a lot gentler than Miss Marchetti."

I stowed my smile as Tracy walked into the room. Maybe her ears were burning.

"All set?"

I pulled ten one-hundred dollar bills from my purse and forked them over to Tracy.

"Can I come back Wednesday?"

Tracy shrugged. "We'll see. Tommy needs to recoup, and I might want Kevin for myself."

I'd fed from Diana three nights ago. She needed to recoup too. It had been a week since the night I fed in the Burial Grounds.

There was no use in complaining to Tracy about it. They were her thralls, and this was my mistake.

I'd fucked up like this before, about sixty years ago. I had to lay off my abilities about a month for the strain of the curse to subside and my color to return. My plan was to do the same thing. That meant no charming gaze, no swiftness, no might, and no shapeshifting.

"Lisa, go hunt. This is stupid. You look fine." Tracy broke me out of my introspection.

She didn't get it. Over my many years, I'd seen our kind submit to their curse so badly that they become little more than walking corpses. All that power while the curse literally rotted their body. And it always started with that first step; that first compromise.

I smiled politely at Tracy. "Thanks for the visit."

"You aren't feeding enough. It's dangerous."

"I'm fine." I managed to keep my smile in place.

"Yea, well, you take more than your share of one my thralls, and I'll rip your throat out."

I let my smile drop. That seemed like a good place to end my stay, so I saw myself out. What really gnawed at me was that Tracy was right. I wasn't feeding enough.

I was hungry.

Episode 3

Brian's House

It wasn't like I fed every day before all this shit happened. I'd skip nights. Even two. Here and there.

But not like this.

I was feeding every third night at best. Even after seeing Tomás, I was still hungry. Like a gas tank half full.

Jesus, what a horrible analogy.

The next night, I tried Brian again. Straight to voicemail. *Who else would have gone to that gathering?* It wasn't like I socialized with many others in the New England bleed. Okay, just Brian.

I called Walter. I called Mark. Straight to voice mail. I grimaced as I dialed Dylan's number. He never missed a gathering. But if he answered, I would have been entreated to his sophomoric charms. He actually called me *sweet thighs* once.

I went to voicemail. Part of me was relieved, but my stomach tightened thinking about Brian. It wasn't like him to not call me back after so long.

I decided to go to his place. Brian's house was in Watertown, just outside the city. But I didn't just need to go to his house. I needed to get *into* his house.

Except that I couldn't.

As a bat, I could enter his home through whatever tollán he had in place. A bat tunnel. All vampires had them. They were a safe and hidden way into our homes. We didn't exactly leave keys under doormats. But staving off my curse as I was, I couldn't use any of my powers. That included shapeshifting. All these nights starving myself would have been for nothing.

I had to at least go to his house to check, so I called a cab. It was an expensive trip and, even at ten thirty at night, over an hour's drive.

When I got there, the first thing I noticed was Brian's car absent from the driveway. I tripped motion sensors and caused the light over the front door to illuminate, but the lights inside the house were off.

That's odd. Chewie should be barking.

I moved up to the door and knocked. No barking.

It smelled terrible. Whatever was inside wafted out and assaulted my nose. I tried to place the smell. It wasn't decay. It was...

"Shit."

If Brian was missing for nearly two weeks, did it mean Chewie had been left alone with no food and water all that time? How long could a dog go without eating?

A rock settled in the pit of my stomach as I realized the poor dog must have starved to death. I'd met Chewie a few times. Big dog, but gentle. He'd always tried to curl up on my lap, completely oblivious to his size.

I felt sick over it, and my worry for Brian spiked to new levels of panic. Brian never would have willingly left Chewie alone all that time.

I put my hand on the door as if to comfort the neglected house. *I should have checked on him sooner. That poor dog.*

A low growl emanated from within.

"Chewie?"

The deep rumble grew slightly in volume.

"Holy shit, you're alive." I grabbed the doorknob. The door was obviously locked.

I had to get in. But a new pang twisted my gut into knots. There was no way I could get into Brian's house without breaking down the door. After that, the door would be ruined, and his house would open to anyone.

I had enough strength I'd amassed over my years to do it, so I didn't have to worry about tapping into my might. But what was the plan? Smash the door in, feed Chewie, and then... what? Leave him alone in a house with a busted down door?

I needed to figure that out.

I shook my head. Either way, I needed to get inside. Chewie was still alive, and I had to get to him.

I squared my shoulder against the door. Once good smash was all it would take. I pulled back and closed my eyes.

One good smash. I stiffened my shoulder and braced for the impact.

"He's not home," a voice called out from across the street.

I stopped and turned to face the man. I must have been pretty distracted to have not heard him open his door and step out onto his lawn. The man approached, crossing the street.

He looked to be in his early thirties. He wore jeans and a tee-shirt that read *Humpty Dumpty was pushed.* His square jaw had two days of stubble and his hair was a mess.

"Yea, I'm a friend of Brian's. I hadn't heard from him," I said.

His timing sucked. Chewie's growling stopped, and I couldn't hear anything coming from inside the house.

"Yea, he went to work some nights ago and hasn't come back."

Telling your neighbors you work the late shift is always a good cover story. "It's almost been two weeks since I last saw him," I said.

"Girlfriend?"

"No, just a friend."

He smiled at that, showing dimples. I really didn't have time for it.

"Listen, his dog is inside, and he was just growling. I think he's been left alone for days. I need to get in there to check on him."

He gritted his teeth with a pained expression. "A dog isn't going to survive two weeks without food. He must have someone coming by to feed him."

"I don't know. With him not returning my calls, I don't think he's on some planned vacation."

"Well, you can't just bust in there. Besides, any dog that's left alone for—"

The growl reverberated through the door once more. The man looked a little dumbfounded.

"See?"

"Okay, I heard that."

"So, what do we do?"

"We should call the cops."

I wasn't keen on calling the police. If Brian's home was anything like mine, it wouldn't be very visitor-friendly to anyone who wasn't invited.

He pulled a phone from his pocket. I really didn't want to use my charming gaze to get this guy out of my hair. Though, I was pretty hungry, and he smelled so...

I shook my head. No, I had to stay focused on Chewie.

"Listen, if you call the cops, Brian could get in a lot of trouble, maybe even arrested."

"That's not exactly a big incentive for me not to call. You're saying the guy's a criminal *and* there is a starving dog inside?"

"It's nothing bad. You'd be ruining this guy's life."

"What's he doing, growing pot in his basement?"

"Something like that. I can't get into it." I was getting frustrated.

"I don't know."

The temptation to charm this guy was getting pretty strong. I needed him out of my hair. But I'd been letting things atrophy for two weeks, I'd lose all that progress.

"Look, if you found a dog in a car with the windows rolled up on a hot day, would you call the cops? Wonder how much time the dog had left? Or would you break the window? It's been days. We need to get in there now."

"It's a house not a car," he said, staring at the front door instead of me. Chewie was still growling. I could tell the man was conflicted.

So, I switched up tactics. Men love to be problem solvers. "It's probably moot anyway. There's no possible way in."

He didn't disappoint. He screwed up his face in thought.

"Well, there might be a way," he said at last.

"Okay." I was all ears.

"He's got one of those old wooden bulkheads out back." He pointed toward Brian's back yard. "I saw it when I was back there. Helping him put one of those pre-fab sheds together. In the middle of the night, no less. Anyways, it's this old wooden bulkhead with a padlock on it.

"I could get my hacksaw and take it off. We could slip in through the basement and check on the dog. Feed him or whatever. Then head back out and replace the lock."

He didn't seem comfortable with the idea and rubbed the back of his neck.

"In and out. We won't disturb a thing. When we catch up with Brian, we can tell him what we did. I'm sure he'll be glad. He loves that dog," I said.

He let out a long sigh. "Fine. Wait here. I gotta get my hacksaw."

I waited for maybe fifteen minutes. It felt twice as long. The guy was so mushy on the entire plan. I didn't want to use my powers to charm him. And I didn't want the police showing up. All I could think of was that he ran back across the street and called the police. Did I want to be here if the police showed up? *Should I duck out and maybe come back later?*

The man opened his front door and came jogging across his lawn toward Brian's house. My anxiety melted away. In his hands was a chrome rectangular-shaped saw with a thin blade at its bottom side.

Holy shit. We were really going to do it. I couldn't believe my luck.

"Come on. Let's just get this over with," he said. I followed him to Brian's back yard.

Sure enough, there was a wooden basement bulkhead with doors that looked like the planks of an old barn. A thick padlock held the two doors together. The man bent over it and started sawing.

"Never got your name. You said you're a friend of Brian's?"

I didn't really want to exchange names with this guy. To *know* him. Twenty minutes ago, I was considering charming him to help me inside and then maybe feeding from him.

"Lisa," I finally gave in.

"Neil."

It didn't take long before the lock was cut through. Neil flung the bulkhead doors aside and started down the stairs into Brian's basement. I followed.

At the bottom of the stairs was a door leading into the basement itself. Neil tried the knob. It was locked.

We were back to where we started.

"Yea, I figured this. We'll just have to explain this to Brian. Saving his dog."

"Explain what?" Wasn't that already the plan?

He ignored my question and began putting his hacksaw to work against the stem of the doorknob. Relief washed over me. I wanted to hug him.

The doorknob fell away. Neil pushed around the inside of the lock and knocked some things out of place. The basement door swung open.

It worked. We were in. I didn't have to use my powers. No police. And we were going to save Brian's dog.

Neil and I stepped into the basement. Blinking lights. Too late.

The room was suddenly bathed in intense white light.

"Holy shit!" Neil shielded his eyes. "That's bright! And hot!"

Sun lamps. Pure focused UV light. Of course Brian would have his basement door boobytrapped.

I doubled over in pain as my skin started to burn.

Episode 4

Chewie

THE UV RAYS OF Brian's sun lamp trap were like a blast furnace. I doubled over and tried to shield the exposed parts of my body. The back of my neck was still uncovered. Searing pain raked through my skin.

"What the hell? Are you okay?" Neil called out.

I knew I had to run back up the stairs and get to the back yard, but if I also knew if I stood up and exposed my face and arms, I'd be in real trouble.

I came up off the floor. The room spun as I was whirled around. Neil had picked me up. In his arms, his body protected me from direct impact of the lamp's scorching light. He dashed up the concrete basement steps and we were both back outside.

"Jesus. You're all sunburned."

"It's my... condition. It's a real thing," I stammered.

My skin still radiated painful throbs of heat. I had rehearsed my bullshit story about some rare light sensitivity affliction I had a thousand times over. I even did some research on it. But *it's a real thing* was the best I could muster.

"Yea. I can see that. Are you alright?"

"Yes. Just give me a moment."

"Stay here. I'm going to go in and try to find the fuse box. Cut the power. We still need to check on Stewie."

"Chewie."

"Right."

I sat up and looked at my arms. They were red with sunburn. That wasn't even what pissed me off the most. The worst part of it was, had my skin not been so pale, had I not drawn on my curse two weeks ago, I would not have been as susceptible to the lamp's light.

I could only imagine how other vampires would have fared in my place. I'd have to remember that the next time Tracy gave me grief for not *drawing on my power*. Had Tracy or anyone else with more of a deathly pallor entered that room, they would have burned a lot worse and a lot faster.

Hell, Jacques may have burst into flames.

It only strengthened my resolve. I had to lay off my abilities and let my curse subside long enough for my life color to return.

The light from Brian's basement went out. Neil showed up a moment later.

"You doing okay, Lisa?"

"Yea. I just needed a minute. Thanks... for that."

"No problem. It was like you were on fire."

"I felt like I was." I got to my feet.

"You still up for checking on Chewie? If you got your phone on you, you can use the flashlight." He pulled out his own phone and fired up the light as if to demonstrate.

The truth was, I saw just fine in the dark. But I turned on my phone's light just the same.

Brian's basement was unfinished and divided into two sides, bisected by a staircase. The half we entered was filled with stacks of plastic tubs. I could see the sunlamps pointed at the basement doorway. Their bulbs were long and thin, like fluorescent lights. Even powered down, heat still radiated from them.

We took the steps. Halfway up, Chewie's low growl rumbled through the house. Worse than that, the smell of his prolonged occupancy permeated the house and seemed to hang in the very air. It was all I could do not to gag.

"Um..., " Neil stopped in his tracks. He seemed more concerned with the growling than the odor.

"Why don't you let me go first. Chewie knows me. I'm sure he's just reacting to the sounds we're making. Once he sees me, he'll be fine."

"Yea... okay."

I stepped past Neil. I could sense his heartbeat. It wasn't something I could hear so much as a pulsing that echoed within me. A shiver ran up my spine as my senses sharpened. Every fiber of my being prickled with awareness that life-giving blood was nearby. The pull was strong.

I paused on the step beside Neil.

"You okay? He doesn't bite does he?"

My hunger pulled on me like a tug-of-war. It would be so easy. We'd been so friendly with each other. The charming gaze would be effortless. My fangs elongated in my mouth. I held my lips tight.

"Hey." He put a hand on my shoulder.

He was smiling when I looked at him.

"I was just saying, Chewie knows you, but I can go first," he said.

I'm not a monster. I need to fight through this to be stronger.

"No. I just... give me a moment." I wasn't looking at him when I spoke. I closed my eyes.

The curse compelled a vampire to do terrible things, but ultimately, it was our choices that made us what we were. And I chose not to let my curse control me.

My fangs receded. I looked at Neil and gave a small smile. "I'm okay."

I ascended the remaining steps. The pangs in my stomach gnawed at me, but Neil was out of danger. So was I, for that matter. My thoughts turned back to Chewie.

I slowly opened the door at the top of the basement stairs. "Chewieee." I tried to affect a sing-song voice to defuse some of his anxiety.

A deep woof came in reply.

I swung the door open. The stench of weeks of house-crapping went up ten-fold. I winced.

"Oh, man." Neil screwed up his face.

"Yea, he's been here alone for a while. I'm sure he relieved himself all over the place."

There was Chewie. The massive, black Neapolitan mastiff had his hackles raised and head lowered.

He was big, even for his breed. His shoulder easily came up to my hip. But Chewie had seen better days. He was emaciated. He looked starved.

"Easy, boy," I said.

Then, recognition. His long tail swiped back and forth like a windshield wiper on high. Chewie lumbered over to me and bumped his head into my thigh.

"Hey there. Nice to see you too."

Neil appeared behind me. "You said two weeks. How is he still... alive?"

"Not gonna look a gift horse in the mouth."

"Is he....?"

"No, he's fine. Just maybe don't get between him and me. You're okay."

I went into Brian's kitchen. Chewie padded in behind me. The entire floor was overrun with his leavings.

"Watch your step. It's like a doggie minefield in here."

"Damn, those are some big piles of crap."

It took me a moment to search around, but eventually I found Chewie's food and filled up his bowl. I also gave him fresh water. Chewie happily ignored us and gorged himself.

"I don't know where Brian is or when he's coming back. Could you... look after him?"

"I'm not really keen on breaking in here every night."

"I mean could you take him? At least until I can get in touch with Brian?"

"I gue—maybe? I don't know." He shifted around and wouldn't meet my gaze.

I didn't want to just leave him again for who knows how long. And I spent most of my nights out, so keeping a pet would be tough. I'm hardly home. I don't know how Brian did it.

Chewie made short work of his food. Neil approached the massive dog. "What do you think, boy? You wanna come home with—"

Chewie made a lunge at Neil. I grabbed his collar and got jerked forward. Neil stumbled backwards and fell on his ass. Chewie halted his charge and looked up at me. He gave single, baritone woof.

"Are you okay?"

"Not exactly. Doggie minefield." Neil showed me his hand. "Aaaand, I think I'm sitting in some."

"Bathroom's down the hall, first door on the right."

"Yea. Great." Neil picked himself up and made his way out. The light from his cellphone disappeared around the corner.

I stooped down. "What was that about?" I asked Chewie.

He licked my face.

The sound of water came from down the hall. "You know," Neil's voice followed. "I don't think I can take him. I may have just lost five years off my life."

"He's just being protective."

He didn't reply. It was moot anyway. I had to be the one to take Chewie.

We got Neil a pair of Brian's pants soon after. We couldn't find a leash for Chewie, but he stuck by my side, nonetheless. He followed Neil and I back out the basement bulkhead and outside. Neil was kind enough to carry the giant bag of kibble for me.

"I'll replace the lock tomorrow. You sure about taking him?"

"Totally. I just have to find Brian. I can watch Chewie until then."

"Well…. good luck. Nice meeting you." He gave me a tight-lipped smile.

"Nice meeting you too." I returned the smile and watched him wander back across the street. He looked back at me once more and shot me another smile before going into his house. I caught myself smiling back.

The next order of business was getting home, so I called a cab.

Since I couldn't stand the smell of that house any longer, Chewie and I sat outside on Brian's front step. I absently pet him while we waited. I couldn't believe how thin he was. I could feel his ribs as I ran my hand across his side.

My stomach pulled at me. I was hungry. It gnawed at me like a chisel inside my stomach. Maybe I could start again from scratch? Tracy wouldn't mind the extra income. Maybe the cab driver...

No. I closed my eyes.

No.

It was forty minutes when the cab driver finally pulled in. I gathered up Chewie's bag of kibble and his two massive bowls. Chewie padded alongside me as I approached the cab.

"Be good, Chewie. Easy."

"What? You can't bring that dog in here," the cab driver said.

This catapulted us into a brief and futile argument over how Chewie was malnourished and needed help and how I had no other way of getting home. The cabbie, for his position, didn't want *hair or smell* in his cab, which I doubted would have detracted from the vehicle's state of cleanliness anyway. It didn't matter. It wasn't a battle I was going to win.

The driver cursed me out for making him drive all the way out to the suburbs and drove off in a screech of burnt rubber.

Real mature.

Chewie looked up at me.

"I don't know, boy," I said.

And I didn't. Until I could figure out my next move, we were stranded.

Episode 5

Meeting With Ivan

I stood on Brian's front lawn and weighed my options. No cab was going to take me and Chewie back to Charlestown. I had no desire to stay in Brian's *pooptropolis,* where Chewie had been left for far too long with no potty breaks. That left one viable option: Neil.

I went across the street and knocked on Neil's front door. Hopefully, he wasn't in bed. No answer. I rang the doorbell.

It took a minute, but Neil came to the door. His hair was disheveled, and he was still wearing his *Humpty Dumpty Was Pushed* tee shirt.

"Hi."

"Hi," he replied, half-awake.

"Listen, the cab driver wouldn't take Chewie. No dogs. Is there any way I could get a ride from you?"

He puffed out his cheeks and let out a long breath. "A ride?"

"I'm sorry. I'm kind of stranded."

"Where do you live?"

"Charlestown." I cringed as the word left my lips.

He cringed too.

"I can pay you."

He waved that off. "No, no... shit. Yea, okay. Charlestown." He rubbed one of his eyes. "Give me a sec."

He closed the door.

A moment later, Neil came out. He had a jacket on, and keys jingled in his hands. He stopped short at Chewie.

The big mastiff looked up at Neil. Even starved as Chewie was, he was still a massive dog.

"Is he gonna be cool?"

"I think he was still jittery when you approached him last time. He's fine."

Neil looked dubious but held out the back of his hand for Chewie to sniff. The dog pressed his nose to it and then licked Neil's hand.

"Okay... so long as he isn't going to maul me or anything."

I followed him to his car. "I really appreciate this."

Neil's car was a very sensible looking Toyota whose prime years were behind it. We loaded Chewie, his hulking bag of kibble, and his two bowls into the back seat. I sat in the front next to Neil.

He was drowsy. His eyelids struggled to stay open. I tried to keep a steady conversation going with him. The GPS said we'd get to my house in twenty minutes. Not terrible, but it was already after midnight and he'd have another twenty-something minute drive back home.

We talked all the way to my house. Neil worked in IT as something called an Exchange administrator. I didn't know what that meant. I told him I worked nights as a nurse. My usual go-to.

We pulled up to my house and Neil stared at the building. "You live here?"

My house was a three-story brownstone on Monument Avenue. I only had the first floor. It was one of many brownstones that lined the street leading up to Bunker Hill.

"Yea," I said a little sheepishly.

"You said you're a nurse?"

"Uh-huh. Yup." I grabbed Chewie's bag of kibble and bowls.

I still didn't have a leash for Chewie, but the big dog stayed by my side without an issue. He'd slept the entire drive and found his energy again once he got out of the car. He jumped up on Neil in an attempt to lick him, and nearly knocked him over.

"Chewie! Don't do that," my scolding wasn't all that firm, but Chewie obeyed.

"Dog's gonna give me a heart attack," said Neil.

"You okay to drive home?"

"Yea. I'm good."

Neil gestured at all the stuff I was holding in my arms. "You got all that?"

"Yea, it's more awkward than heavy. Thank you for driving me. It was really sweet of you."

"Yea..." He shrugged and bobbed his head a little.

"Listen..." I set the dogfood bag down and fished in my purse and pulled out a business card. "Call me when you get home. I want to make sure you got back alright."

He took my card. "You're giving me your number?"

"Well... yes?" I wasn't really thinking of the connotation. I was honest about being worried.

"Yea." That put a smile on his face. "Sure."

"Well, thanks again." Things suddenly felt wonky. I grabbed all of Chewie's crap and went into my house. Neil waited for me to get inside before he drove away.

I set Chewie up with a full dish of kibble and a fresh bowl of water. It was no surprise that he was still hungry, as emaciated as he was. He dove right in and glutted himself with no prompting. I scarcely had time to pull my hand away from the bowl once I had set it down.

The light was flashing on my answering machine. I still kept a land line with a classic answering machine. A lot of the people I dealt with still only called me on my home phone. I couldn't really blame them. For decades, it was the only number I had, and they weren't exactly people who adapted to change swiftly.

I hit the button and Ivan's voice came over the little speaker.

"Siobhan. Call me when you get this."

I let out a sigh. Ivan MacAlistair, the lord of the New England bleed, never called to chit-chat. He also still called me Siobhan, which was my mortal name. Siobhan McQueeney. It was a name I hadn't used in nearly a hundred and fifty years. But Ivan *knew me when*, as they say.

Ivan either wanted me to do some shit or to give me some shit. Either way, I was going to have shit in my future.

I would have taken ten of Brian's *pooptropolises* over whatever Ivan had in mind for me.

I dialed him up.

"Siobhan," he said in lieu of a greeting.

"How are you, Ivan?"

"We have a problem. I need you to come see me."

"What's going on?"

"It's nothing I care to discuss over the telephone. The others are already here. I will see you when you arrive."

He hung up before I could say anything else. Not that I had anything more to say.

Ivan had a place in the Back Bay area of Boston. Not far, but I had to get a cab. And I had to leave poor Chewie alone.

"No going to the bathroom in the house, okay?"

Chewie looked up at me and dipped his head. His eyes never left mine. *Did he just... nod?*

As peculiar as that was, I didn't have time to puzzle it out. I called a cab and tried not to get all worked up over whatever Ivan wanted to talk about with the entire bleed.

The cab ride was around thirty minutes in total, but halfway there, my phone rang.

"Hello?"

"Hey, Lisa. It's Neil."

He sounded sleepy.

"You made it home alright?"

"Yea. Listen... tonight was weird. And crazy. But fun. Can I call you some time? Again?"

"Yes." I caught myself smiling. "You may." Why was I smiling? Why did I say yes?

"Cool." There was a smile in his voice. "I gotta sleep, but I'll definitely call you. Maybe we can do something that doesn't involve B&E and vicious dogs?"

"Chewie's not vicious." I laughed.

He laughed too. "Good night, Lisa. Thanks for the adventure."

"Good night, Neil."

He rang off. I found myself staring at my phone. I hated when this happened. When they got close. But Tracy was right. I hadn't been feeding enough and I had no blood thralls of my own. Neil was a nice guy. And he liked me. And unfortunately, that made him perfect.

Life was so much easier the less you had to hunt.

I spent the remainder of the ride contemplating what a horrible person I was.

Ivan lived in an old brownstone on Commonwealth Ave. It was older than my own and originally served as a luxury apartment complex in the mid-1800s. Ivan had converted into a high-price condo. The secret was that every tenant in his building was his blood thrall. He had dozens to feed on at his disposal. He scarcely needed to hunt.

Ivan's residence took up the entire third floor. I don't know how he did it. I always hated sleeping too far away from street level. Anyone who has ever had their home invaded knows a street level escape is essential. I imagined he must have had a safe room or perhaps a sleeping chamber in the basement.

I knocked on his door in four even beats. Then two. Then three. It was old school speakeasy stuff, but Ivan loved the pomp and circumstance behind it. The door creaked open, and a short thin man peered up at me.

Úll Buachaill stood at around three feet tall. He was rather homely, with a bulbous nose, cauliflower ears, and a patchy beard. Despite his unfortunate visage, he was a snappy dresser. He had on tight blue leggings and a red waist coat. On top of his head was a blood-red cap.

Úll narrowed his eyes at me. "Yer late, Lisa Coopah," he said in an Irish brogue.

I honestly didn't have time for his shit. Not that he was wrong. I pushed past the little redcap and entered the room.

Úll trotted beside me as I made my way to Ivan's study. I opened the door, and Úll ran out in front of me. "Ivan MacAlistah, Lisa Coopah here ta join the meetin'," he blurted out.

Tracy, Jacques, and Richard were already in the study. Ivan looked at the redcap evenly. "Thank you, Úll. That will be all."

The little fae ran out of the room and closed the door.

Ivan sat in a leather chair flanked by two short couches that faced one another. Tracy and Jacques were seated on the couch to my right.

Tracy was dressed up for the meeting and wore a blazer and skirt ensemble. Jacques, no surprise, was dressed in one of his shiny Italian suits. Tonight, was purple pinstripes accented with a red vest and white patent leather shoes. His sunken eyes reflected the smile he casted at me. Black blotches pocked his deathly pale hands and face. He may had been good looking once, but his curse had festered his body to the precipice of rot.

Richard sat at the couch to my left. His style was more casual, but no less fashionable. He wore a black silk shirt, dark blue jeans, and those boots that came up to the ankle and zipped up the side. He called them his *Beatle Boots* and always insisted they were still in style. Richard was quite pale, but in his centuries, he had staved off the curse from wracking his body.

With dark hair, dark eyes, and a square jaw, Richard was conventionally handsome, but I couldn't help frowning at him.

Ivan leveled his gaze at me as I looked over the room. The tension was almost tactile. Ivan was turned in his forties. Tracy sometimes called him the silver fox, but never to his face. He wore a three-piece suit with a checkered Prince of Wales pattern. A style that was popular in the early 1900s.

"Nice of you to join us, Lisa," remarked Richard.

"You are aware that when I call you, I do not expect to go to your answering machine," said Ivan.

"I was out. I gave you my cell. You should be calling—"

"I cannot keep track of a bevy of telephone numbers for you, Lisa. Simply forward all your calls to whatever telephone you use."

He called me *Lisa* in mixed company. Or when he was annoyed. This counted for both.

"It doesn't really work like... sorry, yes. Of course." I figured there was no explaining things to him while he was in this sort of mood.

I took the open seat next to Richard. "What's this all about?"

All eyes were on me.

I looked at everyone. "What?"

"Several members of our bleed have been missing for two weeks," Ivan began. His piercing blue eyes drilled into me. He held up a small stack of papers. "I did a little digging and asked a contact to look into whom they had been in contact with."

I was all ears. If he had a lead, I was eager to hear it.

"It seems you called Brian Sommers the night he disappeared. The night they all disappeared from that little soirée that Dylan was throwing." Ivan waved the papers in his hand. "And you had tried to contact him several more times since that night."

Richard chimed in. "Have you had any contact with your creator recently? Isn't he from our rival bleed in New York? What was his name again? William something?"

"You know damn well who William is," I snapped at Richard. "You think New York is behind this? You think I'm involved? Are you kidding me?"

Ivan looked annoyed with the interruption. "Lisa, what do you know about these disappearances?"

Richard leaned back against the couch and smiled.

Episode 6

Thirsty

"I don't know anything about it," I said.

Ivan didn't say anything. He just looked at me. Jacques' eyes bounced between me and Ivan. Tracy looked bored. Beside me, Richard held a smug smirk.

I wanted to slap it off his face.

"Brian called me two weeks ago about the get-together. I wasn't interested, so I didn't go. I called him later that night and he didn't answer. I kept trying him over the past two weeks and got nothing. That's it."

"And William?" asked Richard.

I glared at him. "I haven't spoken to him in years. And if you must know, he and I aren't on good terms. We haven't been for decades."

Ivan leaned back in his leather chair. He laced his fingers together with his elbows upon the armrests.

Richard wouldn't let it go. "The New York bleed has been encroaching on our territory for years. Just last summer, we found one of them hunting in Northampton. Come now, Lisa, you can't tell us you wouldn't jump at the chance to reconcile things with your dear creator." He tried to affect an earnest smile.

"Are you honestly accusing me of working with William to... what exactly? Smuggling vampires over the border to hunt? They've been hunting in western Massachusetts for over a century. If they were really moving against us, they'd be hitting further east."

"You think so?" asked Richard. "Maybe start by taking out some vampires at a get-together?"

"Oh, fuck you, Richard." I was done keeping my cool with that asshole.

"Alright, that's enough," Ivan spoke calmly. "Four of us are missing. I want to hear theories."

Richard began again. "I'm just saying we can't easily dismiss—"

"You know what, Richard?" Jacques spoke up. "Our Lisa is probably the most honest and loyal among us. The girl has clung to her moral compass like a life raft in this sea of sin we live in."

Tracy rolled her eyes.

"If Lisa said she's not working with William then that's that," Jacques concluded.

"Please. Lisa is a sentimental creature. She would jump at the chance to reconcile things with William," said Richard.

Tracy shook her head. "No. Not after what he did to her."

"Can everyone stop talking like I'm not here?"

I appreciated their defense, but the entire line of questioning had me fuming. I wanted to break the coffee table over Richard's head.

Tracy waved me off. "Does anyone know where the gathering was?"

"Dylan's," I said.

"And has anyone gone over there?" asked Tracy.

Silence fell over the room. Jacques gave a subtle shake of his head.

"Honestly, I've only found out they were missing last night. We don't exactly *hang out*, you know," said Richard.

Tracy looked at me. "You've been keeping tabs more than any of us. You never went to Dylan's?"

A pang hit my stomach. I should have, but what was I going to say *Sorry, no. Dylan is a skeevy asshole, and I was only worried about Brian*. But Tracy was right. To find Brian, Dylan's was the place to start. "I went to Brian's. He wasn't there. But no, not Dylan's."

"Then we should at least start there," said Tracy.

"Very good," said Ivan. "Tracy, see what you can find. Lisa, stay behind, please."

Him asking me to stay behind was an indication that the meeting was over. Tracy shot off the couch and strode out of the room. Jacques smiled at me before he followed her out. Richard rose slowly and smirked at me.

"Good luck, Lisa," he offered.

"Fuck off."

Richard laughed and left the study.

A silence settled into the room between Ivan and me.

"You look a little pale. Have you seized more power for yourself? The fair complexion looks good on you."

"I needed to exert myself, but I'm staving off my... gifts until I can gain back the color of life."

Ivan frowned. "You look hungry. Have you been feeding enough?"

"Tracy has been helping. Her thralls."

"These games you play to keep the balance; they're dangerous, and it isn't worth the price of blending in with the living."

"With all due respect..."

Ivan put up a hand and spoke evenly. "I won't rehash this with you. But if you aren't feeding enough, you'll be susceptible to losing yourself. Risking our exposure. You understand that is not a position I want you to put me in?"

"I'm handling it."

Ivan looked unconvinced. "Have Úll take you to 210. There are two gentlemen in that suite. One pint each. Yes?"

"Yes. Thank you." Two pints? To hell with my pride. I wasn't going to say no to that.

"Now then. About our missing vampires."

"I told you everything I know."

Ivan pierced his eyes into me. "I have to ask. When was the last time you heard from William?"

Fucking Richard.

"Three or four years ago. I told you about it. He offered me a domain in Manhattan. A ten-year occupancy where he'd share his hunting grounds with me. Then I would take Queens for myself. Naturally, he wanted information on our bleed in exchange."

"And you turned him down."

"Do you see me living in Manhattan?"

Ivan frowned. I didn't care. His questions were over the line.

"Sorry, this is all really insulting. You know me, Ivan."

"I do. And in many ways, I think of you as my own scion. I often wish I found you before William." He offered a smile.

"Me too."

Ivan leaned back into his chair. It indicated a topic change. I let the silence settle back in and waited for him to speak first.

"Four vampires disappearing at once. It's troubling. And I fear this is bigger than we realize."

I bobbed my head in response. The only thing I could offer was my agreement.

"Tell me...," he leaned forward. "Your special friends... witches? Can they be of any help here?"

"I could try them. Not sure they would be keen looking for vampires. They generally don't like our kind."

"You're the exception."

"Believe me, that took some doing. But yes... I'll see what I can find."

He leaned back in his chair again, stroking his chin.

"What?" I asked. I already knew I didn't want to know.

"The seiren."

"Lucy has been out of town for years. Florida, I think. She moves around like we have to, else the neighbors get suspicious of the young lady who never ages. But no, Lucy is out of town."

"You could call her? Could her clairvoyance extend all the way to Boston?"

"I don't know. But she sees the future, not the past. She wouldn't be able to see what happened to Brian and the others."

"But she might be able to see what will come to pass. Yes?"

"Maybe. I'll try her. What about the fae?" It was my turn to put the matter back on him. Elders like him had pacts with the fae. I never really understood them, save for the fact that our origins date back to ancient Ireland.

"My resources among the fae are limited, Siobhan. Redcaps make fair servants and work wonders at disposing of things, but it isn't like I have pixie scouts at my beck and call." He gave me a bemused expression.

Looks like the investigation was back on me again. "Fine. I'll call around and see what I can dig up."

"Good. Then I won't keep you. And remember, see Úll about suite 210."

"Suite two-ten, Lisa Coopah." Úll announced as he wrapped on the door.

We were invited in by a man named Raphael and a man who I *think* was his live-in boyfriend, Roger. Raphael looked like he may have been mixed ethnicities. He had rich brown skin and a tight, thin shaven beard. His eyes were dark brown and innocent, which almost belied his brawny athletic build.

Roger, on the other hand, was short and wiry. Though, his features were striking with high cheek bones and piercing green eyes.

Their apartment looked like it had jumped from the pages of a Pottery Barn or maybe a Bombay Company circular. I miss Bombay Company. These two were probably too young to have heard of it.

"I always joke," began Úll. "When Ivan Macallistah comes down here. *Goin' for a little R&R?* I say. Get it? R&R? Raphael and Rojah?" The little redcap laughed.

"Hi, Úll," said Roger. "You want something to drink?"

"I'll have a feckin' beer if ye have one."

Roger left the room and I shook Raphael's hand. "I'm Lisa. Ivan said I could…"

"Lisa Cooper. Of course." He smiled. "Anyone in the bleed is welcome. Been weeks since Roger and I had anyone come by, so we're good."

"All filled up!" Úll explained.

"Úll, can you leave us? I think we're all set," I said.

"Not without me feckin' beer. And 'sides, Ivan Macallistah always wants me to supervise. It's a policy, Lisa Coopah."

I sighed. Raphael laughed a little and took my hand. "Wow, your hand is so warm. Let's go sit on the couch."

He took a seat on the couch and faced his back to me. I sat behind him.

This was so much easier than hunting. I thought about the merits of having a thrall of my own again. My mind went to Neil. Guilt rolled through me for even thinking it.

There was always something awkward about drinking from a willing participant, even though I preferred it. Even after all my years, I hated taking blood from the unwilling.

Roger appeared with a beer and offered it to Úll who broke into a wide, crooked smile.

The pulse of Raphael's carotid artery pulled at me. My stomach tightened. I hadn't been aware of how hungry I was. My fangs elongated.

I leaned into his neck.

"I don't think we've met before, are you from—"

I sank into him.

"Oh, you get right to it," said Raphael.

Copper tinged with... citrus? Had Ivan been keeping him on a steady diet of fruit? Bless his soul. The taste was noticeable. I instinctively held onto him.

"Whoa, ease up. I'm not going anywhere."

I kept drinking. Tracy and Ivan were right. I hadn't been feeding enough. I needed more.

"Okay, that's...," Raphael said.

Raphael kept talking, but I tuned him out. There is a certain peace that comes from drinking, like calming a beast. I wanted to enjoy it, to only focus on that feeling. His blood flowed through me, and the aching emptiness within me subsided.

Pinpricks prickled my body. I was one with my curse. It was no longer a burden. Blood was immortality, and I was in perfect harmony with it.

Everything was quiet. It was strange. My senses were always so sharp, but all sound slipped away. The only thing I could smell or taste was blood.

No.

I could hear something.

There was shouting.

Roger sounded like he was under water, yelling with tears streamed down his face. His muffled cries were difficult to make out.

"Get off him! You're killing him!"

More Trouble

RAPHAEL'S BLOOD FLOWED THROUGH my lips. After two long weeks, my hunger would finally be satiated.

"Get off of him!" Roger's shouts sounded miles away.

Was I taking too much?

How long had I been drinking?

I was grabbed by the shoulders. Raphael struggled in my arms. Úll's small arms wrapped around my waist and pulled at me. They were fighting me.

Fighting *me*?

I pulled my fangs from Raphael's neck. The pang of hunger bit back at me in retribution, but it was so much weaker than before.

Raphael slumped in my arms.

"Oh my God, I'm so sorry."

"Get off him!" Roger cried. Tears stained his cheeks.

I let him go and got to my feet. "I... I didn't mean..."

"Feck sake, Lisa Coopah!" Úll scolded me. "Look at this feckin' mess!"

"I'm sorry." My heart sank. I felt sick. I'd lost control. I'd hurt someone.

Raphael groaned on the couch. The color had drained from his flesh.

"I'm so sorry."

I ran from the apartment. I ran down the stairs and burst through the door and into the street.

I hadn't lost control like that in years. Tracy was right. She tried to warn me.

I had to get out of there. I was disgusted with myself. I lost control.

I lost control.

The next night, I trudged up the stairs from my basement sanctuary. The altercation with Raphael still weighed heavy on my mind.

I checked my answering machine and found no messages from Ivan. I didn't know if that was good or bad.

Chewie was there to greet me in an instant. Dogs were such a miracle. No matter what horrible things we did, they loved us unconditionally. Chewie bumped into my legs and wagged his tail vigorously. I stooped down to scratch his head and back. He rewarded me with huge licks and I was too weary to ward them off.

After I fed him, I took him out for a walk. I used a length of rope as a make-shift leash. Massachusetts had a leash law, after all.

While he did his business, I rang Tracy. I wanted to know what she found out last night at Dylan's.

No answer.

"Hey, Tracy. It's Lisa. Curious what you found at Dylan's. Ivan asked me to poke around with some of my contacts, so I'll let you know what I find."

I could hear the melancholy in my own voice.

I wanted to call Ivan and ask how Raphael was, but I also didn't feel like getting screamed at.

Before I had the chance, my phone started ringing. I checked the name on the display. Restricted.

Normally, I don't pick up calls from numbers I don't know, but with everything going on, I answered the call. "Hello?"

"Lisa Cooper?" came a male's voice.

"Yes."

"Lisa, this is detective Pierce, I had some questions about a missing person – well, persons. One of them is a friend of yours. At least that's what I can surmise from his phone records."

What's with everyone searching mine and Brian's phone records?

"Okay," I replied.

"Have you had any contact with a Brian Sommers recently?"

"Brian? No. Not for days. Is he okay?"

"Well, he's missing," he said in a *no-duh* kind of tone.

I wasn't sure how much I wanted to share. Going missing at a vampire party wasn't something I wanted to be linked to if Pierce was actively digging into this case.

"That's awful." I opted to feign ignorance.

"You've been trying to reach him for weeks with no luck. You didn't think to call in a missing person?"

"He travels for business now and then. We're friends, but he doesn't share his schedule with me or anything."

"You tried him several times after he went missing. Do you usually call him so frequently when he doesn't get back to you?"

I didn't need this aggravation. "No. I just had news I wanted to get in touch with him about. Time sensitive stuff."

"Care to share what that news is?"

"Um... no. Sorry, it's personal."

"Lisa, this is an investigation. Four people are missing, and I have your phone calls repeatedly trying to contact one of them. *And* you called each of the others. Do I need to talk about withholding information and all that?"

"They're all mutual friends. They went to a party together at Dylan Walker's place in Brookline. I wanted to try them to see if they knew where Brian was. But I only called them each once."

"Well, we may need to have you come down to answer some questions, so sit tight. Anything more you can tell me? Were they into anything? Anyone you know might want to hurt them?"

"No." I answered too quickly.

"Yea, well, you remember anything, give me a call."

"I will. Thanks."

He rang off with that.

Stress settled into my chest. I didn't want to be connected to any of this, whatever *this* was. Though, on the plus side, any detective worth his salt would be bound to turn up something. Maybe he'd find Brian. Then again, maybe he might turn up *too much*. And if he hadn't gone to Brian's house already...

Oh, shit. Neil.

Pierce would definitely be asking neighbors about each missing person. I still had Neil's number in my phone from when he rang me last night.

Chewie pulled at the rope, and I jerked forward a bit. He'd done his business and seemed eager to move on. He was a lot stronger than I expected him to be. He was a big dog, but I was a vampire. Yet, I still lurched forward under his strains.

"Sorry, boy. You want to go for a proper walk now?"

A single woof was my reply.

I scrolled to Neil's number as I walked Chewie up Monument Ave toward the Bunker Hill monument.

"Hello?"

"Neil? Hi, it's Lisa. From last night."

"Oh, hey..." He put on that *smooth guy* tone.

"Listen, there may be a detective looking into Brian being missing."

"Oh," he replied with a more sobered voice.

"I don't want to tell you to lie, but maybe leave off the bit about us going into his house?"

"I'm not gonna volunteer that, are you kidding?"

"Okay, good. Just tell him what you told me about him going off to work and not coming back."

"What's going on, Lisa? Am I involved in some kind of bullshit?"

"No. No bullshit. I only know he's been missing. I swear. If there's something else behind that, I'm not involved in it. Neither are you."

"Okay." He sounded guarded for a moment.

"You know…" the smooth tone returned. "I'm not saying this is quid pro quo, because I'm not going to give the detective more than he needs, but maybe this favor earns me some points? Maybe enough to go out for a bite?"

I nearly snorted at his choice of words. Chewie chose that time to yank me forward.

"Gah!"

"Is that a… no? Are you okay?"

"Sorry, yea. I'm out walking Chewie. Or should I say he's walking me."

He laughed. "Oh, you might need two hands on that leash. He's huge. Even for a mastiff."

"Yes, well, he's also strong as hell."

"So.... was that a clever subject change, or…?"

"What? Oh, dinner! Right. Sorry, I'm a little all over the place. Can we raincheck?"

"I mean, we hadn't actually set a date to reschedule, but yea. I can ask you later?"

"Sure." I caught myself smiling.

"Okay, well… cool. Talk later?" asked Neil.

"Yea. And be cool with that detective."

"Right. No telling the police detective about our B&E and dognapping escapade," Neil joked.

I laughed. "Just be cool."

"Alright, alright. Bye, Lisa."

"Bye, Neil."

By the time I had hung up with Neil, Chewie and I made our way up toward the end of Monument Ave. Monument Square was ahead of us. The towering Bunker Hill obelisk rose from the horizon.

"A whole park to pee in, Chewie," I told him.

He bellowed a deep woof in return.

Tracy came around the corner.

"Tracy? What are you doing here? I just tried to call you."

Chewie growled. He lowered his head and his hackles raised.

"Chewie, no." I looked at Tracy. "Sorry about him, he's still a little..."

Something wasn't right. Tracy seemed off. Even her posture seemed wrong. Her shoulders slumped and knees bent as if holding up some unseen weight.

She just stared at me.

Chewie's low growls caused me to tighten up on his rope.

Tracy walked toward me. She didn't say a word. She didn't react to Chewie.

Her expression was vacant. Her eyes were... milky.

"Tracy?"

She bared her fangs and charged.

Episode 8

Tracy Bespelled

TRACY BARRELED AT ME. Chewie reacted before I realized what was happening. He pulled free of my grasp and charged her.

Tracy never broke her stride. She dipped down as she ran. She punched Chewie in the chest and sent him flying through the air.

Chewie crashed into a set of brick steps to the apartments at my left. He let out a painful, high-pitched yelp on impact.

A few tourists who were out for an evening stroll on the freedom trail ran away when they saw the wild murder-lady punch a giant dog. That was probably for the best.

I put my hands up to fight, but Tracy was like a freight train. She plowed into me and knocked me to the sidewalk.

Years of staving off my curse has cost me in the way of power, and that included speed and might. Tracy easily pinned me down. Being able to say that I could last longer in the sunlight than she could didn't really hold a lot of weight in times like this.

She stared at me through glassy, vacant eyes.

"Tracy! Snap out of it! What are you doing?"

I struggled in vain. She was a lot stronger than me.

She started to get to her feet and pulled me up with her. She held me fast.

Chewie crashed into Tracy. The impact knocked her off me and into the street. The big mastiff followed through and leaped at her.

Tracy got to her feet. Chewie sailed harmlessly past her.

She turned to face him, her fangs bared.

Everything moved faster than I could react. I got to my feet in time to see Tracy and Chewie clashed together.

Tracy pounded her fists into him. The massive dog clamped his teeth down on her arm. He shook his head vigorously. Tracy screamed.

Chewie brought her down and continued to tear into her arm.

Small trees lined the street in little square planters along the sidewalk. I knew I had to finish this, so I tore a branch off the closest one.

A stake through the heart wouldn't kill Tracy, but it would prevent her from using her powers. If the heart can't pump blood, we cannot use the abilities our cursed blood grants us.

I turned in time to see Chewie slam into a telephone pole. My chest seized.

Chewie slid down the pole and slumped into the sidewalk.

Tracy came at me again, running like a blur. A couple of pedestrians somewhere screamed, but I couldn't afford the time to look behind me. Hopefully they had the good sense to run while they could.

The wind was knocked out of me as Tracy tackled me to the street. The make-shift stake went flying out of my hand. Though her fangs were bared, she made no attempt to bite me. She only pinned me down.

"Tracy!"

Her vacant eyes stared back at me. She got to her feet, pulling me up with her, grappling me so I couldn't break free.

Low, booming barks thundered across the street. Chewie leaped onto Tracy's back and sank his teeth into her neck. The three of us toppled down onto the street in a heap.

I couldn't believe what I'd seen Chewie survive thus far, but I had no time to mull that over. I struggled and kicked at Tracy, wrenching myself free from her hold.

Chewie held Tracy's neck firm in his jaws and shook her violently. She was a rag doll caught in his massive canine maw.

I reached the branch. I had to stake her. She was too strong for me to fight.

Tracy screamed and wailed in pain. She pulled herself up wrapped her arm and a leg around Chewie. She fought to break free.

I kneeled down and pulled on Tracy's shoulder to give me a clean shot at her chest.

"Lisa! Help! Lisa!" she screamed.

"Tracy?"

Her eyes no longer looked glazed over.

"Get him off me! Is that... is that a stake? What the fuck, Lisa?"

I tossed the branch aside and grabbed Chewie's rope.

"Chewie! Chewie, let go!"

I pulled on him. One sharp yank and he let go.

Tracy cradled her mangled arm. There were bites all over from her forearm to her shoulder. Her neck was bleeding.

"Fuck!" Tracy yelled. She sat up.

Chewie, for his part, sniffed at her. Satisfied over whatever he sensed, he sat on his haunches and wagged his tail.

"You attacked me," I said. "You looked possessed."

"Yea. I think your... dog broke the spell."

"Spell?"

"I went to Dylan's. They ambushed me."

"Who?"

"Dylan, Brian, and Walter."

"What? They wouldn't."

"They weren't themselves. They took me back to some house in Somerville."

I frowned a little. I didn't like where this was headed.

"He was one of the guys at their fucking get-together. Some kind of wizard. He used magic to control them. To control me. He sent me here to capture you."

"Me? Why?"

"I don't know. Something about our blood. He needs a lot of it."

"Where is this place?"

"You can't go there. Are you kidding? We should go there together."

"Your arm is mangled. It'll take you at least another night to heal and you'll need to spend most of that time feeding. Besides, I have Chewie."

"What the hell is he? That's not a normal dog."

"Yea... I'm not sure." I looked at Chewie. He tilted his head at me and increased the speed of his wagging.

Tracy got to her feet. "You'll need more than Chewie."

"If this guy is sending us out against our own, we don't have much time. Also, they may be out trying to capture the others, which means the wizard could be alone."

Tracy gave a dubious nod.

"Fine," Tracy said at last. "He's up on Madison street. I don't know the number. Blue house. He had an AC unit hanging out the second-floor window over the front door."

"Thanks. You should probably get off the street."

"Yea, I'm gonna go feed. You sure about this?"

"I don't think we can wait. He's actively hunting us."

"Well... good luck."

I went back to my house to grab my gun before leaving to hail a cab. It was a Remington R51, a small 9mm job. I kept it in a concealed holster at my left front hip. When you aren't as fast or strong as the other things that go bump in the night, keeping a gun isn't a bad idea.

I trekked down the end of Monument Ave and turned left onto High Street, where the traffic was more plentiful.

Chewie was at my side, calm and patient as I held his rope.

I really needed to figure him out one of these nights.

A cab pulled up soon enough, but he took one look at Chewie and shook his head.

"No dogs," he said as he put his car back in gear.

I leaned over the passenger window. "Take me and my dog to Somerville and you'll get your meter plus five hundred dollars cash."

"Get in."

The ride was shorter than it felt. My anxiety was going through the roof. Was I really about so storm some necromancer's house? Was that my plan?

I had to act before things got worse. What if he had gotten Ivan under his spell? Could Chewie protect me from Ivan?

Then again, if he could get Ivan under his spell, couldn't he get me?

My stomach tightened into a knot. What the Hell was I doing?

Chewie pressed his nose against me. Then he sprawled himself on my lap.

"Mind reader," I mumbled.

I stroked Chewie's fur. I'd faced other supernatural stuff before. Other vampires. Even a werewolf once. And besides, Necromancers weren't bulletproof. I hoped.

"Right here," I announced, when I spotted the blue house.

The cab pulled over, I paid my faire plus the five-hundred-dollar tip, and I got out.

The house was two stories. Tall and thin, it probably dated back to the 1920s. A turret-like window bay took up most of the first floor. Three windows were on the second floor. The one above the front door sported an AC unit. A single window at the peak of the house marked the attic.

Quaint.

I stepped up to the front door. Chewie padded alongside me.

This was it. I wasn't going to knock. I was going to break in and find my friends. I was going to end this bullshit.

I'd use my powers. If cops came, I'd have to charming gaze them.

I looked down at my hands. My color had returned, at least in part. Perhaps I didn't need to stave off my abilities for the full month? It didn't matter. I couldn't hold back anymore.

"Ready?" I asked Chewie.

He answered with a single, sonorous woof.

I kicked the Goddamn door in.

The wood around the lock splintered and the door swung free. I'd nearly taken it off its hinges.

The front door opened into the living room. I don't know what I expected when I walked in, but I was not prepared for what I got.

The entire place was decorated with cats.

Porcelain cat figurines adorned shelves. Statues of cats flanked the walls and sat in corners. Pillows with embroidered cats lined the couch. I counted three actual cats in the room. Two on the couch and one curled up in a platform atop a scratching post.

A framed wedding picture was hung on a wall above one of those plug-in fake fireplaces.

But the pièce de résistance was a portrait, a professional photo, sixteen by twenty, of the same man and woman from the wedding picture. Superimposed in the background was the giant disembodied headshot of a cat. It looked like a younger version of the scratching post cat.

What in the fuck had I just walked into?

The Rescue

MUFFLED VOICES PULLED ME out of the bewilderment I felt regarding the cat décor that furnished the necromancer's living room.

I pulled my Remington from its holster at my hip. Chewie's ears pricked up.

I followed the voices. I moved from the living room into the kitchen. There wasn't any cat décor to speak of. Though, the appliances looked like they hadn't been updated since the 1980s. The olive-green refrigerator and dishwasher were the flagships of the kitchen's outdated look.

I rounded on the door to my right. Whispers.

Chewie padded silently beside me.

I threw the door open and pointed my gun through the entrance. Stairs led down.

The voices went silent, but it was far from quiet. Feet shuffled. Someone was breathing.

They knew I was there.

I waited.

No one came to face me. No one attacked.

I descended the stairs. Chewie remained steadfast at my side.

There they were. Brian, Dylan, and Walter stood in front of a fourth man. He was the same man in the wedding picture and cat portrait I saw upstairs, but he was older. Gray had claimed his temples and spotted his beard.

Two tables were behind them. Each had a body on top. Each body was connected to an IV. There was a small refrigerator against the back wall next to a washing machine and dryer. On the left wall were cabinets and a bookcase.

I turned my attention back to the missing members of my bleed. All of them had that same milky-eyed vacant expression Tracy had.

Their faces were gaunt and held a pale to them betraying the absence of sufficient blood. Brian's pale had washed out his freckles. His red hair had sprouted tinges of white. Daryl's carefully styled hair was unkempt. His clothes were a mess. I wondered if seeing his reflection in a mirror would snap him out of his haze. Walter's brown skin looked pallid and sunken. I barely recognized him.

"It's over," I said.

I wished I had rehearsed something cooler to say.

"I can't believe you actually came here willingly." The man smiled. He waved his hands around and spoke words in Latin. I couldn't make out what he was saying. I never did get the hang of Latin.

I tried to get a clear shot on him, but Walter blocked my path. He and the others just stood there like a barricade between me and the necromancer.

I stepped to my right.

The man's voice rose as he spoke. I felt a tightness in my chest. My heart stopped. Pain wracked through me and my knees buckled.

Chewie bumped against my hip and knocked me upright again.

He shouted, "Sanguis! Sanguis! Sanguis!"

My chest was on fire. Chewie bumped into me again.

"Come to me," the necromancer said.

The pain subsided. My heart beat in my chest. My hands were no longer pale.

"No," I said.

He looked at me, perplexed. "How did you...?"

"I've always been pretty light on the *dead* side, as far as undead go," I chided.

He scoffed. "Kill her!"

The boys charged me.

Chewie moved in front of Brian. Unlike with Tracy, he didn't attack straight away. He made himself a barrier between me and his master.

Brian kicked his faithful mastiff, sending him sprawling into the staircase behind me. Chewie crashed into the wooden steps and let out a yelp.

I fired my gun. I shot Dylan, swerved to Walter, and shot Walter. Perfect shots to the chest.

It didn't do a damn thing.

Chewie slammed into Brian and knocked him off his feet. He growled and snapped at his arms as Brian tried to fend him off.

I couldn't get off another shot before Walter and Dylan were on me. They knocked me down. They each sank their fangs into me.

I struggled. I wasn't strong enough to break free, but I made it hard for them to keep a good bite on me.

Dylan extracted himself and took to punching me instead. He pounded his fists into my abdomen as Walter kept trying to gain purchase on my neck.

Dylan's fists were sledgehammers. Pain tore through me. My insides screamed. Bones broke.

Brian went sailing through the air and slammed into the bookcase.

Chewie.

I brought my pistol up, but Walter pinned my arm down.

Walter slid off me. Chewie had him by the pantleg and pulled him backwards. He released my arm as he turned his attention toward the massive dog at his foot.

I brought the pistol up and shot Dylan. One clean headshot.

He crumpled on top of me. That would keep him out for a bit.

I pushed Dylan off me and got to my feet.

The necromancer was chanting again. My heart seized, and I dropped to one knee.

"Why can't I control you?" he shouted.

I had a few theories, but if the return of my life's color was any indication, I supposed staving off my curse left this asshole with no means to use it against me. I'd have to rub in Tracy's face later. If I ever got out of this.

I got to my feet and leveled my pistol at him.

Brian came at me from the left. I swerved the gun at him, but then...

An idea.

I swerved back to the necromancer and shot him in the leg. He went down and wailed in pain.

Brian crashed into me.

Walter was on top of Chewie. He pounded into Chewie as the poor dog let out painful cries with every blow.

The scent of blood filled the air.

My mind wandered to it. My damn curse. Here I was about to be beaten to death, and the smell of blood roused me to feed, despite it all.

Brian looked away from me. He looked at the necromancer.

Walter halted his assault on Chewie and looked at the necromancer.

To my left, Dylan stirred.

Brian and Walter left their targets and moved toward the man I had just shot.

"No! Stay back! Stay back!" he cried.

I got to my feet and went to Chewie. He was bleeding and whimpered in my arms.

"Wait..." It was Dylan. He got to his feet. Walter and Brian looked back at him, bewildered, but no longer glassy-eyed.

"He's mine," Dylan said.

"Who is this guy?" demanded Walter. "He was at your party."

"He was one of my thralls. Him and his wife but..." Dylan frowned.

"My wife is dead!" the necromancer spat. He clutched his bleeding leg. "When she became sick, I came to you. You did nothing! So, I took matters into my own hands. I was given a book. I taught myself the craft."

Given a book?

"Mark?" Brian looked at the man on one of the tables. "Mark's dead! He took all the blood from him!"

"I was still refining my technique! You were going to bring my wife back. You fucking monsters! I loved her, and after years of serving you as your blood bags, you didn't do a damn thing for her."

For Dylan's part, the man's soul-bearing fell on deaf ears. "Lisa, did you shoot me in the head?" He rubbed at it, then inspected the blood on his fingers.

I frowned at him. "Yes. You're welcome."

Dylan turned back to the necromancer. "Frank, you done fucked up."

"You have to understand! I was trying to save my wife! I would have released you once—"

"Enough talk." Walter leaped on Frank and sank his fangs into him. Frank screamed.

"Wait!" I shouted. But it was too late. I wanted to know who gave Frank the book.

"Ah, well." Dylan shrugged.

Brian was over at the other table. He'd pulled back the sheet on the second body. "This must be his wife. Jesus, she looks two months dead."

"Yea, that's Jane," said Dylan. There wasn't a hint of emotion in his voice.

Brian looked shaken over it. Compassion. There was still hope for him.

Walter gorged himself, and Frank's wails went silent.

"I'm calling in the redcaps," said Dylan.

We sat in the living room while we waited for the redcaps to arrive. Brian reached out to Chewie from a distance, but he stayed at my side and growled at him.

Dylan poked at the porcelain cat figurines. "I'd never been here before. If I had known Frank and Jane were this weird, I never would have invited them."

"I think we owe Lisa our thinks," said Walter. After feeding from Frank, his color had returned. Though paled from his curse, he looked like himself again.

Dylan turned to me. "You're right. Thanks, Lisa. But why didn't you get captured?"

"The spell didn't work on me. I guess it helps being not as dead as you lot," I grinned.

"You see? You see what she does? Cheeky. And here I was thanking her," Dylan pleaded to Walter.

"Chewie, come on boy. It wasn't me. I wasn't in control," said Brian.

It didn't stop Chewie's low growls at him. For his part, Chewie was doing a little better after the pounding he took from Walter. He sat curled at my feet like nothing happened. Except that he was decidedly pissed off at Brian.

"Give him time," I said.

"Maybe you should hold on to him until... or if he comes around," said Brian.

"Sure."

"And thanks. For coming after us." Brian gave me a wan smile.

"What are friends for?"

Walter peaked out the window. "Van's here. I'll show the redcaps where to go. They'll eat everyone and everything, right? Even the IVs?"

"Everything," Dylan assured. "Well, no. They won't eat Mark. We'll have to leave him in front of a window or something. Let the sun do its work."

"That could set the house on fire," I said.

Dylan shrugged. "It's gotta be done."

"Nobody says it has to be done like that. Have the redcaps drag his body out and dump it in a sand pit. It'll be gone by morning."

"That'll cost more."

"I don't care. Just do it."

"You're very free with my money, Lisa."

Dylan was dancing on my last nerve. "I won't risk a neighborhood fire over this. People could lose their homes. Don't push me tonight. I'm not in the mood."

"Okay, okay." He laughed and put his hands up.

"Don't fuck with her, man." Walter grinned.

Dylan put on his best smile and affected a posture of surrender.

I ignored him and turned to Brian. "Hey... I've been wondering. What is Chewie anyway? He's more than mastiff."

"Oh. Yea," said Brian. "You don't know?"

I shrugged.

"He's part mastiff. Half, I think. But he's also part barghest."

"Barghest? As in the fae dog?" My jaw went slack. I knew we vampires had ties to the fae, but a barghest was a new one for me.

"Yep. He was my creator's. He left him to me. His name used to be some old Irish word I could never pronounce. It meant hunter. I named him Chewie. I think he's.... around seventy?"

"Years old?" I asked the obvious, mostly because I was so incredulous.

He laughed. "Yea. Smart as hell. Loyal." He shook his head and frowned. "I fucked it up."

"He'll come around."

"No, he won't. Lisa, barghests... they aren't pets. They choose you. I never would have been able to take Chewie from my creator if he didn't want me. He chose me. My creator and I really didn't have a say. I think... he's with you now."

I needed moment to digest that. Chewie no longer growled at Brian, but he hadn't left my side, either.

"Chewie?" I felt like I had to ask him if all this was true.

A single woof was my only reply.

Episode 10

The Deadly Rumor

Everything changed after that night with the necromancer.

The biggest shift in my life was that I had a half-barghest, half-Neapolitan mastiff living in my home. The huge fae-dog and I had become thick as thieves. I tried to spend as much time with him as I could, which was tough considering how long I was awake each night. So, I made some changes.

The first thing I did was hire a dog walker who would come into my house, feed, and walk Chewie. Amy had no idea that I was sleeping in a secure chamber in my basement all the while. She thought I was at work.

I also got a car. I never really wanted to own a car in the city. With nearly a hundred years of driving under my belt, I still hated to parallel park. But with Chewie, it was a necessity. A big dog like him needed room to run and explore. The city wasn't very accommodating for that.

It was a Friday night and about a week after my run-in with the necromancer. Chewie and I piled into my new Toyota Camry and hit the road. We took route 16 out of Cambridge and onto route 2 heading west. Our destination was about a half hour away. Walden Woods.

We meandered on to Sandy Pond Road, which cuts right through much of the preserved area of the woods where miles of forest were still untouched.

Once we pulled over, Chewie waited patiently as I undressed. It's always a pain the in ass to shapeshift when I still have clothes on. I folded my clothes neatly and stacked them in the front passenger side seat. Oncoming headlights forced me to slam the door and crouch behind the car until they passed. I really didn't want to be caught out there naked. I would have had to use my charming gaze and it would be a whole thing.

Bathed in darkness again, I smiled at Chewie. "Ready for our run?" I asked.

He gave a deep woof in response, sending his jowls swaying.

I let the shift take me, dropping down to my hands but keeping my feet flat on the ground. It was only a moment in that awkward position as my limbs evened out. Fur sprouted from my body. My face elongated into a snout. Triangular canine ears took the place of fleshy human lobes. Claws. Teeth. A tail.

Even in my grey wolf form, Chewie dwarfed me. He butted his head into mine, and we nuzzled a moment. His long tail whipped back and forth. He was always excited when I took my wolf form. It meant it was time to play. Time to run.

My sense of smell captured what I couldn't see. A rabbit. Damp earth from a nearby stream. And the scent of a thousand pines.

I ran. Chewie kept up beside me with no effort. So, I poured on the speed. With my power, I can run faster than any normal wolf or dog, but Chewie kept up just fine.

Chewie caught the scent of the rabbit as well and tore off in its direction. The small creature darted out from under its thicket, and Chewie gave chase. Being part barghest, Chewie was a bit more primal than your average domesticated dog. When he could, he would hunt for his own food.

I chased after him. The rabbit was nowhere near fast enough.

The little animal zig-zagged to try and throw Chewie off, but the huge dog matched him beat for beat. Unable to outpace Chewie, the rabbit soon found himself within his jaws.

I padded over to Chewie, but I really didn't want to see him eating. I don't care how old I get or how much darkness I've seen in my life. I never really could get used to watching animals get eaten. I can't even watch the Discovery Channel.

Chewie nosed some bits toward me. It was kind of him to share, but I let out a chuff indicating I wasn't interested. Being what I am, I can't process solid food, and animal blood does nothing to satiate my curse. It has to be human blood.

So, instead, I curled up next to him while he ate. I ignored the carnage and treated it like cozying up to a dear friend. I never knew I needed Chewie in my life until he entered it. I feel like he rescued me and not the other way around. I felt like I was living again.

I put my clothes back on after a good hour or so of running and sniffing everything in the forest we could get to. Chewie had marked everything he laid his snout on. I could have stayed in the forest all night, but I still needed to dedicate part of the evening to feed.

I checked my phone and saw that I missed a call from Neil. No voicemail, though.

We got in the car and drove off before I rang him back. The magic of Bluetooth.

"Hello?"

"Hey, you." I kept my flirty voice on when I talked to Neil these days. I was still priming him to be my thrall. On one hand, I hated bringing anyone into my life for that purpose, but more thralls equaled less hunting and I'd been playing it fast and loose for too long. Besides, less hunting meant more time with Chewie and doing the things *I* wanted to do.

Still, I really liked Neil and leading him on like this made my stomach roll. I needed people like Neil in my life to keep me from becoming a monster hunting the streets, and I'd been without a thrall for nearly three years.

"Lisa, hey. I was just calling to see what you were up to."

"Not much. Out with Chewie."

Chewie's big, floppy ears pricked up at the sound of his own name.

"You free tomorrow night?" asked Neil.

"I should be. What did you have in mind?"

The last time I hunted was two nights ago. I really needed to hunt tonight. I especially needed to if I was going out tomorrow night. I always try not to let myself get too hungry.

"Thinking about playing some pool."

I sucked at pool, but I loved to play. "Sounds like fun."

"There's a decent hall in Allston. Halfway between us. Want to meet me there, say eight o'clock?" Neil offered.

Eight was still light out this time of year. "Can we do nine? My shift."

Neil was still under the impression I worked random hours as a nurse.

"Nine? Yea, sure," he agreed.

I could hear the smile in his voice.

"Cool. See you then." I hung up before he could keep the banter going. Better that way.

Chewie gave a deep, sonorous woof from the back seat.

"Yea. I like him too."

About forty minutes later, I pulled up to my brownstone and parked. I gritted my teeth the entire time, pulling the car back and forth to align with the damn curb. I got it on the seventh try. I really did hate parallel parking.

I woke up the next night feeling refreshed and satiated. After I dropped Chewie off at the house, I did a quick hunt. I used the old *hail a cab, charm the cabbie* routine. The trick was to find a lecherous enough cabbie so I didn't have to push too hard with my gaze. I found one on the third attempt.

After what happened last time with my charming gaze, I'd become extra cautious with how much I push my charms.

I made my way upstairs and greeted Chewie. Amy had left me her typical note.

"Chewie fed and went potty. He's such a big love. – Amy"

I went to the bathroom to get washed up. Tonight, was my date with Neil.

My phone rang as I was getting out of the shower. I wondered if it was Neil. I hoped he wasn't cancelling. This whole thrall thing aside, I really wanted to see him.

That only made the *thrall thing* harder.

I checked the caller ID before picking up. Unknown number.

"Hello?"

"Siobhan."

Only two people in the world still called me by my given name. Ivan, and…

"William." My tone was dour. I couldn't believe the bastard had the gall to call me.

My creator and I were not on speaking terms, at least from my position. And not for his lack of trying. But I had nothing to say to him.

"You continue to surprise me, my dear. Just when I thought you could never forgive me."

"What the hell are you talking about?"

Chewie gave a low growl at the phone. His hackles raised up. I put a hand on top of his head to ease him. It tempered him, but he kept his eyes locked on my phone.

"With your friend, Mark, dead, Cambridge is free territory. Prime hunting ground. Such a delicate balance, New England. I'm told you had a small part in Mark's death. It makes sense for you to expand from Charlestown into Cambridge."

Mark had died at the hands of a necromancer. Since his death, Ivan had talked about the open territory in Cambridge. Of course, I wanted it. But it also neighbored Brian and Walter's territories. Then there was Dylan, who controlled Brookline, across the river. He said it would be *cool to hunt college girls at Harvard*. Ugh.

I had nothing to do with Mark's death, and I wasn't in the mood for William's vague sentiments. "I'm hanging up now."

"You should have come to me directly, Siobhan. Though, I can't blame you for wanting to cover your tracks. Still, after all these years, I never thought you would be keen on delivering Connecticut to me."

"Wait, *what*?"

I don't know where William was getting his information, but his accusation made my blood run cold.

"Siobhan, please—"

He started again with that condescending tone. I hung up.

Even a rumor about treason or conspiracy can quickly turn deadly within any bleed. We vampires didn't exactly have an *innocent until proven guilty* society. Our judicial system was a bit more... Spanish Inquisition.

I needed to get in front of whatever bullshit William was talking about. A stone brick of dread settled into my stomach just thinking about it. I needed to call Ivan.

Episode 11

The Vanishing Dog

"You will need to lay low for a while."

Ivan's advice only made me feel worse. I was grateful that he was on my side after I told him about William's call and the inane rumor about how I was giving Connecticut to the New York bleed, but hearing Ivan say *lay low* instead of something like *don't worry* or *I'll handle it*, made me feel sick to my stomach.

Did I really need to worry about being hunted? Brought up on some charges?

Ivan may have been the Lord of the New England bleed, but he wasn't the only elder among us. The other elders would also weigh in. Richard, for example, was always a rival of William's, and now that rivalry had passed on to me.

Kenneth, who had the whole of Connecticut as his territory, would surely have an opinion on this situation. Not to mention Clive in Rhode Island and Theresa in Vermont. I wasn't too much worried about Seamus. He was pretty old, but he lived way up in Maine and was more interested in living among the wild than politics.

"You think I should leave town?" I asked.

"I think you should leave Massachusetts. At least until we can get a handle on things," Ivan replied.

"This is ridiculous, you know I'd never—"

"Siobhan, you have rivals. The truth does not matter to them. They'll use this to put you on trial. And our trials aren't designed to discover the truth. You know this."

I gritted my teeth. Ivan was right, of course. Our trials were about as just as the Salem witch trials.

"You think Richard is behind this?" I asked.

"I don't know. Let me do my own digging. In the meantime, go find a place to hunker down until we can straighten this out. I can tell you this – if it is Richard, he will pay dearly."

"Thanks, Ivan." With that, I rang off.

Chewie bumped his head into my thigh. I absently reached down and scratched him. He could always sense my distress.

I needed to pack a few things and blow out of town. My mind went to Neil.

Shit.

We had a date planned tonight. If anyone came looking for me, I couldn't risk Neil getting pulled into things.

I got to packing. I had no idea how many nights I'd be away, and I wanted to travel as light as possible. I also had Chewie to consider. He needed to be fed and watered during the day, and I couldn't exactly invite Amy on this trip to my safehouse. Which reminded me I also needed to call Amy and put her services on hold for a while.

This whole mess was a clusterfuck.

I packed in record time. A few changes of clothes, toiletries, and yes – my 9mm Remington.

All things considered; I was as ready to go out on the lam as I was going to be. I planned to call Neil and Amy from the car.

Doorbell chimes pulled me out of my brainstorming.

Chewie's ears perked up, and he tilted his head at me. I returned his perplexed look.

I opened the door and found Neil standing there. A small bouquet of flowers was in his hands. Tulips, daisies, and carnations.

"Neil?"

I was supposed to meet him at the pool hall in Allston. Actually, I was supposed to cancel our date via phone on the way to my safehouse.

He smiled, showing off his dimples. "Hi. I hope you don't mind, but I wanted this to be a proper date. Me picking you up and all that."

I smiled despite it all. I really liked this guy. But this complicated the hell out of my plans.

"But we agreed on Allston because it was half-way. We could have picked some place closer to you or me if you were going to pick me up," I said.

"I know, but the more I thought about it, the more I wanted to come down and surprise you."

"Oh…" I put on a smile. "You shouldn't have. Really."

"I don't mind. Oh! And I brought you these." He thrust the flowers toward me.

Sure, I'll just dig out a vase for them in my copious free time.

"Thank you… come in." I didn't know how to handle this curve ball, but I knew I didn't want to stand there with my door open.

I found a vase in the living room. It was a decoration, but it would work in a pinch. I took the flowers into the kitchen and got them set up. I wasn't looking forward to breaking off our date. Neil had driven all the way from Watertown.

I set the vase back on its pedestal.

"Listen, Neil…"

Chewie let out a low growl. He was facing Neil but somehow didn't seem entirely focused on him. Something other than Neil had his hackles up.

"I thought he liked me," said Neil.

"He does. This isn't you."

"It sure feels like it's me."

"No... he senses something. Maybe outside?"

Shit. My stomach tightened at the thought Richard or maybe some of his goons were outside looking to question me or worse – take me in.

Neil stepped out of Chewie's angry gaze. The fact that Chewie didn't follow Neil seemed to alleviate his worries.

Neil looked at me. "Are you okay, you look worried."

I had to get rid of Neil. The last thing I needed was for him to see any supernatural juju.

"Listen, Neil, I meant to call you—"

Chewie disappeared in a cloud of black smoke. The thick fog hung in the air where he stood for a few moments before it dissipated.

"What... the... fuck was that? What happened to Chewie?!" Neil's distress was palpable.

His reaction only fed my own shock. Chewie had just vanished into black mist, and I had no idea how or if he was okay. Panic tightened my chest.

I froze, watching the last of the black smoke waft away.

"What the hell happened?" Neil's voice was almost shrill.

"I-I don't know," I confessed. I suddenly became very aware that a very mortal guest in my house had just witnessed something very supernatural.

I didn't have time for any of it. I could call Brian and ask him about Chewie. Maybe this was some barghest thing. I focused on Neil. I needed to settle him down before I could leave and head to my safe house. I couldn't afford him babbling about vanishing Neapolitan mastiffs.

And in Neil's panicked state, using my charming gaze would have been a heavy lift, and I didn't care to push on my curse enough to force it on him.

I turned to him and spoke gently. "Neil... listen to me. Chewie is very special. And right now, it isn't safe to be in this house. We need to leave. Now."

"How? What the F—." He could only blink at the place where Chewie once stood.

"Neil."

He looked at me. His eyes were like saucers.

"We need to leave. It isn't safe here. You just saw something, and I can't explain it here. We need to go."

"Is Chewie okay? Is he... dead? Is that why he was able to live with no food for two weeks? Is he a ghost?" Neil fired off questions too quick for me to answer.

"He's fine," I lied. "He's just a... vanishing dog. I'll explain everything. But we need to go."

I couldn't believe *vanishing dog* was the best I could come up with on the spot. But I couldn't leave Neil alone with what he saw, and I needed to get out of Massachusetts.

Maybe I could have him drive me to his house and I could fly to my safehouse from there. Explain whatever bullshit reason for Chewie's smokeshow as best I could.

Yea. Great plan.

Neil's face was screwed up in consternation.

"Neil. Take me out. Just like we planned. I'll explain on the way."

"Yea... yea.... did he really....?"

"He's fine. We need to go."

Any reservations I had about making Neil my thrall went out the window in those moments. He was in it now. And it would be dangerous for him to just cut him loose with what he witnessed. But I wasn't ready to bring him all the way into that life.

Not yet.

Poor Neil

NEIL GRIPPED THE STEERING wheel. His knuckles were white. "Okay. Explain it again."

Telling Neil that Chewie was a vanishing dog was not my greatest improvisational cover for the weird supernatural crap that permeates my life, but that's what I blurted out, so that's what I stuck with.

"Chewie is... he's magic." I felt like I was digging myself deeper. I kept telling myself at least I wasn't revealing there are vampires in the world.

"Magic." Neil repeated.

Neil had reluctantly agreed to drive us out of Charlestown and stick to our original plans to play pool in Allston.

"You see the thing is—," I began.

"Wait... is that why Chewie survived for two weeks without food? He's... magic?"

"Well, yes."

"Are you a witch?"

Am I a what?

I felt my mouth fall open. I was flabbergasted. But the longer the silence drew out, the more Neil's anxiety became palpable. I could almost feel it. Like a thick fog of panic settling between us.

"Yes," I said.

Great, Lisa. Just keep digging.

"Okay, so let's say I believe all this. I mean, I *did* just see your dog disappear. What's going on? Why were you in such a rush to leave your house? Wait, is Brian a witch too?"

Brian was Neil's neighbor and Chewie had originally lived with him.

"No, no... Brian had no clue," I lied.

Neil looked at me, taking his eyes off the road for a split second. I hadn't answered all his questions.

"There is a rival... coven. And I've been accused of conspiring with them against my coven."

"So, what's that mean?"

"It means I'm in trouble until we can get this sorted out."

"This is nuts." Neil shook his head. "He disappeared. He just vanished in smoke. I saw it."

I put a hand on his arm. I felt awful. Mortals aren't meant to see the strange and terrifying things of the supernatural world. He tightened at my touch and it only made me feel worse.

"I'm sorry."

He didn't answer. That thick silence fell between us again.

"So now what?" His question broke the quiet.

"I don't know," I said softly.

"We go play pool and I take you back to your house? Are there really people after you?"

I bobbed my head a few times. "Yes."

"I don't even know what to say to this. Witches? Am I crazy? I saw him disappear."

"Listen, maybe under the circumstances, you should take me someplace else."

"Like where?"

"I have a place in New Hampshire. You could drop me there and head home and..." I was going to say reschedule, but I wasn't sure Neil wanted any part of seeing me again after everything that happened.

"Where in New Hampshire?" He answered at last.

"Londonderry." I winced as I said it. Londonderry was an hour each way.

"Okay, but if you're in trouble, I can't just drop you off and leave."

"I'll be fine. I can call you tomorrow."

"You'll be up there with no car. Do you even have groceries up there?"

"I have some stuff, nothing in the way of perishables, but I have food stores," I lied, "I'll run out and get some things. I just need to lay low for a while."

I hated lying to him, but with everything going on, it was too dangerous for Neil to be around me.

He let out a long sigh. "Alright. Fine."

It took the better part of an hour to get to Londonderry. I tried to serve up small talk or any sort of conversation to take Neil's mind off everything he'd just been dealt.

I may have been planning to make him my thrall, but this was not how I wanted to introduce Neil into my world. I debated coming clean with him, but that would mean making him my thrall then and there. I couldn't do it. Not with all the crap I had going on.

Pangs of guilt stabbed into my stomach. At some point, I needed to wrestle with the realization that I really liked Neil. Perhaps more than I should. But I couldn't afford to explore that until I got my situation within the bleed sorted out.

We pulled into the driveway. I hadn't been to my safehouse in months, but it looked no worse for wear.

"I don't like this," said Neil.

"Nobody knows I'm here. I'll be fine."

"I don't mean that. I mean... I don't feel right leaving you. If you're really in trouble. If people are trying to hurt you. Can't you call the cops?"

"No. It's too complicated. I can't call the cops on my own coven." I almost forgot to say *coven*.

Neil kept his grip on the steering wheel. He stared at the house as if it were a powder keg ready to blow.

"Neil." I put a hand over his.

He breathed in a little and looked at me. I gave his hand a squeeze.

"I'm fine," I said.

He got out of the car.

"What are you—" I got out of the car.

He came around to my side, but he didn't say anything. He just stared at me.

"What?"

"I'm sorry," he said.

"What are *you* apologizing for?"

"You have people after you. When I came to your house you were literally trying to run away. Then the Chewie thing happened, and I freaked and you've spent this whole drive trying to calm me down when I should've been there for you."

"Neil..."

"No, I mean it. Tonight was fucked up. And I still need to get my head around this, but I haven't been a good friend... or... friend."

"Friend or friend?" I smirked.

"Yea... " He rubbed the back of his neck. "I mean, this was supposed to be like a date? Maybe? It's... that's not what I'm trying to say. What I'm saying is that I'm sorry I haven't been here for you tonight when you're going through this," he stammered.

He was cute, all flustered. He could barely make eye contact with me.

I kissed his cheek. "Neil. You've been great."

He got that trademark goofy grin on again. "Well… still… " Then he looked at the house again. "You sure you'll be okay?"

"You want to come in? Come on. I'll show you around."

I figured maybe I could ease his mind a little when he saw how secure my house was. Sure enough, when we crossed the front lawn, the motion sensor triggered the porch light.

"See? Motion lights."

I unlocked the front door, and we stepped inside. I turned to a control panel on the wall and shut off the nagging beeps by entering in my security code.

"Alarm system." I smiled. "If anyone busts in, breaks a window, or whatever, a call goes out to the police."

I had other boobytraps in place for the more supernatural concerns in my life, but I didn't need to show him those.

Neil looked around my living room as if waiting for some ninja to jump out from behind the sofa. My Londonderry house was furnished much different than my place in Charlestown. Rough chiseled wood gave a rustic and hand-made look to all my furniture. Irish tchotchkes and baubles hung from the walls. It was as close as I could come to the sort of simple design I grew up with in Boston when I was a girl. This was my safe house. And the old nostalgia lent itself to help me feel secure.

"Let me at least run out and get you some groceries. Can't have you living off canned goods while you're here. You can give me a list."

I wanted to tell him it was dangerous for him to be around me. But in that moment, the name of the game was assuring him that I was safe so he would leave. If I tried to rush him out the door, he'd get suspicious.

My phone rang. Saved by the bell.

Another unlisted number. It had *burner phone* written all over it. I hoped it wasn't William.

"Hello?"

"Lisa?" He sounded exasperated.

"Jacques?" A cocktail of relief and confusion spread through me at the sound of his voice.

"Oh, thank God. Are you okay? I heard the awful rumor. It's terrible!"

"You heard... what?"

"Ivan gathered Richard, Tracy, and I, and he told us some nonsense about you and William plotting together."

I was guarded. Jacques always liked me, but I learned a long time ago to watch your back when there was a target on it.

"Well, I'm certainly not working with William on anything," I said.

"Of course not. But Ivan says it isn't safe for you. Are you home?"

"Jacques, I really don't want to discuss my whereabouts over the phone."

"Ooh, yes. Good thinking," he replied.

"So how did everyone take the rumor?"

"Oh, you know. Ivan said it was *rubbish*, Tracy agreed, and Richard thought it would be helpful to explore the possibility."

"Typical Richard." My tone was laced with arsenic.

"*And* Ivan mentioned some heinous notion about you plotting with that necromancer to kill Mark."

"Oh, that came up too? Jesus."

"More insanity if you ask me! Everyone you rescued said so. Though, it's quite a tragic story. All he wanted was to resurrect his wife. Macabre business."

Neil was looking at me with concern. I needed to get off the phone, calm him down, and send him on his way.

Before I could extricate myself from the call, Jacques followed up. "Did you know the poor devil asked Dylan for help while his wife was sick? Dylan can be so heartless. Then he went to Richard to beg him for help."

That got my attention. I moved away from Neil and into the kitchen. "Hold on. Richard knew the necromancer's wife was dying?"

"That's what he said tonight."

"Someone that desperate may not have stopped at Richard. I wonder if he somehow got connected with William."

"What do you mean?"

"This rumor about me working with William and me engineering Mark's death came along at the same time. They've got to be connected. If it's not William, it's someone else in common."

"Like who?"

"I don't know. But I remember the necromancer saying something about how he was given the spell book he used. I thought that was unusual. People don't just hand out stuff like that lightly."

This wasn't just a couple of unfortunate rumors. I was being set up.

"Jacques, I really need to go. I'm safe, but I need to deal with this."

"Okay, Lisa. But call me at this number if you need anything. And stay safe."

"Will do." I hung up.

I walked back into the living room. Neil was looking at me with his eyebrows raised.

"Yes," I said to him.

"What?"

"Your idea. If you were serious. To get groceries. It would be a huge help. I need to lay low here."

"This is real isn't it? You're in danger."

"That's why I'm here."

"I don't want to leave you."

"I'll be fine. Go for groceries and come back. I'll be right here."

It took a little more convincing, but I ultimately used Neil's argument against him. There were no groceries in the house, and I shouldn't leave to go shopping on my own.

I finally got Neil out the door. That bought me some time alone, but my next big problem would be finding a way to ditch him before sunrise.

Neil was right, though. I was in danger. I needed my Remington R51.

I also needed my car.

What a mess.

My stomach constricted when I realized what I had to do.

I had to go home.

Episode 13

The Intruder

I LEFT A NOTE for Neil before I left. It explained that I grabbed a cab to run home to pick up some things, and I didn't think it was safe for him to come with me.

He wasn't going to be happy, but I left my house so quickly that I left behind a lot of stuff I needed. Including my car.

The next thing I did was call Amy, Chewie's dog-sitter. It was a quick conversation, but I asked her to hold off on her daily visits for a while. I told her I was taking a vacation.

That business managed, I went into the bedroom. I stripped down, folded my clothes, and put them away.

I melted down into my bat form, everything got huge. Leisler's bats may be the largest species of bat in Ireland, but they can fit in the palm of a hand.

It's bullshit what people say about a bat's eyesight. I could see just fine in my bat form. My sense of smell and hearing? Off the charts. Even as a vampire.

My tollán was in the kitchen behind a backsplash tile on the wall. I fluttered through the house and landed on the counter. Like all bats, my wings had small digits that could grasp onto things. I gingerly pulled off the tile and placed it on the counter. Even if Neil found it and popped it back in, I could knock it out from the other side.

There is a bit of a maze within the wall of my house in Londonderry. Lots of false turns and traps. Many of the dead ends triggered UV lightbulbs.

Even knowing my way through the vertical labyrinth took me time to navigate. Some of the spring traps I had installed were quite sensitive.

The tollán spilled out into a plastic flap on the side of my dryer vent. I bumped my head into it, and it swung open. From there, I hopped into the vent and flew outside.

I fly much faster than a mortal bat and the forty or so miles to Charlestown took me just over a half hour. I love flying. The wind and sky beneath my wings is so liberating. And sonar! I love the tingles of sound vibrating through my ears as I navigate around other flying creatures of the night.

I kind of wish I had sonar in my normal form. But then I'd have to scream at people all the time.

My home in Charlestown had a tollán too. It was accessed through a tiny trap door under the soffit of my roof. From there, I had to climb down to the first floor and pop out through a false section of baseboard.

I grew back to my human form. Tiny wings elongated into arms. Stubby feet sprouted long legs. I was still naked, but that was the deal with shapeshifting.

I half expected Chewie to come bounding at me when I appeared, and my heart sank when he didn't. I stared at the spot in my living room where he had growled at some unseen threat before vanishing.

I hope he's okay.

I went into my bedroom. This wasn't really my bedroom in the sense that I slept there. I changed the comforter and pillows out now and then for the different seasons, but that's about it. I only used the room for its walk-in closet. My actual bedroom was in my basement.

I got dressed. Jeans and a tee. I figured they were practical. I really didn't need to be running around in heels and a skirt while I was on the lam, thank you very much.

The duffle bag I packed for the trip, and subsequently forgot when Neil showed up, still laid on my bed.

A noise caught my attention. Like glass being disturbed on its surface before rocking itself steady and into silence.

Someone was here.

I stepped out of my bedroom, padding quietly on the balls of my feet. I sniffed the air. I listened.

Nothing.

I moved into my living room. There was a white Lennox vase on top of a pedestal that seemed to be the culprit of the noise. It still bore the flowers that Neil brought me. I looked around it. I stooped down and looked under the couch.

"Chewie?"

There was only silence.

A new scent caught my attention. Blood.

I turned to see a couple of drops of blood on the floor leading to my kitchen. I was pretty sure those weren't there before.

I stooped over and dipped my finger into one of the drops. I tasted it. It had the unmistakable tinge of fae. Like citrus.

"Chewie?" I whispered.

Nothing.

A sinking feeling gripped my chest. I slowly made my way back to my bedroom, with frequent looks over my shoulder.

I had my Remington packed in my duffle. But when I started searching for it, it occurred to me that I didn't need my neighbors reporting they heard a gunshot. I needed something quiet.

I went back into my walk-in closet. That's where I kept my shillelagh.

The old wooden stick belonged to my father. He'd made it and brined it himself back in Ireland. It had seen its share of scraps in both my father's hands and in mine. It was a sturdy weapon and, combined with my strength, was deadly in my hands.

I held it aloft, not unlike a sword. The shillelagh was more of a fencing weapon, after all.

I moved from my bedroom and went room to room. I couldn't hear anything, but the smell of blood had become more potent. I followed the scent.

There, in my kitchen, bloodied and torn, was a redcap. He was alone.

"You feckin' bitch," he breathed.

"Who sent you? Richard?" I pointed my shillelagh at him.

He ignored my question. "You feckin' bitch."

"Where's the rest of your *drong*?" I looked around, expecting more redcaps to leap out at me.

"Dead! As if ye don't know!" He drew a knife from his belt. "And I'll kill ye! I'll kill ye!"

The little fae charged me as best he could. He limped on his one side. His leg was as bloody as his cap.

I worried more about his bite than his knife. Redcaps can bite through bone.

I stepped back and jabbed him in the chest with my shillelagh.

He spun and ducked and came at me again, slashing wildly with his knife. I moved out of the way with little trouble. He was fast, but not faster than me. And, without the support of his drong, I couldn't be surrounded.

"You can't win this, redcap. Tell me who sent you."

He bellowed and charged me again. The wounds on his leg produced more blood the harder he exerted himself. The smell was intoxicating. Mortal blood smells like copper, but it sets off that dark urge within me, nonetheless. Fae blood? Fae blood was fragrant on top of every urge I had to feed. It smelled delicious.

I was beginning to care less about who sent him and more about what he tasted like.

The distraction almost got me sliced by another wicked slash from his blade. "They were me brothers!" he cried.

I wrapped him across the face with the stick's ferrule.

His bloodlust was unabated. He kept coming at me, swinging wildly. I had to end it.

I stepped back and parried, my free hand on my hip. Father would have been proud of my form. I tossed the shillelagh up within my hand and caught it by the ferrule. Then I swung the butt end like a club and walloped the little biter across the skull.

He fell to the floor, and I leaped on him, pinning his dagger hand to the floor with my shillelagh.

The smell of blood only grew stronger.

"Who sent you!"

"I can't tell you for me bond! But even if I could, I wouldn't. May the Morrigan feast your bones, you feckin' devil."

A bond. That meant he'd entered into a contract with the one who sent him. But who?

He struggled against me in vain as the realization hit me that he was no longer of any use to me.

And he smelled delectable.

He cried out when I sunk my fangs into him. Rich, sweet blood ran over my tongue and down my throat.

It's rare to drink from fae. They don't like it, and it pretty much deters them from ever wanting to work with us. But moments like these – when some little shit crosses the line, a vampire can have a taste of the forbidden. There are no laws, vampire or faerie, that can protect a fae who tries to kill a vampire and gets caught.

I could feel his death approach before I'd finished drinking. His heartbeat grew infrequent and weak. It took an effort of will, but I pulled back and let out a breath. I don't feed from dead bodies, fae or otherwise.

Besides, I needed what little blood he had left for something else.

I left the incapacitated fae on my living room floor while I rummaged around through some cabinets, finally settling on my junk drawer in the kitchen. From out of an ensemble of pens, rubber bands, a screwdriver, and unorganized papers, I dug out a plastic test tube.

It was messy, but I squeezed the fae's blood into the tube and topped it off. I resisted the urge to down the contents for myself.

I looked at the bright red blood swirling around within the vial.

This would come in handy.

I'd collected my prize just in time too. The little fae had bled out and his body shimmered and faded away, leaving behind only stains of blood on my hardwood floor. I could only presume He'd gone back to Otherworld, the land of the fae.

This was more than just someone framing me. Someone wanted me dead.

But someone was also protecting me. Who killed the rest of that redcap's drong?

Questions flew around in my head as the rush of fae blood whirled inside me. I felt fuzzy, and a little giddy. But I still knew I had to get out of the house.

I grabbed my duffle bag and kept my shillelagh on me when I left.

I threw everything into my car and sped off into the night.

It was shortly after 2am when I arrived back at the house in Londonderry. Neil's car was in the driveway, so I entered the house as quietly as I could.

I found him asleep on the couch. I also noticed some groceries on the kitchen counter.

It was monumentally sweet, but I still needed a way to get rid of him. I'd needed to be in bed before five, and I didn't want to have to explain why I was sleeping in the basement in some light-less saferoom.

Shit, I hope he didn't wander into the basement while I was gone.

He stirred as my mind was concocting ways to give him the slip.

"Lisa?" he sat up and rubbed an eye with the heel of his hand.

"Hey," I plastered on a weak smile.

"Lisa, what the hell? I was worried sick about you! You're being hunted, and you leave some note and don't take your cell phone?

Oh, good. We get to do it the hard way.

Episode 14

Kenneth

"I don't understand," said Neil.

"I'm sorry," I said. "I needed to get some things at home and it's not safe there right now."

"I would have gone to your house with you."

"I know. But I didn't want to put you at risk."

"This is so messed up, Lisa. Did I really see Chewie vanish?"

I couldn't answer. Part of me didn't want to confirm any supernatural crap he witnessed. I just gave him a thin-lipped smile.

"So, listen, tomorrow—"

"Neil," I interrupted. "Thank you. For everything. Driving me up here, getting groceries. And I'm sorry I took off with just a note and worried you."

"I sense a *but* coming."

He was right. Pangs of guilt knotted my stomach. This was the part where I needed to send him on his way.

"But, I think you should spend the night and then leave in the morning."

"Maybe I should just leave now."

"No. It's almost three. You're tired. Spend the night. Take the spare bedroom."

"No, it's okay. I'm gonna head out."

He didn't look angry. He looked crushed.

"Neil..." How could I tell him? Tell him I was jumped by a redcap in my own home, tell him that more redcaps could be coming for me from

Otherworld, or tell him about the plethora of other supernatural threats I was in danger of? And he was in danger as long as he was near me.

The truth was, him leaving would be the best thing for him. I just felt awful.

"I really wanted to play pool with you tonight," I said. I meant it.

"Yea." He answered quickly. Then he strode out the door. And just like that, he was gone.

My heart sank. I wanted to chase after him, but I knew letting him walk out the door was for the best.

My mind went to Chewie. Was it better that he wasn't here? Was he safer wherever he vanished to?

And that made me think of Brian. Chewie wasn't the only thing I wanted to ask him about.

I pulled the burner phone out of my bag and ran him up.

"Hello?"

"Brian. It's me." Even on a burner phone, I don't like saying my name. Call me paranoid, or maybe I watched too many spy movies.

"Lisa?"

Oh, well.

"Yea. I can't talk long."

"Are you okay? Where are you? No, don't tell me."

"Brian, listen. I'm being framed."

"Yea, no shit. I know you'd never cut a deal with that asshole."

I knew Brian had my back, but it was nice to hear it. I could feel my shoulders untighten at his affirmation.

"I need to know if that necromancer, Frank, told you about his wife dying," I said.

"The necromancer? No. I barely knew him. I'd seen him at Dylan's a few times. He was one of his thralls. If he had come to me for help, I probably would have done something."

"Apparently, he asked other vampires for help with his wife, not just Dylan. Richard and maybe others. Have you heard anything about that?" I asked.

"No. But I'll keep my ear to the ground. Why?"

"Because whoever is framing me; whoever is behind these rumors of me working with William and getting Mark killed, is likely the person that dealt with Frank."

"Jesus," said Brian.

"One more thing. Chewie... vanished."

"Vanished?" His surprise showed in the higher pitch of his voice.

"Yea. He growled at something. And then... poof. He just disappeared."

"My creator said something about it, but I've never seen him do it. Chewie used to belong to my creator, Angus. Well, not *belong*, but..."

"Sorry, I need to know if he's okay and what's going on with him." I was surprised at my impatience, but I didn't want to be kept on the phone longer than I had to. Ivan once pulled phone records on me, who knows who else had access to our records?

"Right, yea, so you know how Chewie is part barghest? He's a fae dog, and he can travel to Otherworld. I've never seen it, but Angus said he goes there to hunt sometimes."

"To hunt? To hunt what?" I asked.

"I don't know. But he might have been protecting you, Lisa."

"Redcaps."

"What?"

"Brian, I gotta go. Thank you. And don't tell anyone I called. No one." I hung up before he could answer.

That lone, bloody redcap that invaded my home accused me of killing his friends. If one redcap survived Chewie's slaughter and Chewie hadn't returned, then he could be badly hurt in Otherworld. Or worse.

I had to keep focused. I couldn't travel to Otherworld, and I couldn't help Chewie. At least not yet. I had to get myself out of the mess I was in. But I wasn't the only one in danger. I had to talk to Kenneth.

Kenneth Megalos was the Lord of Connecticut. I had only met him a few times, as he seldom came to Boston. He was also young for a Lord with so much territory. Around Brian's age.

I didn't have his phone number, and the trip from my safehouse in Londonderry to Kenneth's place in Connecticut was over two hours one way. It would have put me too close to sunrise for a visit and round trip.

I needed to go the next night.

It was around eleven o'clock by the time I arrived in Waterbury. I spent most of the trip thinking about Neil and Chewie. I hated how I left things with Neil, and I was desperately worried that something awful happened to Chewie.

Waterbury is a quaint Connecticut city. Quaint has a particular meaning in Connecticut. Typically, the more quaint something is, the wealthier the populace. Waterbury had its share of wealth, but it was more *conventionally* quaint. Like a city carved out of surrounding woodlands.

Kenneth's mansion was on the outskirts of the city. It was built in the colonial style with white clap board, black shutters, and multiple dormers that jutted from its roof. It was flanked by twin chimneys on either side and sported a porte-cochère held up by pillars where one can drop off passengers underneath its shelter if it was raining.

Quaint.

The gravel driveway was circular with a grassy island at its center. The lawn and accenting hedges, bushes, and skinny trees were well manicured.

There was an older Lexus parked to one side. I assumed it was Kenneth's, and it was the only car in the driveway. I pulled up behind it.

Kenneth answered the door himself. He wasn't expecting me, yet he still wore a blazer and a white button-down shirt. Pressed slacks matched his blazer.

Kenneth was a stocky man with black hair and a few days' worth of stubble that he'd have to live with for eternity. If his creator had been polite, he would have let him shave before turning him.

"Lisa. What an unexpected surprise." He eyed me wearily.

"I would have called, but I don't have your number," I said.

"I only give it out to people I associate with. Well, come in. You've come all this way." He turned and walked into his foyer, leaving the door open for me.

I followed him in, shutting the door behind me.

We walked in silence past a twin, twisting staircase that rose up to the same landing. It reminded me of the iconic staircase from the Titanic, only it was much wider.

The foyer itself was mostly undecorated, save for a mirror flanked by sconces and, on the opposite wall, two swords crossed over an embroidered coat of arms that read *Megalos*.

Kenneth led me under the landing into a sitting room where he took a seat behind his desk and gestured to a chair in front of him.

Something about the mansion seemed... off. It was quiet. Very quiet. I dragged my finger across an end table on my way to sit. I brought back a fair coating of dust.

"To what do I owe the pleasure?" asked Kenneth.

"There are rumors about me floating around. They aren't true, but I'm worried William is on the move."

"William Donovan? Your creator?"

"Yea. He says he's going after Connecticut."

"You came all this way for nothing. William won't move against me." He was nearly scoffing at the notion.

"Kenneth," Kenneth was always *Kenneth*. Never Ken, "he called me personally."

"And you came all the way down here to... warn me?"

"Yes." It came out a little more exasperated than I wanted.

"Lisa, I'm going to help you understand how politics work. We vampires keep our territories through a clever balance of bargaining and deal making. Shows of force? Not so much."

I frowned. Kenneth was around Brian's age. Maybe seventy or eighty years old. I didn't need him mansplaining how vampire politics worked.

"Did you know that this house was actually built in 2001? Most people think it was built in the early 1900s for its style, but no," Kenneth said.

"Super. So, what sort of *deal* do you have with William that'll keep him out of Connecticut?"

It was his turn to frown. Clearly, we were supposed to move on to the part of the conversation where he brags about his house. A mansion where he answers his own door and lives alone, apparently.

"I don't care for your tone, nor your insinuation. I am the Lord of Connecticut." He tried to stare me down with a hard gaze.

He had me outranked, sure. If you control an entire state, you get to be a Lord. But he was a lot younger than me.

Kenneth relaxed a little. "If you must know how I keep William at bay, I give him intel by way of my scion."

"I didn't know you had a scion," I said.

"Most don't. He's in a Pennsylvania bleed now. Philadelphia. And he's been giving me information that I pass along to William. He's much more interested in eastern Pennsylvania than my tiny state. That keeps him at bay."

"For now."

"Lisa, you're old. And I respect that you've survived so long, but vampires like you and William have lost touch. They don't understand how information moves. They don't understand how the law works or how the police operate. Your creator is powerful, yes. But he can't keep up with me."

What an insufferable asshole. I rolled my eyes.

"Lisa. All this nonsense. The rumors. Stirring up Ivan. Trying to stir up me. He's playing you. He's trying to deteriorate our bleed from within."

"I thought you said he was leaving the bleed alone."

"Connecticut, yes. But who is to say what he's going after in New England? Do I really need to educate you on this?"

I stood up. "Alright, we're done here. I'd have your butler show me out but clearly you can't afford one, what with all the groundskeeping and twenty thousand square feet of small dick energy. Good luck."

"Lisa."

I stopped but didn't turn around.

"First of all, it's twenty-one thousand five hundred square feet. And, second, to show you I'm not so heartless, I'll throw you a bone. William isn't the one spreading rumors. You know that. He doesn't talk to people in the bleed. These rumors, all this trouble, is coming from one person."

"Richard." His name was poison on my tongue.

I fucking knew it.

Episode 15

Richard

IT WAS AFTER ONE in the morning when I arrived in Worcester. With all my driving around between territories, I'd been watching the clock like a hawk. The last thing I needed was to be on the road when the sun came up. But I had plenty of time.

I was seething at the prospect of Richard being involved in all this. He'd accused me of conspiring with William before, but he'd never gone this far. Accusing me of orchestrating Mark's death? Working with William to award him Connecticut? I was so angry, I was shaking.

I wanted to confront him, but I had no plan. I'd be on his territory. I was driving to his house. He'd have every right to go on the defensive, but he wouldn't try to kill me. That would be against our laws. I kept telling myself that.

Richard never seemed to have a goal behind his little plots. He just liked fucking with me. He did the same with William before he left the bleed and weaseled his way into New York.

I pulled into his driveway. His enormous house loomed over me. Richard lived in a mansion in Westwood Hills. The houses in this part of the city were nice, but Richard's mansion stood out like a ridiculously lavish sore thumb.

As I made my way to his front door, I had to pass a phalanx of cherub statues, water fountains, and topiaries. The house itself was three stories of brick straight out of the late eighteen century playbook on mansions.

I thought it looked like an old library.

I pounded on the door. If I was going to confront Richard, I wasn't going to show him any weakness.

The door swung open, and I was met by an actual butler. I can't remember the last time I'd been at Richard's estate, but it still floored me. Maybe I forgot. He had an actual butler.

The man wore a navy-blue suit and was balding at the top of his head, probably prematurely. He didn't look much older than his early thirties. The eyes gave it away.

He quirked an eyebrow at me. "May I help you?"

"I'm here to see Richard."

"Is he expecting—"

I pushed past him. I wasn't in the mood to deal with any gatekeeper.

He grabbed my arm at the elbow. "I'm sorry, miss. But I didn't invite you in."

He was strong, much stronger than he should have been. This man was a damphyr, and it was clear from his strength he'd been drinking a lot of Richard's blood.

I stopped and looked back at him. "Fine. Go get him." I wasn't in the mood to brawl with Richard's butler. I had *some* decorum.

He appraised me a moment. I'm sure he was weighing the likelihood that I was a vampire. Then he stiffened his jaw, released my elbow, and closed the front door.

"And your name is?" he asked.

"Lisa."

He frowned at me. "Wait here."

While I waited, I took in the opulence before me. It looked like a Louis XIV era palace threw up in the foyer. A crystal chandelier hung from the ceiling, gold leaf crown molding ran atop the walls, a sweeping staircase curled upwards to the second floor on one side, and on the other...

I shook my head. The asshole had his own elevator.

The butler appeared from a doorway to the left. "Mister Davenport will see you now."

I strode into Richard's office. I still didn't have a plan, but I knew he was the one behind all of this. He had to be.

"Lisa! An uninvited pop-in? I love it! And look at you. You look like you just ate a lemon."

Richard sat behind his mahogany desk. Brass baubles and fancy pens were arranged neatly on its surface. He wore a blue button-down shirt with his sleeves rolled up and one extra button undone at the chest. His often-neat hair was skewed into a devil-may-care mess across his forehead.

For Richard, he looked unkempt. Off guard. It was all an act.

"It's more of an expression," said Richard. "I'm not sure I've ever actually eaten a lemon. You look upset, Lisa."

"You've gone over the line, Richard. You know damn well I would never deal with William, and you know I'm not behind Mark's death."

I guess cutting to the chase was my plan.

Richard let out a sigh. He shook his head, making a bit of theater about it. "I hate when you do this," he said.

It was an odd moment of sincerity from Richard. He was serious. For a brief spark of a moment, he dropped his little act and looked... disappointed.

I frowned.

"Hate what?" I spat.

His smug smile returned. He reclined in his chair. "You never want to do the dance, Lisa. You just want your dance trophy."

"No. I'm just not interested playing your stupid games."

"Politics *is* games, Lisa!" He shot out of his chair as if passionate over his declaration. "That's something that oaf, Kenneth, doesn't understand."

"How did...?"

"Honestly, Lisa. You think I don't know you've already spoken with Kenneth? I know you better than you know yourself. Let me guess, you wanted to warn him? A waste of time. He's a snake and not worthy of your concern."

"That's rich, coming from you."

Richard shrugged. "I can be snake-like, I suppose. But there are rules, Lisa. Even our kind can't exist in a society without rules. Kenneth is a *páiste* in charge of a fiefdom. But, I digress. You came to throw accusations at me. Please, continue."

He sat back down.

I hated when he did this. All his theater and deflection. Kenneth being a *páiste*, a child, wasn't entirely relevant. Everyone knew he was young. Richard bringing it up was just more distraction and misdirection.

"You've been accusing me for years of making deals with William, this whole mess I'm in has your stink all over it."

"Does it now?"

"You sent redcaps after me!" I balled my fists at my hips.

"Did I?"

My blood was boiling. I'd driven all night. Chewie was missing. I had fucked up things with Neil. And now this asshole wanted to play coy with me.

"Let me see if I follow," said Richard. "Because I chide you about your past connection to your creator, you think I'm behind some elaborate plot in which you are accused of... what? Conspiring with William to deliver Connecticut right from under Kenneth's feet and... what? Conspiring with a necromancer to kill Mark in order to... I'm sorry, what was it you were supposed to have gained from Mark's death?"

Actually, that was a damned good question. I had been so upset over the accusation; I hadn't really thought about that. Why would I want Mark dead? What would I gain? My territory was adjacent to his and Mark always let me hunt there. There was plenty to go around. Plus, Mark was young and had less station within the bleed than I did. I caught myself frowning.

Richard smiled.

"This is a plot to discredit me. Maybe get me banished, or at worse destroyed," I said. "There doesn't need to be great logic or some sensible connection between Mark and Connecticut. It's not like anyone in the bleed will be investigating my innocence. So, it doesn't matter what anyone thinks I may or may not gain."

"I agree. Though, Devil's advocate says you would gain something from Cambridge being all yours. Wouldn't it be *cool* to hunt college girls in Harvard?"

I narrowed my eyes at him. "You've been playing this little *dance* with me for years. Putting me in binds and plots. Before me, you pulled the same shit with William."

"Not entirely true. I hated William."

I shook my head. "This is just one more of your schemes. I can't prove it yet, but I will."

Richard clapped his hands together. "That's the Lisa I love! The tango between us. The give and take." He beamed at me. "So much excitement for my long, tired life."

"You have a problem."

"Go! Go, the night is still young. Get out there and investigate. Dig up clues. Hang me out to dry! Though, next time you confront me, let's step it up a bit, yes? I want sparks. Verve!"

Richard may have had a screw lose, but he had a point.

I had nothing on him.

I shouted a string of nonstop profanities in my car halfway home. I was no further along than where I began, and I'd learned nothing. I was no closer to finding out who framed me.

I hated that Richard could be right. Richard liked the game. He wouldn't want to see me dead or banished. I honestly believed him when he said he had a long, tired life.

God, I hope I never get that way.

I frowned at my brush with sympathy toward him. No. He was an asshole. And what was that weird jab about hunting college girls in Harvard?

Wait.

Wouldn't it be cool to hunt college girls in Harvard? That's what Dylan had asked me.

Son of a bitch.

Episode 16

Besieged

It was nearly three in the morning by the time I got back to my place in Londonderry. I was frustrated and my anxiety weighed on me like an anvil on my chest.

As coy as Richard was being, he had given me a clue. I'm sure it was on purpose. His little way of stirring the pot.

He connected Dylan to all this.

Why would Dylan move against me? Would he really risk an accusation this dire just for the Cambridge territory? The risk was too great. It didn't add up. If I could prove he was behind it all, he'd be banished. Or worse.

Finding Dylan was my next order of business, but he could be anywhere. I didn't have enough hours of darkness to drive around looking for him.

I needed outside help.

I wasn't completely lying about witches when I fed Neil all that stuff about covens. There really was a coven in Peabody. It was too late to call on them now, but if anyone could find Dylan, they could.

I flitted around the house a while, trying to watch TV and doing anything to take my mind off the mess I was in. Nothing worked. That anvil on my chest constantly reminded me that I had to solve this before I wound up dead.

I tried to take my mind off it. I watched late night TV with my shillelagh on my lap and my Remington at my side. Small comforts.

Eventually, I went to bed.

My basement sanctuary was a small alcove built up with cinderblocks from floor to ceiling, creating a near lightless cement cell. A metal door clanked shut as I walked in.

There wasn't much to the chamber. A decent bed and a nightstand. No decorations or knick knacks. I had a small lamp on the nightstand, not that I needed much light.

I'd left my main phone there too, traveling only with my burner on me. It showed I had a missed call and a voicemail.

Neil.

I tapped to play it, feeling that anvil press down a little heavier. I hated how I had left things with him.

"Lisa, hey it's me. Neil. So, hey, I wasn't trying to get in your business or anything. I was just worried. You said yourself you're in danger and... I don't know if I crossed a line or something, but I really got worried. I like you, Lisa. You know? Okay, so that's it... call me. I'd love to know that you're okay. Bye. This is Neil, by the way. I already said that."

It wasn't the most articulate message in the world, but at least he wasn't angry at me. Though, him taking the blame for how short I was with him stirred up some guilt.

I shook my head. Him saying he liked me complicated things. I already knew it, but now it was out there.

I forced myself to put it out of my mind and placed my phone back on the nightstand next to my shillelagh and Remington. I slipped under the covers and tried to fall asleep as best I could.

One would think living on the lam and trying to prove my innocence would be all that consumed me that night, but Neil's voice message eclipsed everything.

I slept like hell.

The first thing I noticed the next evening is that the door to my secure chamber had gouge marks, scratches, and damage to the door frame. I'd slept through it, but someone was trying to force their way into my room last night.

I backed into my room and retrieved my pistol and shillelagh. Whoever tried to get to me last night might still be in the house and the gut dropping realization hit me that I had to go upstairs and flush out an intruder.

As if I didn't have enough fucking problems.

My heart seized when I got to my living room. Chewie lay on the far side of the room, dried blood matted his fur. He looked broken. Deflated.

He lay under a net which covered him from snout to tail. His breathing was ragged and his abdomen rose and fell in quick, stuttered intervals.

Beside him stood a redcap. The little fae was dressed like a renfaire reject, accented with the obligatory bloodied cap atop his head and a blue scarf around his waist.

I keep my curse at bay behind a wall of willpower and humanity. But rage can plow through that wall like tissue paper. My anger was an open invitation for the curse to flow into me, to promise revenge. Justice. Anything I wanted.

I seethed as my eyes locked on the redcap and my curse was like an old friend whispering in my ear, promising strength, speed, and death.

I could nearly feel my skin going pale as I considered it.

"Oy! Let's not be too hasty, love," the redcap said. "Your wee doggie is prone, and a scuffle could land him dead, I reckon."

Three more redcaps came from other rooms and flanked me. One from the kitchen, one from my bedroom, and one from the guest room. Each of them had the same blue scarf tied around their waist.

"'Sides," the fae continued. "You're outnumbered."

"The fuck I am." I raised my pistol and shot the fae through the head. He crumpled to the floor beside Chewie.

"Get her!" the redcap who had been in my kitchen shouted. The three little fae leaped on me at once.

I shot again, this time at the new ringleader. The redcap was fast, and he had closed in before I could steady my aim. My shot went wild.

The interloper from my guest room came at me on the left. I had my shillelagh ready for the little bastard and I jabbed him hard in the chest. He bleated out a yip and stumbled backwards.

That was all I could get off before I felt a knife cut into my right thigh. My knee buckled and the kitchen redcap slammed into me, knife held high.

I went down hard.

I brought my shillelagh up to block kitchen boy's knife attack. I looked around to get a bearing on the other two.

I raised my pistol up to find a new target, but a knife lodged itself into my forearm.

Searing pain coursed through my wrist and hand up to my elbow. It felt like my entire lower arm was on fire.

I dropped the gun.

"We gonna kill her?" the one to my left said.

"Nay, just hack her up a bit. She'll heal," said kitchen boy. He was still fencing with me as he lay on top of me.

Terror seized me. *Hack me up*? I was awash with fury and fear, and it was a cocktail ripe for my curse to pull on. It almost begged me, dangling all the power I needed. All I had to do was take it, to drift down that dark spiral, and eviscerate every last one of these little fu—

A blade plunged into my side. I screamed and the grip on my shillelagh faltered. Kitchen boy stabbed down into my chest.

My mind swam. Fire ripped through my body. Every inch of me shrieked in pain. I couldn't concentrate. I reached out for my curse, but I felt it slipping away. Everything was fuzzy. The cries from the redcaps sounded like they were under water. All the light began to dim.

But then...

Blood.

The smell of blood hit my nostrils and something primal and horrible awoke within me. I was hurt and I needed to feed.

I was aware of the one who stabbed my side. He let himself get too close. I grabbed him by the neck and tossed him across the room.

My body screamed in protest, but the little fae sailed through the air and slammed into the far wall.

I rolled over on top of kitchen boy, pinning him down. I sank my fangs into him.

His screams beckoned my curse to the surface, like a beggar wanting to glom onto my newfound energy.

"Lisa!" a pounding came from the door.

I ignored it. Nobody knew I was here. I kept drinking. Sweet faerie blood hit my tongue. I was lost in his slowing, rhythmic heartbeat. With the aid of liquid life, my wounds fought to knit themselves back together.

A knife plunged into my back. The third redcap was still up.

I screamed out as I crumpled on top of Kitchen boy.

"Lisa!" came the shout again.

Neil?

I was going to die. I was too wounded.

"Lisa!" the door slammed. The windows shook.

He was trying to break in.

"Neil! Help!"

The door shuddered again, bracing against its lock and hinges.

The third redcap ripped the knife from my back and strode toward the front door.

I screamed out again. Electric throbs of excruciation wracked through my spine. I gritted my teeth to bite back the pain. It didn't work.

The little fae and everything around me looked bleary and spotty. Flashes of light clouded my vision.

The redcap brandished his knife and crouched by the door.

I fumbled around for my gun. It hurt to move my arm, and I was bleeding bad.

Neil burst through the door, and horror took over his face.

The redcap lunged at him.

I raised my pistol and fired.

A loud bang and the little fae crumpled to the floor.

Neil stared wide-eyed at the scene before him. Panic took over his expression.

The one I'd thrown against the wall collected himself and moved at me, knife held high.

With my side skewered and my back stabbed through, I couldn't twist to him in time.

"Neil!" I slid the gun across the floor to him.

Neil picked the pistol up.

The redcap slammed into my back and another horrifying bout of pain seized my body. I cried out again.

A blast from my pistol rang out through the room.

The redcap collapsed on top of me.

If I were a mortal woman, I would be dead by now. As it was, the telltale itchy, stretching sensations let me know my body was fighting to mend itself, but without blood, I wouldn't be able to close up as much as a paper cut.

I lifted my head to look at Neil. He had dropped the pistol. He took a split second to survey the bloodbath with the appropriate amount of horror before rushing to my side.

"Lisa... oh, God."

"Neil. Get Chewie. Use my shillelagh to remove the net."

He wasn't listening. He fumbled around his pocket and produced his phone.

I couldn't let him call anyone. "Neil. See to Chewie."

"What?" he surveyed the room. "Holy shit."

"Use my…"

Neil reached for the net and pulled his hand back as sparks erupted from the mesh. Chewie let out yelp.

"Ow! Shit!"

"Use my shillelagh." It hurt to crane my neck in his direction, and it was too painful to try and sit up.

"What?"

"See the club looking thing lying on the floor over there? Use that to pull the net off. Don't touch it with your bare hands."

Neil did as instructed. I could only imagine how I was going to explain this one to him.

And as if the universe plotted against me to ensure Neil was aware he was dealing with *more* supernatural bullshit, the four redcap bodies vanished before our eyes.

Neil looked this way and that, taking in all the places where the redcaps had lain.

Chewie stirred and his tail wagged, despite his injuries.

Neil looked at me and tightened his jaw. "I'm calling 9-1-1."

"No," I said. My eyes looked into his. "Come here."

I was hungry.

Episode 17

Crossing Lines

BLEEDING ON THE FLOOR and laying on my stomach were not ideal conditions to use my charming gaze.

The only thing that made it viable, was that this was Neil. And his feelings for me made him susceptible.

"Come here," I repeated. I needed to feed. I'd lost too much blood and the knife wounds in my back were agonizing cries for help that my curse was all too willing to answer.

Neil's arm went slack, his phone held limp in his hand.

"Lisa," he breathed, "I need to call you an ambulance."

His genuine concern for me was making this harder. I had to get creative.

I moved my lips, speaking softly.

"What? I can't hear you."

I let my head loll downward, still muttering.

My pain and hunger overshadowed any guilt I could feel for what I was about to do.

Neil crouched in front of me. "Lisa, what is it?"

I raised my head and peered into his eyes.

"Oh." Neil's expression went a little goofy.

I hurt all over. It was everything I could do to hold his gaze. Throbs of fire pulsed through my body, and it took every ounce of will not collapse into a blubbering heap.

"Neil..." It was all I could get out.

"Lisa, I need to call someone."

It wasn't working. I literally couldn't charm him because he was too worried about me.

I met his gaze again. "I'm sorry I tried to ditch you the other night."

"Lisa, stop."

"No, you've been amazing, and you saved my life." I winced as I shifted my weight to get a better look at him.

Neil frowned at my pain. "Don't move."

"Just listen to me." I had to tell him before I lost my nerve. "I got your phone message."

Neil had the understandable expression of someone who was confounded as to why the bleeding lady was making small talk.

"I like you too," I said.

That shook his ambulance quest for a second. "Like? Like, *like* like?"

I laughed and instantly regretted it as searing pain wracked through me.

"Lisa. Shit. Hold on."

I met his eyes again.

Something instinctive took over. In that pure, honest moment of expression, my curse slithered itself into my psyche like a snake and wrapped itself around my mind. I was wounded. I had to feed. I had to heal. And here, right in front of me, was a human who cared for me.

My charming gaze went off again. I couldn't recall if it was me or my body's instinctive reaction.

Neil leaned toward me.

His lips brushed against mine.

I angled my head away. I couldn't kiss him. Not like this. I needed to feed. I needed to heal.

I let my lips trail away from his and journey across his jaw and down his neck. Neil let out a breath as my lips parted and settled on his warm skin.

My fangs elongated.

Was I really going to do this? To Neil?

I pierced into his neck. Warm blood rushed through my lips.

My wounds pulled against themselves, seeking neighboring tracts of broken flesh to knit with. The healing process was painful, but I kept drinking. The further along it went, the less it hurt.

I had to be careful not to take too much.

Neil's arms wrapped around me. He lifted me up to a sitting position and he held me in his arms while I drank from him. He was enraptured. He was oblivious.

A tug pulled on my pantleg.

How much had I taken? How much did I need? The last time I fed was from that redcap Sunday night.

I struggled to reason how much I required while my curse beckoned me to take more. I had to stop.

A stronger tug on my pantleg nearly pulled me out of Neil's arms.

What was that?

I withdrew my fangs and found Chewie pulling me off Neil.

"Chewie?"

I hugged him, and he panted in my ear. "I was so worried about you."

"Lisa?" Neil moaned.

Shit.

I turned to face Neil and made eye contact again. "Hey, it's okay. I'm okay. You just got a little dizzy there."

My wounds were still hard at work mending themselves closed, but at least I could move. I got to my feet.

"Chewie's here," I said.

"Chewie? Hey." Neil smiled and came out of his haze.

I needed to get out of my bloody clothes, but first I needed to tend to Chewie. Though his wounds were days old, he was still horribly injured. Dried blood matted his fur.

"Lisa, I need to call you an ambulance." Neil got to his feet and followed me into the kitchen.

Thank God Neil had gone shopping for me. I ransacked the fridge and found some hamburger and strawberries.

"I'm okay, Neil. They're scrapes."

Neil frowned at me.

I showed him my arm, then I lifted my shirt slightly to show him my side. The wounds were there, but they looked like fresh, wet scars. "See? I'm not going to the hospital for this."

I didn't enjoy gaslighting Neil any more than I did feeding from him. Though, now that I was out of danger, the weight of my actions settled into my chest like a ton of bricks. I felt sick over it.

But I had to play it like everything was fine.

"I need to change out of these clothes. Can you heat up some hamburger and give Chewie some of those strawberries? He loves those."

"Well, yea… but, Lisa, we gotta talk."

"I know, and we will. I just want to get out of these bloody clothes."

He gave a distracted nod, looking just as worried as when he walked in the door.

'Out o' these *bloody* clothes!" I repeated, but in a cockney English accent.

He either didn't get the joke or it just didn't land. Either way, comedy fail.

"Yes, well… be right back," I said.

Pulling my bloody tee shirt off was not only gross but a little painful. A lot of the blood in my open wounds stuck to the fabric when my slashes closed up. I threw on a black tee shirt to hide what might still be bleeding. I still had a bit more healing to do.

When I got back into the kitchen, Chewie was eating from a bowl and the smell of ground beef hit my nostrils.

Neil gave me a tight-lipped smile.

The conversation that followed was something I had been dreading for a while. Neil had a lot of questions. I had a lot of lies.

Now wasn't the time to tell him I was a vampire. I had a lot left to sort out and he was in danger while he was around me. I had to keep my secrets to protect him.

I slung the bullshit I had to.

Neil had gotten worried when I never replied to the voice mail he left me last night, so he drove up. When he knocked on my front door and got no answer, he decided to wait in his car in my driveway. Then he heard gunshots.

But Neil never saw redcaps, and I never corrected him. His mortal eyes saw grown human men attacking me. The redcaps were glamoured. It's an illusionary power faeries had to befuddle humans.

When they disappeared, I simply told him they were wizards who teleported away.

I figured if he was still hung up on me being a witch, I'd stick with that same supernatural category and not introduce anything else.

I had to explain that Chewie, my magical dog, had been jumped by my assailants and placed under a magical net. Most of that was basically true.

As to why I recovered from multiple knife attacks?

Magic again.

After about a half hour of explaining, we sat at my small kitchen table in silence. Chewie happily chowed down on a second heaping bowl of hamburger.

The clock on the wall showed nine-thirty.

I still needed to take my investigation to the next level but having Neil around would be dangerous for what I had planned. And there was no way I was leaving Chewie behind.

Although...

"I need to give Chewie a bath. You want to help?" I asked, breaking the silence.

Neil bobbed his head. "Yea, I'll help. Sure."

One thing I didn't have was dog shampoo, so I improvised and used hand soap. Neil asked if I had any dish soap, which I didn't. It's not like I clean a lot of dishes in my life. I just told him I ran out.

Neil helped with the bath too. We both sat on the bathroom floor with Chewie in the tub. Brownish red water ran from him as we washed the dried blood from his fur.

"Please don't shake and get blood everywhere. Just wait until we get you clean."

I'm sure he understood because he didn't shake at all.

"So, we like each other," said Neil.

"Hm?" That caught me off-guard.

"We um... like each other. I said it in the voice mail I left you. You said it tonight."

He remembered that? He was under my charming gaze when I told him that.

I nodded slowly. "Well, yes."

"So maybe when things settle down, we could try that date again? Pool or whatever. Doesn't have to be pool."

"I like pool," I said. And I caught myself smiling. "But things do need to settle down. I can't really get involved right now."

"Yea, I understand."

The shower head blasted the remaining suds off Chewie. The last colors of red swirled down the drain, escorted by an entourage of bubbles.

"Did we kiss?"

I searched his eyes looking for some certainty in the question he asked. He looked unsure. His mind should have been fruit loops when our lips grazed.

"No. You got a little dizzy. Remember?"

"Right. Though, I think I remember holding you."

The charmed were not supposed to have this level of recall. I shook my head. "Well, yea. You were worried."

Neil looked at me as if to puzzle something out.

Chewie soaked us both with a torrent of water as he shook off the last of his bath from his fur. Neil and I were sprayed from the waist up.

Neil and I sat, drenched and incredulous staring at each other.

Neil was the first to start laughing.

"Chewie!" I laughed.

He gave another shake for good measure. His tail whipped back and forth at record speed.

It felt good to laugh. After nights of rumors and plots and getting stabbed, it was such a wonderful relief to finally have a moment of fun. Even if the fun was getting soaked by an enormous barghest-mastiff, I'd take it.

Still chuckling, Neil brushed a wet lock of hair off my cheek. "You okay?"

"Yea." I grinned.

He leaned in toward me. Slowly.

"Wait." I cut him off.

He stopped and withdrew his hand from my hair.

"There's still a lot of weird shit going on. Magic. Whatever. I can't explain all of it. I actually need to head out to see some friends. More weird stuff."

Neil looked crestfallen. "So, you want me to go."

I shook my head. "No, I want you to come with."

I'd made up my mind. Neil was in it now. There was no more debate over him becoming my thrall. He'd seen too much. I had to bring him under my care to protect him.

I was doing the right thing, all things considered.

So why did I feel so horrible?

Episode 18

The Coven

FORTUNATELY, MY DOOR WASN'T completely destroyed. Neil smashed the deadbolt through a chunk of the frame when he forced the door open, but the door could still close. Push on it with a little force, however, and the door would swing open.

I didn't have time to deal with that in the moment.

"So where are we going?" asked Neil.

"Peabody," I said, opening the back door for Chewie. Chewie had regained some of his energy after some food and a bath. He bounded into the car without even a questioning head tilt.

"And that's where your coven of witches is?"

"Not _my_ coven. Friends." It was the truth. But I left out the part about asking them to help me track down Dylan. Richard's little slip of the tongue implicated Dylan as the one behind all these rumors.

I always knew Dylan was of questionable moral fiber, but I never figured he'd cross me like this.

Neil screwed up his face. "So, you have your coven, some enemy coven, and this other coven? How many covens are there?" He moved to the passenger side door, but didn't get in.

He was still latching on to the bullshit story I fed him when he asked if I was a witch. I had no intention of going deeper into the dishonesty. Witches were real, and I wasn't keen on spilling their secrets to cover for mine.

"I really can't go into it, but once I square away things with them, I'm in the clear," I said.

"How? Those guys just attacked you in your home."

"I can't go into it. But suffice it to say, we beat them and that's it." I rounded my car to the driver's side.

"Wait... were *they* the enemy coven?"

"Neil." I couldn't help but chuckle.

"Okay, okay. I'll drop it. As long as you're safe." He smiled at me.

"Come on. Get in." I smiled back. "Let's get this over with. You still owe me a night of pool."

Peabody was north of Boston and about forty minutes south of the New Hampshire border. It's one of the many towns along Massachusetts' North Shore, and it happens to border the town of Salem.

Andrea McShane lived in a raised ranch on Birch Street. The pale-yellow house was adorned with black shutters and had a built-in garage. I wasn't sure what Andrea did for a day job to pay for a three-bedroom house on the North Shore, but I was fairly certain it wasn't witchcraft.

"So, we just wait in the car?" asked Neil.

"It shouldn't take too long. And you're kind of a *civilian*, if you know what I mean. We're going to be talking about some supernatural stuff that you shouldn't hear."

It was true.

Neil bobbed his head a little. "And Chewie."

"Yea, they're doing me a favor, and I'm not sure it would be okay for Chewie to go in." I flashed Chewie a tight-lipped smile. "Sorry, buddy."

Chewie dipped his head and then slapped his snout against Neil's cheek.

"Oof! Hey..." Neil started.

A laugh escaped me. "See? He'll keep you company. I won't be long. I promise."

It hit me when I started up the walkway to the front door. I felt like I was wading through water. Each step had weight to it, resisting me. I plodded my way up the walkway with the house's protections pushing back at me.

I knocked on the door, then pressed a button on the door frame. It wasn't a doorbell. The button turned on a light inside the house that Andrea could see.

The door opened and Andrea's fourteen-year-old daughter greeted me with teenage apathy pooled in her eyes. "Hello?"

"Hi, Katie," I said. Was she fifteen? No, I was pretty sure she was fourteen. "Is your mom home?"

"It's Kathryn. Who are you?"

"I'm Lisa.". She was dreadfully ill-mannered, but I kept a smile on. "Your mother is expecting me. We've actually met a few times."

"It's eleven-thirty at night," Kathryn said.

"I know it's late, but I'm here to see her... *club*."

"God." Kathryn rolled her eyes. "Come in."

All at once, the weight dissipated, and I was able to step into the house with no difficulty. It's an old wives' tale that vampires can't enter a house unless invited. But in Andrea's case, there was a ward cast on the threshold of her front door.

Kathryn led me downstairs to another door. The room was very quiet inside, save for the rustling of clothing. There were people inside. They were moving, but not speaking. The pleasant smell of sandalwood filled the air.

Kathryn hit a button on the door frame.

A moment later, the door opened. Sophie Hunter stared back at me. She had her strawberry blonde hair pulled back in a ponytail. Sophie was barefoot and dressed in what I like to call a *wiccan dress*, the flowy ankle-length dresses popular among modern witches who liked to put on a Celtic look.

But Sophie wasn't a witch. She called herself a druid. Frankly, I didn't know the difference.

"Lisa, hi. We were expecting you. Come in."

Sophie eyed me up and down, her heartbeat increased slightly. She was nervous.

"Hi, Sophie. Thank you."

Kathryn took that as a cue to slip away.

"Thank you, Kathryn!" Sophie called after her.

"Yup," came her response from the top of the stairs.

The room beyond Sophie didn't scream coven. Andrea appropriated the downstairs den for her meetings and magic. Six other women were in the room. Some were milling around a counter with snacks. Two sat on a couch. Another sat on the floor, arranging tarot cards on a coffee table.

The room was adorned with those fake wood-panel walls and an old tube-style TV.

Andrea rose from the couch and smiled at me.

Andrea was in her early forties these days, but she looked young for her age. She had curly, shoulder length hair and bright brown eyes. Her smile was kind and a little mischievous. I always liked Andrea. A long time ago, she gave me the benefit of the doubt when no one else would.

Andrea signed to me, her hands flitting back and forth in a language I only partially understood.

"She says hello," Sophie said. But my hands were already signing out a greeting in response. I understood that much.

All at once, the other women greeted me. Some more friendly than others. Not everyone in the coven was keen on doing business with me.

Andrea's power to combine dissimilar magics made the coven a vibrant tapestry of ethnicities and cultures. Nearly every woman in the room had their own way of making magic.

Sophie was a druid. Marisol had some sort of Caribbean magic I never really understood. She said it wasn't voodoo, but some other thing. Jennifer was probably the only actual witch in the coven. Su-Hyun was something called a Mudang. I didn't understand that one either. It was some sort of Korean magic. Brenda was apparently descended from the Wampanoag tribe and called herself a healer. Alice was the one with the tarot cards. Her magic was about divination and seeing the future.

Alice was the one I was here for.

It took a moment to get all the signed greetings out of the way. For the other six women, they spoke as they signed.

Andrea began signing again, but so did Jennifer. It was hard to follow what Andrea was saying because Jennifer spoke as she signed.

"I don't want to seem rude, but we should probably get the matter of payment out of the way," Jennifer said. She never really trusted me.

Sophie spoke up. "Jen, Andrea was saying we should discuss Lisa's question she needs answered."

Andrea turned to Jennifer and signed at her. Her gestures were sharp and strong to drive her point across.

"What's happening?" I asked Sophie.

Sophie sighed. "Andrea is reminding everyone that you were the one that brought us the vampire blood so that we could build our ward. She's reminding them about the time you protected our territory from a werewolf. And... she's talking about that book you brought in."

"The necromancer's book? I gave you that book so you could destroy it."

Sophie gave a nod. "We did." Then she peered at me. "It's weird, you being a vampire and working with us. We all think so. But you've been a good ally to the coven."

"I was hoping *friend* would be the word."

Sophie shrugged. "You are still a vampire, and we have to be guarded. Su-Hyun gave us all talismans in case you ever get dangerous."

Sophie signed as she talked to me, and Andrea gave a frown and signed forcefully at Sophie in return.

Sophie translated Andrea's words with some reluctance. "Andrea doesn't appreciate my inference. She says she considers you a friend."

"Please sit," Andrea signed. I got that one.

There were a few stools by the counter and a recliner. Each of us found a place to settle in. I grabbed a stool.

Sophie did all the translating, though I tried to sign words when I knew them.

I pulled the vial of redcap blood from my purse. "I want to come on good faith and give you something in return for the help I'm asking for."

I held the vial aloft. "This is redcap blood. I took it from someone who attacked me recently. You can add this blood to your threshold ward and keep out another group of unwanted nasties."

"I still think blood magic is dangerous," said Marisol. But she came forth and took the vial from my hand.

Marisol was from Puerto Rico and, for some reason, I think it was her magic that built the wards.

Her dark curls fell about her face as she examined the vial. The red liquid made a striking contrast against her brown skin. She whispered words in Spanish that I mostly escaped me, but I caught the word *sangre*.

Blood.

Marisol nodded then turned to her sisters. "This is what she says it is."

Andrea smiled and began signing again. "What can we do for you, Lisa? You said something about finding someone?"

I told them everything. I told them about the bogus rumors, the lies with William, the possible ties to the Necromantic book and Mark's death, the idea that Kenneth's territory in Connecticut might be at stake, and that Dylan's designs on the Cambridge territory might make him a suspect.

It took a moment for them to digest what I said, and I was asked to wait outside while they deliberated.

I checked my watch. Poor Neil and Chewie might be in for a longer stay in the car than I anticipated. I never understood magic.

The door opened and Sophie invited me back inside.

Alice was back to sitting on the floor next to the coffee table. She was shuffling her tarot deck.

Sophie translated as Andrea signed. "This divination you seek, to find the ones doing this to you, will take an investment from the spirit world. It will cost a bit of power to accomplish."

"Can you help?" I was able to sign the word *help*.

Andrea gave a swift nod and signed. "Yes. We can. But you can only ask three questions."

The Three Questions

A WHILE BACK, ANDREA had explained magic had a cost. It wasn't that the coven didn't want to help more than three questions worth. It was more that three questions answered was the cost they were able, or willing to pay.

Whatever that cost was, I didn't ask.

With only three questions, I had to make them count. There was a lot I wanted to know and a lot of moving parts to the predicament I was in.

First, there was a rumor I wanted to defect to the New York City bleed. This included a rumor that I planned to give the Connecticut territory to William. But Kenneth assured me that William wasn't after Connecticut because of some deal that involved trading intel on the Philadelphia bleed.

Then there was the rumor that I arranged Mark's death to claim the Cambridge territory for myself. On top of all that, I needed to know who was sending redcaps after me. Dylan certainly wanted Cambridge for himself, but would he really send redcaps after me?

And then there was Richard. Richard always seemed to be in the thick of whatever mess I was in.

I supposed the first question I had was easy. It encapsulated all the questions I had.

I turned to Alice, who sat with tarot cards at the ready. "Who is plotting against me?"

Sophie signed my question for Andrea to see.

Alice began laying down cards. I was never familiar with the tarot. I knew there were cups and swords and things. There were pictures of people; Death, the Hanged Man, a Queen maybe. But I didn't know what they all meant.

The cards were put down in a pattern. Some crossed one another, some made a T-shape. Some were upside down. Alice's expression changed with each new card.

The rest of the coven gathered around Alice. They joined hands and closed their eyes. Alice continued to lay down cards.

"Okay," Alice said at last.

The women released hands. Sophie signed to the group while speaking out loud. "Alice is ready."

I stiffened my lip. This was it. I was going to find out who was behind it all. Maybe I didn't even need the other two questions.

Alice looked up at me with sympathy in her eyes. Her hands were still full of cards, so Sophie signed for her. "Lisa... there are too many. There are plots against you from many, many people. I stopped reading after I got to five. I don't know who any of them are. I think your question was too vague."

My stomach tightened. Five people plotting against me? I knew I had rivals. Enemies even. But five? I didn't know what I felt worse about: the idea I had that many enemies or the fact that so many people didn't like me.

"Okay," I said at last.

Two more questions. I had to narrow this down.

"Try to be more specific," offered Alice.

Perhaps there was more than one person involved with the trouble I was having. There could also be additional plots I wasn't aware of. There were too many unknowns, and I needed to focus on the problem at hand.

"Who sent the redcaps after me?" I asked.

Alice gathered her cards again. After a quick shuffle, she laid them down once more. New cards came up. New patterns. New expressions across her face.

Like before, the other women joined hands and closed their eyes. For a moment, I could have sworn the hair on the back of my neck stood up.

"Okay," said Alice.

The pattern repeated. The women let go of their hands and Sophie signed to Andrea.

"You have an enemy from the southern territory who sent them," said Alice.

"Territory?" That word stood out to me.

"Yes, that was very clear. A territory to the south."

Dylan's territory was just south of mine, over the Charles River. He wanted the Cambridge territory. This entire debacle has been about territory. And Dylan's comment about hunting college girls in Harvard made it all the way to Richard. It was Dylan.

"Son of a bitch," I muttered.

"You know who this is?" asked Alice.

I nodded. I had one question left.

"Tell me where Dylan Walker is. No!" I caught myself. I still needed time to get to him. "Tell me where Dylan Walker will be in one hour."

"Sorry, sorry, sorry," I said as I got into the car.

"That was almost forty minutes," Neil gave a half-hearted smile. "I don't mean to complain, but I still need to drive home after we get back to your place in New Hampshire."

Chewie banged his head against Neil's. It was affectionate, but it sent Neil lurching forward.

"I know. I didn't expect things to take so long, but... I can't drive you back to New Hampshire yet." I winced.

"What? Are you still in danger?"

"No. No, it isn't that. I just need to go confront the guy who's behind it all."

"Are you sure that's a good idea? Is this the guy that sent those... wizards after you?"

"Yea. But this will finish it. I just need to call him out."

I didn't have time to drive back to New Hampshire. I knew where Dylan would be in one hour and I needed to leave now.

Neil made a face.

"You wanted to keep me safe, right? Get me out of this? Come with me. You and Chewie both. No waiting in the car."

It would be risky confronting Dylan with Neil in tow, but time wasn't on my side.

"I suppose I could call out sick tomorrow. Catch up on all the sleep I'm gonna miss." Neil gave another weak smile.

I was going to have to make this up to him.

I leaned across the seat and kissed his cheek. It was probably a bad idea. I'd dragged him into the thick of a supernatural clusterfuck, and I was still planning on making him my thrall. But in that moment, he was being so kind.

No.

Neil busted down a door and saved my ass after he'd driven up from Watertown because he was worried about me. And he'd insisted on coming with me to Peabody to ensure I was truly out of danger.

He earned the kiss.

"What was that for?" Neil smiled at me.

"For you. For being great. For sticking by me through all the weirdness."

"I gotta say, my life's been an adventure since I met you. Rescuing magic dogs, breaking down doors, witch covens..."

"Plus, you shot a wizard."

"I... yea... wow."

Chewie let out a sonorous woof.

"And you helped give Chewie a bath." I laughed.

"Well, I sure as hell can't quit now. Where are we going?"

"I had them divine where Dylan would be an hour from now. He's the guy who sent the um... wizards after me. The one who started all these rumors."

"And where is that?"

"Harvard University. Where the college girls are."

We trekked across the Harvard University campus. Neil was at my side, and I held on to Chewie by a bungee cable from the trunk of my car. From a distance, it would pass for a leash. It was the best I could do for what I had on me.

The campus was peppered with a collection of red-brick buildings with white-trimmed windows. The buildings were generally around four stories and sported three to four chimneys a piece. Most of them were built around the 1800s, but some were much older.

I had to convince Neil that all I wanted to do to Dylan was talk to him. That might be true, but I wasn't sure if things were going to get physical when I confronted him. Neil's being human brought another level of complexity to the situation.

It behooved me to keep things civil, but deep down I wanted to throw Dylan a well-deserved beating.

The good news was this nightmare was almost over. I could go home, and things would go back to normal.

At a little past one in the morning, there weren't many people around the grounds. A few students stumbled from one building to another for some frat party or drunken hookup, but nothing that drew any attention to us.

We made our way to a part of the campus called the *Old Yard*, which was beyond University Hall and where many of the freshman dormitories were.

The Old Yard was a grassy partition that ran from Holworthy Hall and flanked other, similar buildings on either side. The small field was dotted with trees, which gave the Old Yard an almost wooded ambiance.

We found Dylan staring into the eyes of some young blonde coed. Her slumped posture indicated she was fully ensnared within his charming gaze.

Neil muttered to me, "Is that the guy?"

"Yea," I said. I let go of Chewie's leash.

Dylan didn't have a deathly pallor, but he was pale enough to pass for someone who had the flu. It was the sort of sickly complexion that many vampires had when they had begun their decent down the dark spiral. Beyond that, Dylan had dressed for his campus hunt in skinny jeans, canvas sneakers, and a gray hoodie. Fucking poser.

Chewie charged at the girl and Neil started forward. "What are you doing?"

"It's okay," I said.

Chewie bounded to the girl and planted his forepaws on her, making her stumble off balance.

"Hey!" Dylan shouted and took a step toward Chewie. "Wait... I know you."

Neil and I approached from the side. Dylan whirled on me. "Lisa? What the hell? I was just about to—" His eyes fell on Neil. "Who's this?"

"This is Neil." I followed with a subtle shake of my head. Dylan's frown indicated he got the message. Neil wasn't in the know.

The young coed was startled out of her haze. "This dog is huge! Where did he come from?"

"It's nearly one in the morning on a school night. Shouldn't you be in bed?" I asked.

"Oh, shit... right. Sorry, Barney. I'll see you later?" she asked Dylan.

"Sure," Dylan gave a distracted wave of his hand.

She frowned at the gesture and hurried off. Chewie sat on his haunches in front of Dylan.

"Really, Dylan? Freshmen? What was she, nineteen?" I asked.

Dylan shrugged. "What are you even doing here?"

"What do you think?" I took a step toward him. "Those rumors about me. You stalking around Cambridge. You tell me."

Dylan laughed. "I'm sorry, Lisa. Am I supposed to be frightened right now? You bring some normie and your pet dog and I'm just supposed to confess to some idiotic—"

Chewie leaped at him, bowling him over and sinking his teeth into Dylan's shoulder.

"Holy shit!" Neil cried.

"He's tougher than he looks. He'll be fine," I said. I moved toward the melee.

Dylan was pounding his fists into Chewie's sides. Chewie responded with a powerful shake, flailing Dylan to and fro.

Dylan cried out and kicked his legs, trying to break free.

Neil was in absolute panic, looking around us and occasionally running a hand through his hair. I didn't have time to calm him down.

I put my foot on Dylan's neck as Chewie pinned him down at the shoulder.

"Yes, Dylan. You're supposed to be frightened right now."

Episode 20

En Garde!

"Have you lost your mind?" Dylan's voice rasped under the weight of my foot on his neck.

"You sent assassins after me!" I snapped back.

"What? That's crazy! Even if I wanted to, I can't afford that!" he wheezed.

"Lisa," said Neil.

Poor Neil had seen Chewie and I go all *Goodfellas* on Dylan. But I couldn't deal with him right now.

"You wanted Cambridge, so you tried to—"

"Kill you?" Dylan cut me off. "Are you insane? I was going to ask if we could share or split the territory."

"Lisa," Neil repeated.

None of this was making sense. Dylan's motives were flimsy. But the tarot pointed to a rival in a southern territory. I eased my foot off his neck. Chewie took my cue and released Dylan's shoulder.

"Have you been working with William?"

"What? No! Of course not." Dylan sat up.

"Lisa!"

I turned to Neil. "I'm sorry, this got out of hand. I just need to—"

"No, I'm done," Neil said. "This is too much. I just... I can't. You're shaking this guy down. The people breaking into your house and... vanishing? This is just too much, and I can't do it."

"Okay." I let out a breath. "I'll just... I'll take you home. Let me just finish up here and—"

"No, you aren't getting it. I'm leaving. Right now. I'm sorry. I'm going to grab an Uber or something. Grab my car from your place. I'm sorry, Lisa. I want to know that you're going to be okay, but this is just too much."

With that, he turned and walked off.

"Neil, wait." I started toward him.

"Redcaps? You said assassins, but you meant redcaps?"

Dylan's question jarred me. I stopped.

Neil turned around.

I stood between the man I had taken advantage of, the man who had been nothing but kind to me and the man who had information about who was trying to kill me.

I could only imagine that Neil saw the indecision in my eyes when he shook his head and walked away.

I stood there like an idiot, rooted to the ground.

"Lisa, I can't afford redcaps. I don't have either the blood or the money for that. Redcaps in the bleed are coordinated through Richard, you know that," Dylan said.

Just like that, Neil was gone. I tried to tell myself that it was better he wasn't around for the things I was dealing with, but it decimated me.

"Hey. Psycho lady, I'm talking to you. You're lucky I don't go to Ivan over this. Not that he'd do anything to his precious step-scion."

I turned to face Dylan. "It wasn't Richard."

"How do you know?"

"Because Richard plays the game. It's a dance to him. Sending redcaps is too overt. Too vulgar."

"So... William? It wasn't me." Dylan rubbed his shoulder.

Chewie was back on his haunches, wagging his tail.

"No, not William. The coven said it was a southern territory. That's why I thought you. You wanted Cambridge and Brookline is south of me."

I screwed my face up in consternation.

Kenneth?

"But why would Kenneth be behind this? He'd never want to give up Connecticut and he's got some deal worked out with William where no one from New York encroaches on his territory. He has no motive."

Dylan looked baffled. "Kenneth?"

I had asked the questions more to myself than Dylan. Then it hit me.

Holy shit.

"Come on, Chewie."

We turned and walked off.

"Hey, you just attacked me! There needs to be some restitution!"

I took hold of Chewie's bungee leach to keep up appearances. I wondered how quickly I could make it to Connecticut.

"I'm going to Ivan over this! You can't just get away with attacking me! We're in the same bleed!"

Dylan's shouts were a little distracting, but I managed to put a plan together. It was no more off-the-cuff or haphazard as my other plans.

"Lisa!"

I parked my car under Kenneth's porte-cochère in case I need to make a quick hop to my car from his front door. The lights were on in his house, so I knew he was home. Since he was alone the last time I was here, I was banking on him being alone now.

My plan simple. Kenneth was a vampire who had committed conspiracy against the bleed and was going to sacrifice me to pull it off. I planned to confront him over it and threaten to go to Ivan if he didn't sort the whole thing out.

Sure, I could have just gone to Ivan, but Kenneth would likely be destroyed for his actions. I wanted to give him a chance to make it right, even if he didn't deserve it. I supposed I also could have blackmailed him over it, but that wasn't my style either. Besides, he had nothing I wanted.

I checked my watch. Three-thirty in the morning. I'd need to make this visit quick to get home before the sun came up.

I knocked on the door. Chewie padded to my side.

The door flew open. Luckily, I saw the stake in time to twist my shoulders.

The wooden weapon slashed my shoulder, cutting through my tee shirt sleeve and flesh. Chewie let out a vicious bark.

I moved to get into a stance, but before I could back off, Kenneth followed up by grabbing my neck and throwing me into his foyer.

I slammed into his tile floor and skidded further inside, rolling like a rag doll.

Chewie charged the doorway but let out a yelp as his paws touched the threshold. Kenneth ignored him.

I got to my feet.

So, that's how this was going to go down.

"You just couldn't leave this alone!" Kenneth shouted.

Chewie barked and snarled outside, seemingly unable to enter the house.

I got in a stance. I took Karate in the seventies and a little Tae Kwon Do in the nineties. I think I was a blue belt. Something like that.

Kenneth was looking paler than usual. He was a lot more pallid for a vampire of his age. Part of the reason he was a Lord so soon is because of the amount of power he'd drawn on. He'd never tried to balance it over time. Dangerous. And stupid.

But Kenneth's long-term effects weren't as relevant as the power he had at his disposal here and now. And I was banking that my age could challenge the speed and strength that came with someone of his deathly complexion.

I wasn't sure it could.

"So, you're just going to kill me? Others know I'm here, Kenneth. It's over."

"That's unfortunate. Or you could be bluffing. But no, I'm not going to kill you. Just subdue you. And have you delivered to your creator in a box."

I scowled. Chewie continued to bark and growl. He gnashed his teeth and frantically scraped his paws against the door frame.

Kenneth cast a look at the massive dog over his shoulder. "I was hoping my defenses would work on him. I heard about your mutt after you concluded that business with the necromancer."

"What did you do to him?"

"Nothing. My front door threshold is pure iron. I deal a lot with fae. Redcaps, mostly. Though I'm sure you're well aware of that by now."

"Fae are repelled by pure iron." I gritted my teeth.

"Very good, Lisa. Yes. And your dog is half barghest."

I was done talking with the asshole. I strode toward him.

He held up a hand. "Before we begin, I want to know one thing. How did you figure it out?"

I didn't break my stride, and I had Kenneth backing up. That was satisfying. "Process of elimination, I suppose. But you're also broke. I remembered my visit here; dusty furniture, no servants, no thralls, and an old car. William wants more than the intel your scion is giving him, doesn't he? So, you agreed to hand over Connecticut in exchange for money. *Money!*"

Kenneth continued to back up. He chuckled. "Almost. I'm giving up nothing. I will remain Lord of Connecticut and New York will hunt here as they please. And if you must know, my scion is dead. He was discovered by his bleed and destroyed two months ago. That sort of... accelerated things between William and me."

I paused in my steps and searched his eyes. Was he mourning the loss of his scion? Was I dealing with a grieving and broken man who had become desperate?

"It doesn't have to end like this, Kenneth."

I saw nothing. Only pools of blackness. Ivan always said I was too trusting.

"I'm afraid it does." Kenneth backed up a bit more until he was at the wall. The pair of crossed swords were mounted behind him, splayed across the Megalos coat-of-arms.

Kenneth took the two swords down from their perch. "I've heard you're quite capable with a shillelagh. A lot of people think a shillelagh is a club, but I know it's used as a fencing weapon. I'm a bit of a swordsman myself. Why don't we settle this properly? Civilized. With proper weapons instead of beating and biting each other like animals."

He dropped one of the swords on the floor and kicked it over to me.

I bent down and picked it up.

Kenneth got in a fencer's stance. One foot out, knees bent, one hand on the hip. "En-garde."

Episode 21

Swimming With Sharks

THE SWORDS KENNETH AND I had weren't made for fencing. They were arming swords, crafted for knights and soldiers during the Middle Ages. But with our heightened strength, we could wield the heavy blades as if they were as light as foils.

My stomach was caught in my throat. This was supposed to be a quick shake down. I was supposed to call him out on his crimes against the bleed, and Kenneth was supposed to back down. What was his plan after he shipped me off to William? I certainly wasn't going to stay in Manhattan.

Either I had seriously underestimated Kenneth, or he'd found himself way over his head and gotten desperate. And stupid.

Either way, I wasn't in the mood to be cut to ribbons.

Kenneth charged me, it was an obvious thrust, and I blocked.

We circled each other a little. The tips of our blades occasionally touched as we measured one another.

Outside, Chewie continued to bark and snap at the scene before him. The front door remained swung open, yet he was still helpless to cross the door's iron threshold.

"It doesn't have to be like this, Kenneth."

"I'm afraid we're both in over our heads, Lisa."

With that, he lunged again. I parried and stepped to his side. I whacked him in the ribs with he flat of the blade.

Maybe Ivan was right about me. I am too nice. But I figured if I gave a compelling display of my skill, I wouldn't have to hurt him.

No dice.

Kenneth swung at me, then became a blur of arm and blade. He was fast, but so was I. This was where it boiled down to my greater age versus someone who'd wrung almost every drop of power he could from his curse.

I took a gash to my shoulder.

Score one for the dark spiral.

Chewie's barks and howls became more frantic. He clawed at the doorframe, splintering wood and gnashing his teeth, but he was still unable to cross the threshold.

We clashed, a blur of blades once more. I was more skilled, but Kenneth was faster. I took a cut to the leg above the knee and staggered. He followed up with a skewer that raked across my side.

I was bleeding.

It's never a good thing when a vampire starts losing blood. My head became fuzzy. Pain seared through my side and my leg and shoulder throbbed in bursts of fire.

Kenneth took a step back and took in a long breath through his nose.

"Perhaps I'll drink of you before I ship you off to your creator."

I raised my blade again. "You can try."

He smirked at me. Somehow my snark didn't couple with my being a bloody mess.

Our blades danced again. This time I kicked him in the shin as I parried. His leg buckled and I thrust my sword into his chest.

He bellowed and staggered back, clutching his bloody pectoral with his free hand.

I advanced and didn't let up.

He parried me strike for strike. I could feel blood running down my body, leaking life, energy, and power. My head swam.

Kenneth ducked a slash at his neck. He swung his counter across both my thighs, and I crumpled at his feet.

"Argh!" he bellowed, still clutching his chest. He paced back and forth in front of me.

My sword clattered to the floor beside me. I reached for it, but Kenneth kicked it away. "I'm going to make you suffer for what you did to me."

Kenneth raised his blade. I scrambled to get away and my legs screamed in protest.

Glass shattered, shards of a nearby window blasted into the room.

Chewie's paws hit the tile floor, and he skidded to a halt.

He had crashed through the window.

Kenneth whirled on him. "Clever dog."

Chewie leaped at Kenneth, clamping his huge jaws around his sword arm. Kenneth tumbled backwards and fell. His sword flailed around uselessly in his hand as he howled in pain.

I got to my feet. It was a painful affair. My legs, side, and shoulder shot lightning bursts of pain through every inch of me. I gritted my teeth and grabbed my sword.

Kenneth grabbed his sword with his free hand and pressed the flat of the blade against Chewie's side.

Poor Chewie let out a yelp and released the arm.

Kenneth crawled off a ways and slashed Chewie across the chest. Chewie let out a high-pitched cry, and he fled from the Lord of Connecticut, tail between his legs.

The young vampire got to his feet.

"Iron. I told you I don't fuck around with fae. These swords are iron."

I limped toward him. I had to finish this.

He advanced on Chewie, putting more distance between us.

"You ruined everything. You know how hard it will be to cover this up?"

"You should have thought of that when you accused me." I said, limping as fast as I could. I nearly slipped on my own blood.

"I tried to teach you about politics, but you wouldn't listen. You should have just taken the deal. Hunted in *Manhattan*. Manhattan!"

"Get away from him!"

Chewie padded toward Kenneth, terrified as he was. His tail still hung low, yet he tried to put himself between him and me.

"Stupid dog."

Kenneth lunged.

Pure iron.

I leaped. My body was a chorus of pain and fire, but I leaped at Kenneth despite it.

My blade slashed through his carotid artery while I was still in the air. I landed and my legs immediately gave out from under me. I tumbled to the floor and Kenneth fell beside me. Blood surged from his neck in pulsed bursts.

"Chewie?"

He licked my face.

As feeding goes, it was one of my more gruesome moments. I crawled to Kenneth and drank from his open wound. A lot of it was off the floor tile, but I didn't care. The ten second rule really doesn't apply when you've lost as much blood as I had.

Kenneth wouldn't die from lack of blood. He'd fall into the *death sleep*. There he'd remain until blood passed his lips again.

I wasn't going to kill him. But pulling him out of the death sleep wouldn't be my problem, either.

My wounds closed. The flesh knitted itself together with a feeling not unlike a part of your body falling asleep. For all my injuries, I felt the pin-prick static all over me.

I had to sit up to let it pass. At least it pulled me out of my feeding. Vampires can't be killed by draining but feeding the last drop of anyone brings you into their soul, and that's something I avoid at all costs.

I glowered at my watch. I had over a two-hour ride back to my house. There was no way I could make it in time before the sunrise. I'd have to speed, and pulling off a charming gaze on a police officer while covered in blood was no easy feat.

Besides that, I still wasn't done at Kenneth's.

Not having enough time to make it back home meant I had to spend the day at Kenneth's. I grabbed one of the many bedrooms in his empty mansion. It did fine, though it wasn't great for keeping out the sun. The room was hot and uncomfortable, and I felt like I was sleeping next to an open flame.

I suppose vampires deeper along in their curse would have found it painful.

When I awoke the next evening, I found Chewie curled up at the foot of my bed. He was looking much better and there were muddy pawprints around him.

"Did you go to Otherworld again?"

He got to his feet and wagged his tail. Then he bounded on the bed and licked my face.

"Okay, okay. I'm fine. I'm up." I laughed.

I got up and dressed myself in a tee shirt and sweats I found in Kenneth's bureau. They were huge on me, but at least they weren't ripped and bloody.

"So, you ate while I slept?"

Chewie let out a woof, and I took if for a yes.

We went downstairs and found Kenneth right where I left him.

"Lisa!" he shouted when he heard me.

I had to stifle a laugh at the scene before me.

Since I hadn't drank him completely, Kenneth never entered the death sleep. I didn't want to risk him recovering after our swordplay, so I had to stake him. That took away his powers; particularly his strength and ability to heal. Then I had to tie him up to keep from taking out the stake. And last, but not least, I had to throw heavy blankets over him to keep the sunlight from killing him.

He squirmed under his blanket like a very angry caterpillar.

"Lisa!"

"Coming," I sang.

He'd wriggled out of one of the blankets, and I pulled the remaining blanket off him.

His face and neck were burned.

"Ooh... you must have kicked the other blanket off during the day."

"I'll kill you for this!" He writhed on the floor.

"I don't think you will. Any toe out of line, and I'm going to Ivan about your little deal with William."

"You're bluffing. You would go to him with that information right now. If you keep it from him, he'll punish you."

"Yea... probably. A slap on the wrist." I crouched down next to him. "Nothing compared to what he'll do to you."

I yanked the stake from his heart.

Kenneth shrieked in pain. He gritted his teeth and kept his eyes smashed closed, probably to find some means of enduring the excruciation. I gave him a moment before continuing.

"Let me explain how vampire politics work, Kenneth. You swam with sharks while you were bleeding, and you paid the price. But I'm going to keep your secrets and you, my friend, you are going to owe me."

It sounded more hard-ass than it was. If I turned him over to Ivan, Kenneth would be destroyed. It was mercy wrapped up in bravado. But Kenneth didn't need to you know that.

"Are you supposed to be the shark?" he spat.

I stood up and tossed the stake aside. "Me? I'm a God damn mermaid. No. William is the shark. You made a deal with a much older, more powerful vampire, and you just lost him the only thing of value he cared about. Me."

"I still have Connecticut."

"Good luck with that."

With that, I left. Chewie padded along beside me.

With his stake removed, Kenneth could break his ropes and heal himself. He'd need to hunt, but he'd be fine.

But it finally hit me when I brought up the GPS in my car. I didn't have to go back to Londonderry. This nightmare was finally over.

I punched in the address for my place in Charlestown.

I was going home.

Episode 22

The Werewolf of Watertown

THE *LET'S GO BACK to your place* strategy had been my steadfast means for feeding since the nineteen seventies. It was uncomplicated, safe, and efficient.

I'd meet someone at a club or bar, chat them up, and do the old cliché *let's go back to your place*. Once there, I laid on the charming gaze, drank my pint, then off I went. It left no witnesses, and my charmed quarry was none-the-wiser.

Easy peasy.

I pulled up behind Gary's Honda Civic. He parked in the street. There were already two cars in the driveway, one behind the other. My first red flag.

"You have roommates?" I said, getting out of my car.

Gary shut his car door. "Parents. Well, mom and a step-dad, but don't worry. They're cool."

Gary's house, or more accurately, Gary's parents' house was a raised ranch. There were lights on inside and by the flickering brightness of the front bay window, I could tell there was a television on.

I grimaced. "You sure about this?"

"Yea, yea... it'll be fine. You'll see."

Gary had to unlock the door, and I followed him inside.

"Hey," he said. "Mom, Lyle. This is Kelly."

They didn't move. Mom and Lyle sat under an afghan blanket staring at the TV. At first, I thought there was something wrong, but then it hit me. They didn't care.

"There's popcorn in the kitchen," Mom said at last.

"Nah, we're good," Gary said. He cocked his head at me to follow him.

"Sorry," I said when I passed in front of their view of the TV. I felt very much like an intruder.

I followed Gary downstairs. His room had posters on the walls. Superheroes, mostly. The live-action versions. The other posters were cartoon drawings of young women. They were done in the Japanese style. Anime? I don't think you can say Japanimation anymore.

"You like Anime?" he asked.

"Um."

He pointed at the posters in succession. "Bubblegum Crisis. Darling in the Franks. Mononoke Hima."

Part of being my age and trying to stay current meant keeping up with pop culture. This wasn't the first time I'd seen anime art, but I didn't know the subject well.

"It's... pretty," I said with a smile.

"Yea. It is. Not enough people appreciate that."

I moved into his line of vision. I wasn't comfortable with his parents upstairs, so I wanted to get this over with. I peered into his eyes.

"So, I've never..." he began.

"It's okay," I said.

"No, I mean, I'm not a virgin, but truth be told, I don't really bring a lot of women down here."

"Gary, it's okay."

He kept looking this way and that, bashful. I couldn't get a lock on his eyes.

"Let's sit," I suggested. I sat on his bed.

Gary sat beside me. "I'm nervous."

"I can tell. Relax."

A woman shouted from upstairs. "Gary? You want popcorn?"

"No, mom. I'm okay," Gary called up at the ceiling.

"How about your friend?" came the hollering reply.

"No, mom. We're okay. Thanks," he shouted back.

Gary's cheeks flushed a little. "Sorry about that. Oh, did you want anything?"

"No." I laughed.

I debated leaving. If mom burst into the room with a bowl of popcorn mid-feeding, things would get ugly. But as I wrestled with my predicament, Gary looked into my eyes.

The predator in me found it difficult to resist.

I stared back at him. "She won't come down here?"

"No." He leaned in to kiss me.

I put two fingers over his lips. I don't mess around with the people I feed from. Instead, I turned on my gaze.

"Gary."

He breathed into my fingers. I saw his pupils shrink.

"Relax," I whispered. I leaned into his neck. My fangs elongated.

He wrapped his arms around me. It was a normal reaction. I didn't dissuade his perception that this was a romantic moment.

The tips of my fangs dragged across his neck. The pulse of his heartbeat thrummed through them as I hovered over the right spot. I sank into him.

His arms tightened around me. It hurts to get bitten, but the charming gaze masks the pain from registering as danger.

I drank. His blood was tinged by the infusion of sugar and alcohol from the rum and Cokes he'd been drinking. It somewhat dulled the copper flavor.

When I'm in control, I can tell when I've taken my pint. It equates to a certain amount of time coupled with the dulling of my hunger pangs.

I pulled back and looked at Gary. He smiled at me.

"The two wounds on your neck will be gone by morning. Probably mosquito bites."

He bobbed his head, still glassy eyed.

I looked around his room, taking in the anime women on his posters. "Try meeting someone that shares your interests. Don't invite her back to your place. Don't try silly pick-up lines in a bar. If you meet someone and you hit it off, ask her if you can call her."

His head lolled around in what looked like charmed agreement.

I gave him a pat on the shoulder. "I can't stay. Sit here until your head clears. If your parents ask, tell them I wasn't feeling well."

I didn't wait for him to acknowledge. I'd already stayed too long and risked too much with his parents just upstairs.

I saw myself out.

I had to walk past Gary's blanket-clad mother and step-father. Lyle paused the TV when I walked in front of it.

"Who are you?" he asked.

"Kelly. Gary just introduced.... It doesn't matter. Your son invited me over, but I'm not feeling well, so I have to leave."

"What's going on?" Gary's mother pulled her attention from the paused television and looked me over.

"It was nice meeting you."

In the nineteen eighties, the term *couch potato* was coined. All I wanted to do was get away from these spuds.

They both seemed bewildered. Lyle appeared to be piecing a question together.

Then my phone rang. Saved by the bell.

I gave them a tight-lipped smile. "Sorry, I have to take this. Have a good night."

I hurried out the door, grateful to be out of that house and into the night air. I checked my phone. It was Brian calling.

"Hey, Brian."

"Lisa, you got a minute?"

"Yea, I'm free. Finally. What's up?"

"I'm not on speaker, am I? Are you alone?" he asked.

"Not on speaker. I'm alone. Spill it. What's going on?"

He made a pained noise like he was revving up to tell me some bad news. "We got a werewolf. He came at me, here in town."

I stopped in my tracks on Gary's walkway. "Are you okay?"

"Yes, but—"

"No, no. Hold on."

I got into my car and started it up. I could hear Brian's protests as I fumbled to get my phone situated.

"Just hold on, okay? I'm putting my phone on the car's stereo thing."

Soon, Brian's voice was piping through my car's speakers. "Lisa, are you there?"

"I'm here. Tell me what happened."

"It was a couple of hours ago. I was leaving my house to hunt, and I saw him out on the street. Wolf form. At first, I thought he was a coyote, but he was too big.

"He stared at me for a while. It was weird. I still thought he was just a wild animal, so I tried to shoo him off, but he didn't budge. Then he charged me."

A werewolf against a vampire is no pleasant contest. "Are you hurt?"

"I'm fine. He never touched me," said Brian.

"He charged you but never touched you? No offense, Brian, but you're not faster than a werewolf. You sure this wasn't a coyote?"

"It wasn't a coyote. Too big. He ran off. I didn't outrun him." Brian started to hem and haw again. "Lisa, I need you to come up here. We can't do this over the phone."

"Brian, it was probably just a big coyote."

"I swear it was a werewolf. I know for certain, but I can't... I need to show you. I can't do this over the phone."

"Brian, if you're that sure it's a werewolf, then call Ivan. He'll send Walter and Tracy and maybe try to find this thing."

"No! We can't call Ivan."

His outburst made me feel even less comfortable.

"There's a werewolf running lose in Watertown and you want me to come up there?" I asked.

"It's not like that. It's more complicated. I need to show you. I wouldn't be asking if this wasn't important and if I wasn't confident that there's no immediate danger. Trust me."

No *immediate* danger.

I let out a long sigh. "Alright fine. I'll see you in about a half hour."

As I drove off, I found myself envious of Gary's mother and step-father and their werewolf-free night of television and couch potato glory.

Episode 23

Not A Coyote

I PULLED INTO BRIAN'S driveway, parking behind his car.

The last time I was here, Brian had been missing for weeks. He was held under the sway of a necromancer. That's when I met Chewie. And Neil.

Thoughts of that adventure flooded back to me. Neil's house was just across the street. His car was in the driveway. His lights were on inside.

Weeks ago, he'd left me after a somewhat violent altercation where I interrogated Dylan over some bullshit rumors about me. I let things get out of hand, and it had been gnawing at me since.

I wanted to go over and knock on his door. To apologize.

Brian's front door opened. "Lisa."

I turned to see Brian in his doorway. He looked from me to Neil's house and back. "What are you doing?"

"Nothing. What do you have to show me?"

I wanted to get this over with and go home and let Chewie out. I'd left him home when I went out hunting. My dog-sitter, Amy, never showed up to feed and walk him. Even though I let him out when I woke up, poor Chewie had been cooped up most of the day.

I followed Brian inside.

There was a woman sitting in his living room.

I glanced at Brian. We had werewolf business to discuss, and the stranger in his room immediately put me on guard.

"Lisa, this is Coyotita. Coyotita, this is Lisa."

"Hello," Coyotita said stiffly.

Despite my wariness, I couldn't help noticing how stunning Coyotita was. Her features betrayed a native American heritage. Her light brown skin was flawless. She had long dark hair that hung in straight locks past her shoulders. Her eyes were a striking brown with flecks of gold that nearly made them sparkle.

She was wearing Brian's clothes. At least, I assumed they were Brian's. A men's tee shirt, baggy on her frame, read *Salt Life*. It sported a giant sailfish bursting out of the ocean. She wore equally baggy sweats. She had bare feet.

I frowned. "What the *fuck*, Brian?"

"It's not what you think." He jumped between us.

I took a step backwards. The borrowed clothes were a telltale sign of someone who had just been naked and no access to their own clothes. As a vampire, I'd been in that position before because I had to disrobe to shift into a bat or wolf. There were other shapeshifting creatures that disrobed before changing their forms.

Like werewolves.

"She's not a werewolf, not truly. And she wasn't the one that charged me," said Brian.

"My mate did," said Coyotita.

I frowned. None of what either of them said made me feel better. "Explain this to me."

"Coyotita is a coywolf," said Brian.

The woman in question sat unfazed on Brian's couch.

"Like a coyote?" I asked.

"Well, yes. Coywolves are hybrids of wolves and coyotes. They're their own species. Been migrating into New England over the last hundred years or so."

I gave Brian an incredulous look.

"I used to watch a lot of Wild Kingdom," said Brian.

"I'm still not following. She's a were-coywolf?"

"Yes, that's it," Coyotita said. She was pulling on the little strings on her sweatpants. "What are these for?" she looked up at Brian.

My jaw fell open a little. "She's an *actual* coywolf who got bit by... what? A werewolf?"

"Another were-coywolf," said Coyotita.

I threw my arms in the air. "Are we in danger here?"

"No. We're helping her and she's helping us."

"How do you figure?"

"When that coywolf charged me—"

"My mate," Coyotita interjected.

Brian gave an absent nod. "Yes, when Coyotita's mate charged me, it was Coyotita who was the reason he fled. She attacked him."

"I didn't want my mate hurting anyone. Once you hurt someone, they hunt you," said Coyotita.

"After the attack, she followed me home and shifted to her human shape. We talked, and she told me how her mate had been acting funny the last couple of days."

"Funny how?" I asked.

"He hadn't been sleeping in our den. He would drive me off when I tried to get close to him. He was trying to hurt me. I was afraid for myself, but I was afraid for him too. He is my mate. How can he be like this?"

Tears welled in Coyotita's eyes as she looked up at me. Her bottom lip quivered. She looked so vulnerable, and nothing like some flesh ripping savage monster.

And there went my heart strings.

I looked at Brian. He knew as well as I did that Ivan had a *kill on sight* rule for any werewolf spotted in the New England territory. I wasn't sure where he'd land on were-coywolves, but I was betting it wouldn't be good for Coyotita.

Brian just shrugged.

"How did you get the name Coyotita? It's a little on the nose if you're trying to keep a low profile." I asked.

"Brian named me. I had no name," she said.

"Really? *Coyotita?*" I cocked my head at Brian.

"It just sprang into my head. I thought it was clever. I like Coyotito – the baby in *The Pearl*."

I rolled my eyes. "If you're such a Steinbeck fan, you'll remember that Coyotito was shot in the head at the end of the book."

Coyotita's eyebrows shot up her forehead and she gazed at Brian.

"It's just a story. It's not you," Brian explained.

"Why couldn't you have told me all this over the phone?" I asked.

"If I told you I had a were-coywolf in my house, would you have come up? Would you have called Ivan? You had to meet her and see for yourself."

He had a point.

"So, what now?" I asked.

"We need to find her mate. I was thinking we go in wolf forms."

"Brian, I need to get home and let Chewie out. He's been cooped up for hours while I was hunting."

"You could bring him. Drive back and get him. We really need to find her mate. She said he wasn't acting right."

It wasn't that I didn't want to help. I had been serious about Chewie. Nighttime was supposed to be the time when he and I hung out. I looked over at Coyotita. I was also conflicted about keeping all this from Ivan.

"Maybe if we go to Ivan—"

"Ivan can find out when we've handled it and Coyotita is safely on her way. Please, Lisa. She's not a monster. I tried to think what you would do in this situation, and I thought you would help her."

Dammit. He went and played the *What Would Lisa Do* card.

I took a moment to look Brian over. He'd been doing well. His complexion wasn't as lifelike as mine, but he wasn't overly pale either. His hair was still a healthy ginger, and his freckles weren't washed out by any deathly pallor. All things considered, he was keeping his curse at bay, and he was trying to be a good person.

I exhaled. "Fine. But I really don't want to keep Chewie cooped up too long. I can hunt with you for an hour."

Brian exhaled in relief. "Thank you."

"And Wild Kingdom? You watched *Animal Planet*. Nobody the age you look is going to remember some seventies show on PBS." I shook my head and grinned at him, despite it all.

Coyotita had told Brian that she and her mate had a den in the woods to the east. After going back and forth with her to pinpoint the location, we narrowed it down to the only possible place.

Whitney Hill Park.

We stepped out of Brian's back door. There was Chewie. Black smoke billowed off him. It was the same dark mist that was left behind when he disappeared on me weeks ago.

"Chewie?"

He gave a deep woof and let his tail wag to nearly a blur.

I ran to him and gave him a hug. "Hey, buddy. Did you *poof* here?"

He smooshed his giant block-like head into mine in response.

"Chewie?" It was Brian's turn to ask.

Chewie looked up. His tail slowed a bit. He peered at Brian, thoughtfully.

This was the first time Brian and Chewie had seen each other since that night all those weeks ago in the necromancer's house. Brian had gone missing, and he left Chewie alone in his house for weeks. Chewie, it seemed, had taken that for neglect.

"How've you been?" Brian asked.

Chewie pulled from my arms and padded to Brian. The big dog still came up to Brian's thigh. He ran the length of his body against Brian, not unlike the affection of a cat. Chewie made a complete circle around him and then drove his head firmly into Brian's stomach.

Brian smiled with tears in his eyes.

"I missed you," he said while scratching Chewie's head.

It was a touching moment. But I couldn't help but feel worried. What if Chewie chose to stay with Brian instead of me? Barghests aren't pets. They choose their companions on their own. Sometimes I joked I was Chewie's familiar.

Chewie looked toward Coyotita and perked his ears. It was interesting that he didn't react to her like a threat or danger. My trust in the were-coywolf went up a notch.

"That's Coyotita. She's a friend," Brian explained.

Chewie simply gave a woof in her direction.

"Looks like Chewie's coming with us to the park," I said.

Brian grinned. "We're gonna make a hell of a pack."

I asked Brian if I could change in his shed. I was over a hundred and sixty years old and undressing before a shapeshift was all very natural vampire stuff, but I still had my modesty.

From what I could tell, Coyotita had no such reservations, most likely seeing her human body as just one more form.

When I loped back to the group, I was surprised how much smaller Coyotita was than the rest of us. Chewie was big, even for a mastiff. Brian and I were large grey wolves.

Coyotita was literally like a big coyote. Did this mean her mate, the one we hunted, was the same small thing?

Perhaps this was a good makeshift pack after all.

Chewie was standing beside Brian. I tried not to feel jealous. He and Brian had been together for years before me, and I wouldn't want to take that away from either of them. But Chewie was as true a friend as any person I'd ever known. And if he left, I'd miss the hell out of him.

A breeze swept through the yard, carrying a wealth of information. A cat. A car burning oil. Some neighbor's cheap cologne.

The smell of suburbia was overpowering. We would be able to glean a lot more when we were in the woods, away from the gasoline, charcoal briquettes, and asphalt.

It was unspoken, but I could tell everyone else reached the same conclusion. Without prompting, we all trotted out of Brian's backyard.

The hunt was on.

A Mournful Discovery

HUMANS TYPICALLY DON'T PANIC when they see a bat in the sky. A wolf on the street is another matter.

In the thousands of years since vampires have been around, the likelihood of seeing a wolf has drastically diminished. And for humans, who never seen a wolf, it can be a scary sight.

With Chewie and Coyotita among us, I hoped that fear could be mitigated. Coyotita could easily be mistaken for a coyote. Chewie, as big as he was, looked like a Neapolitan Mastiff. I hoped the odd assortment of canines would befuddle any onlookers to rationalize that maybe we were a pack of stray dogs. Big huskies maybe.

I didn't think anything of it when Brian took the lead. It wasn't an alpha thing. We weren't truly wolves. But this was his town. He knew the way to Whitney Hill Park on foot. Or paws, I guess.

Brian loped out in front, and the rest of us formed a neat group behind him. He made his way to the street. Even at this hour, the traffic was busy, so we had to be careful about crossing.

Coyotita pushed forward and nipped Brian. Not hard, but it got his attention. She turned from the street and made her way through someone's yard. She only paused to see if we were following.

Brian looked at me, ears perked. I gave a nod and swished my tail.

Body language was all we had to work with in these forms, but Brian got the gist. We all turned and followed Coyotita.

The coywolf knew this town differently than Brian. She knew which yards to slip through. She knew where the small patches of trees were and who had wooded backyards. It was a longer way toward the park, but the path she took was privileged with shadows, tree cover, and vacant streets.

Soon enough, our motley ensemble of canines meandered our way to Whitney Hill Park, doing a commendable job at avoiding the notice of humans.

The woods were small. They amounted to a small strip of forest preserved in a conservation area. Nearby houses could be seen in almost every direction. There weren't a lot of places to hide for Coyotita's mate.

We stayed off the trails and continued to follow Coyotita. She led us to a hole in the ground dug into a the side of a slope. It was heavily obscured by brush, and it wasn't something someone would see if they casually walked by.

Coyotita went into her den alone and came back out a moment later. I could tell by her posture that she was disappointed. The den was empty.

We continued our search. We traveled up and down the park's two short trails. Like many parks, no one was allowed in after dark.

Coyotita stopped and sniffed the ground. After a moment, she raised her head and let out a call for her mate. It was odd seeing a coyote's cry coming from a wolf-like body. Her yipping was an eerie cacophony of cries and half-howls that somehow sounded like a chorus of animals instead of just one.

Her cries carried into the night and then faded into silence.

We waited.

There was no response.

Coyotita's tail hung low, and she continued down the trail.

The smell hit me a moment later. Coyotita must have smelled it first. The stench of death and decay. Brian bobbed his snout up and down. He'd caught the scent as well. Behind me, Chewie let out a low growl.

It didn't take long to find him. The coywolf's body lay in a ditch at the edge of a clearing. It looked days old.

We stopped in our tracks.

Coyotita padded forth a few steps but stopped short of the body. She yipped a few times and barked at her mate. She was met with only silence.

She seemed to accept the sad reality as she began to whine. The mournful canine cries seemed to be the only sound for miles.

Coyotita closed the distance between her and her mate. She curled up beside him and rested her snout on his flank. Her whines continued. Her ears went limp, and her entire posture deflated.

I didn't know what to do. I wanted to comfort her, but in that moment, I felt completely powerless.

Brian shifted about on his paws beside me.

I glanced at him. His ears were flattened. I knew what had him fidgeting. Coyotita's mate had been dead for days, yet Brian claimed to have seen him only a few hours ago. Even Coyotita claimed it was him.

Brian gave a chuff. It was a prompt that we had to continue looking.

I gently jawed at his snout. I thought he was being insensitive to Coyotita.

He lowered his tail, submitting to the gesture, and we remained at Coyotita's side a little longer.

Coyotita never stirred. Her eyes stayed open, but she remained curled up with her mate.

At last, I had to concede to Brian's desire to keep hunting. I didn't want to disturb Coyotita's mourning, but we also couldn't stay here all night.

I swung my head back to the direction we came. Brian and Chewie followed me. We weren't sure where we were going next, but we had to find whatever it was that Brian saw.

The three of us padded away from Coyotita, leaving the tragic scene behind.

I was glad Brian had convinced me not to call Ivan about this werewolf sighting. Coyotita would have been pulled into the conflict, and I had resolved that she was no threat. I really didn't want the bleed to give her any trouble.

We hadn't made it all that far when a sharp bark yipped out behind us. It was Coyotita.

Her hackles were raised. Her ears were flattened. Her teeth bared.

Her body language could have been mistaken as a threat toward us, but among our little misfit pack, we knew otherwise. She was pissed off.

I stepped away from Chewie and Brian to break ranks. It was a gesture that opened up a position back within our group.

Coyotita trotted into the open space. Then promptly ran off ahead.

What the hell?

We ran after her. Chewie, Brian, and I kept up with her well, but Coyotita was speeding up. She ran as straight as she could, winding around the occasional tree.

Her determined pace made it clear that she'd caught the scent of something.

Coyotita had already demonstrated that her sense of smell was greater than ours. I was certain she'd found what we were looking for.

New scents hit my nose. Denim. The rubber soles of sneakers. But, oddly, nothing else. When I'm in my wolf form, the smell of a human is a myriad collection of scents. Clothing is a great part, but there are also soaps and shampoos and their natural odor. I smelled none of those things in conjunction with the clothing.

Could it just be a pile of clothes laying in the woods?

We continued to follow Coyotita.

Movement. Up ahead, a man walked through the edge of the woods.

He smelled off. He smelled wrong.

Coyotita flanked to the left. I pulled ahead of Brian and Chewie and flanked right.

Seconds later, the man was surrounded.

Coyotita had her teeth bared. I wasn't entirely sure how to present myself. What was our plan? We couldn't interrogate him in these forms, and I wasn't about to maul some random guy walking through the woods.

The man didn't react like a human would. Three wolves and a giant dog had him surrounded and he didn't look at all scared.

He looked intrigued.

That unnerved the hell out of me.

Coyotita growled at the man. It drew his attention to her.

A shift in wind hit my nostrils. New scents. New information. I smelled the curse on him. But weak and watered down. He wasn't a vampire. He was damphyr.

I didn't recognize him, and I couldn't recall who in our bleed would have a damphyr or why they would be wandering around Brian's territory.

Yet, he still smelled... off. A damphyr mixed with something else. I couldn't put my finger on it.

The wind died down, and I lost the scent.

Frustrating. In my wolf form, I should have gotten a wealth of sensory information off this guy, but I got nothing.

Brian growled. He must have picked up on the same scents. A foreign damphyr was more than enough to raise his hackles.

Brian's reaction must have been all Coyotita needed to see. She leaped at him, jaws bared.

The man caught her and tossed her away. She hit a nearby tree, letting out a cry.

We moved on him.

He batted Chewie away. He was strong. Too strong.

He dodged Brian.

I bit into him at the forearm. He tasted wrong. He was foul, like rotten meat. I resisted the urge to release him, to get that taste from my jaws, but I fought through it. I shook him, trying to take him down.

Brian and Chewie were on him again.

The man picked me up while I was still clamped onto his arm. He ran, breaking free from Chewie and Brian. He slammed me into the trunk of a tree.

The crushing blow sent a course of pain through my ribs. I released my jaws.

The man backed away from us. He looked around, no longer intrigued but decidedly annoyed.

Coyotita was back on her paws and charging.

The man frowned, but simply rooted his feet to the ground and closed his eyes.

He burst into flames.

The human-shaped column of flame lit up the woods like it was daytime. The heat backed us all off and away a few paces.

Then he was gone. No flames. No man. Not even a scorch mark on the forest floor.

Episode 25

Clash With Authority

Brian drummed his fingers on his kitchen table. The three of us sat in silence. Chewie was curled up on the floor at Brian's feet.

Despite a dead werewolf and a damphyr who burst into flames in my recent repository of things I needed to worry about, I couldn't help but feel a little jealous. Why wasn't Chewie curled up at *my* feet?

I'm sure he missed Brian, but it still stung a little. And it bothered me that it stung. I was being selfish, and that made me feel guilty on top of everything else.

I should have been spending more time thinking about the werewolf and damphyr.

Coyotita broke the silence. "Can we go over it again? It's all so confusing."

Brian bobbed his head and ceased his drumming. "We both saw your mate earlier tonight, or at least something that looked like him."

"And smelled like him," Coyotita added.

Brian nodded and gestured at her to acknowledge her point. "Yet, we found his body. And he'd been gone for days."

"Gone. Such a word for such a thing." She hunched over and let out a whine.

I could tell she was hurting. Water pooled in her eyes and her cheeks flushed. She sat, slumped over.

"Do you want some water?" asked Brian. "I don't have much in the way of food here."

"No. Please continue."

"Well, that's it, really. After that, we found the damphyr. And you saw him burst into flames and disappear."

"What is a dam-feer?"

"Someone who drinks vampire blood and gains a bit of their power. They cannot vanish in flames. Not even a vampire can do that," I said.

"Yea, we burn like anyone else." Brian gave a thin smile.

For a moment, the table fell back in silence once more.

"Whatever that thing was. The dam-feer. It must be responsible for killing my mate," Coyotita said.

"That or the imposter we saw earlier tonight," said Brian.

"Likely both. It's too much of a coincidence," I said.

"So, what do we do now? I want to hunt!" Coyotita snarled.

I rose from the table. "I won't keep you from it, but I have to go. I need to drive home and settle in before daylight. I can come back tomorrow night and check in."

"Thanks, Lisa. I knew you'd understand," said Brian.

"Call me if anything changes."

With that, I turned to leave. Chewie raised his head and wagged his tail but did not follow me. My heart sunk.

"I, um… it looks like Chewie may stay here," I said.

"Oh." Brian looked down at the enormous dog at his feet as if just noticing him. "Well, he's always welcome here."

'Yea." The awkwardness was tangible. "Well, talk soon."

I walked out of Brian's house Chewie-less. Once more, I found myself more upset about Chewie than the impending threat of a coy-werewolf doppelgänger and combustible damphyr.

Chewie had only been with me a couple of months. He'd been with Brian for years. And he'd left Brian over a misunderstanding.

The sound of scraping plastic on asphalt pulled me out of my consternation.

"Neil?"

Neil was pulling his trash can to the curb. It was late. I was surprised he was still up.

"Oh, hey." Neil looked up, noticing me at last.

Neil's garbage-toting outfit consisted of plaid sleep bottoms and a tee shirt from what I assumed was some heavy metal band from the 1980s. One of the ones where the letters looked sharp and pointy.

His hair was unkempt, and he needed to shave.

I smiled at him. "How are you?"

"Good. Good." He set his trash can upright and rubbed the back of his neck. "You?"

"Good."

"Hanging out at Brian's?" He asked while I was still standing in Brian's front yard.

I turned around and looked at Brian's house before answering. "Yea."

A silence settled between us.

"You uh... out of danger? Got all that stuff settled?"

"Yea. I resolved things with the guy spreading rumors. It's done." I put on another smile.

I could feel the pull of my curse roiling inside me. It latched on to my emotions, as it always did. I'd never traversed far down my own dark spiral, but its outer rim would often beckon me. It tempted me to use my power to simply take Neil. Charm him. Enthrall him.

I missed him, and my curse knew it. It was an almost sentient thing whispering in my ear, enticing me to leverage my powers to take what I wanted.

"You okay?" Neil asked.

I shook it off. I was stronger than that.

"Yea, sorry."

"Kinda spaced out there for a sec."

I wanted to ask him out. To try to get to that game of pool we never played. But I was too afraid he'd say no.

"Well, I gotta..." He jabbed a thumb behind him in lieu of finishing.

"Yea, me too." I gestured at my car like an idiot.

I ambled to my car, watching Neil leave and walk into his house.

My car felt empty without Chewie, and the nagging regret over how things ended with Neil continued to gnaw at me.

The lonely ride home was a visceral reminder of what I'd lost.

The next evening, I awoke to get an early start with Brian and deal with our werewolf and damphyr problem. It was a little past dusk.

The receding rays of the sun were like standing next to an open fire, but it was nothing I couldn't handle.

A man got out of a car from across the street and walked toward me. He wore a worn brown leather jacket over a shirt and tie. Dress slacks completed the ensemble. The man looked to be in his early forties, with some salt and pepper around his temples and a mustache that had gone completely white.

"Miss Cooper?"

I stopped a few feet in front of my car. Was this guy waiting for me? "Yes?"

"I'm detective Pierce. I'm not sure if you remember me. We spoke on the phone a while back."

I remembered. He called me when Brian and the others were missing. He was sniffing around looking for suspects to the missing persons case attached to their disappearance.

"I remember. What can I do for you?"

"You're a hard woman to get a hold of. Your neighbors say you work days, yet your car has been here all day. And you haven't been answering your phone."

Parking was a premium in Charlestown, and it was definitely a plot hole in my story about working days. But I didn't want to engage him on that topic.

"Is there something I can help you with, detective?"

"Amy Wagner was found dead this afternoon. In her apartment."

Amy was my dogsitter. My stomach dropped. She was dead?

"How?"

"Strangled. When was the last time you saw her?" The detective produced a small notebook from his jacket.

I almost had to steady myself on my car. Was he really questioning me over this? Amy was such a kind person. She loved animals. She loved Chewie.

"Miss Cooper?"

"This is awful. You can't possibly think I had anything to do with this."

"Miss Wagner had a small circle of friends. Some family in town. Some family out of state. I'm talking with everyone and getting statements. That's all."

"She was my dogsitter. She took care of Chewie during... while I was at work."

"When was the last time you saw her?"

"Maybe a month or so ago. We usually just talk on the phone. She comes by when I'm not home."

"Even though your car is here?"

I frowned at him.

"I asked some of your neighbors," he said.

"I take the bus to work. Easier. Parking is tight."

"And where do you work again?"

"Brigham and Women's Hospital," I lied.

Detective Pierce jotted a few things down. "Where were you between the hours of seven a.m. and nine a.m. yesterday morning?"

"I... was getting ready for work and then I commuted in."

"On the bus."

I narrowed my eyes at him. "Yes."

"Can anyone corroborate this? Any neighbors, witnesses, coworkers?"

"I don't know," I answered tersely.

"It's funny, Miss Cooper. This is the second time our paths have crossed. In my experience when a name hits my desk more than once, there is usually something interesting about that person."

"I didn't kill Amy Wagner." I gritted my teeth.

"They're just questions, Miss Cooper." He gave me a smile and tapped his pen on his notebook.

"Will that be all?" I asked.

He handed me a business card. "For now. If you think of anything, please call me."

I snatched it out of his hand and got in my car.

I needed a moment before I started up the engine. Amy was dead. Just the other night I'd awoken to a note telling me about her fun visits with Chewie and the walks they take at Bunker Hill. Sometimes, when she took him out, she'd send me pictures of him enjoying their outing together.

Who would do such a thing?

I wiped tears from my eyes with the back of my hand.

I noticed Detective Pierce was still across the street, watching me from within his car.

Asshole.

I fired up the engine and drove away.

Once I got on Washington Street, I fished the burner phone out of my purse. I rang up Ivan's number. I had to deal with Detective Pierce's snooping around.

After a few rings, I got his voicemail.

"Ivan, it's Lisa. My... dogsitter, Amy. Someone killed her." I took a breath. It was hard to say that last part out loud. "There's a detective snooping around. I need someone to corroborate that I was working at the Brigham yesterday morning."

I spent the rest of the drive stewing. Whatever supernatural threat I was driving toward seemed to fall by the wayside as my thoughts dwelled on Chewie, Neil, and now Amy.

Before long, I pulled up to Brian's house.

There was a new car parked in front, a silver SUV. It took me a moment, but I recognized it.

Walter was here.

Walter Garvin wasn't the type to make social calls. More importantly, Walter was one of Ivan's enforcers. If he was here, it was *bleed* business. And in light of everything going on with coywolves and a flaming damphyr, this didn't bode well.

It was Brian who answered the door. That was a good sign. He had a pained expression on his face.

Walter sat in Brian's favorite lounge chair. He swiveled it toward me when I entered. The last time I'd seen Walter was after I'd rescued him from the necromancer's basement. He'd gotten much of his color back since then, though his typical pale pallor still muted his brown skin.

In the far corner of the room, Chewie sat on his haunches, glaring daggers at Walter.

"Lisa." Walter rose from his chair with a smile. "How did I know you'd be here? Oh, right. Your dog is here."

He gestured toward Chewie.

Chewie growled.

"What's going on?" I asked.

"You tell me." His smile melted into a frown. "I'd damn sure like to know about this werewolf in town and why you've been keeping this from the bleed."

Episode 26

Ivan's Ire

WALTER WAS LESS THAN pleased. Being one of Ivan's enforcers, he admonished us over the irresponsibility of ignoring a possible werewolf threat within the New England territory. We tried to explain that we wanted to investigate the issue before reporting it. It was a lie. We were never going to tell Ivan.

It didn't matter. The cat was already out of the bag, and the next night, we found ourselves in council with Ivan. He had called a meeting of what he called the *Boston Core,* all of us who had territories in Massachusetts: Richard, Jacques, Brian, Dylan, Walter, Tracy, and me.

Fun.

I was the second person to arrive. As usual, I was led in by Úll Buachaill, Ivan's redcap butler, for lack of a better word. He was dressed in a purple waistcoat with tails, a garish lime-green tunic, and white leggings. I was pretty sure the getup passed for a high station among redcaps. I couldn't imagine why else anyone would dress like that.

Tracy was already there, seated in her usual spot at the corner of the one of the two couches that faced one another. Ivan's chair sat empty.

She looked up at me, shook her head, and returned her attention to her phone. I watched as she vigorously swiped at whatever video game she was playing as I took a seat at the opposite corner of the couch.

We sat in silence for a while until Jacques was shown in. I was thankful to see a friendly face.

He rushed over to me, taking a seat opposite from me on the other couch.

"Lisa, thank God. Are you okay? Werewolves? Nasty things. Are you hurt?"

I smiled a little. Jacques was looking not as dead as usual. His deathly pallor remained, but he'd lost much of his rotting pock marks.

"I'm fine." I gave him a tight smile. "You look good. Are you fending off your curse a little?"

"The power, I could deal with. But did you see what it was doing to my complexion?"

"Good for you. If you ever need—"

He waved me off. "I appreciate it, Lisa, but I can't afford to do this whole..." he waved his hand in my general direction. "...thing. I just don't have it in me."

Brian was shown in soon after. He looked nervous. He gave me a quick nod and sat between Tracy and me.

"You okay?" I asked.

"Yea. How much trouble are we in?"

"Save it for Ivan," Tracy interjected. "If I were you, I'd keep my mouth shut on any werewolf business until he gets here."

"Oh, don't listen to her. She's trying to scare you," said Jacques.

"I'm trying to help him," Tracy replied. Her eyes never left her phone.

Next came Richard and Walter.

I arched my brows.

Walter seemed to pick up on my unspoken question. "We just met outside and chatted a little before coming up together."

"Or maybe we've formed an alliance!" Richard jeered at me.

I rolled my eyes at him.

Richard and Walter took the remaining seats on the couch with Jacques.

"We're one chair short," I said. "Dylan."

Richard shrugged.

Across the room, two ladder-back chairs flanked a small table and chess board. The pieces were scattered mid-game. I grabbed one of the chairs and placed it at the opposite end of the couches.

Richard shook his head.

"What?" I snapped at him.

"I'm sorry, but it's just such a metaphor for your lot in life, isn't it? Poor Dylan doesn't have a place to sit, so Lisa, one of the eldest vampires in this room, gets up and moves furniture around like a servant."

"Wow, you're quite the psychologist. Is that what you gleaned from this little scene?"

"Lisa, my observations—"

"Jesus, can we get through one fucking meeting without you two sniping at each other?" Tracy cut in, still never taking her eyes from her screen.

She had a point. Bickering with Richard was useless. I returned to my seat. Richard chuckled quietly to himself.

The door opened again, and Dylan entered. With his skinny jeans and faded, faux-retro rock band tee shirt, he was dressed about ten years younger than the age he looked.

Richard shook his head, giving an indication he disapproved of Dylan's casual attire.

"What?" Dylan confronted the looks he was getting from the boys. Tracy was still feverishly dragging her thumb across her screen. "Ivan said I could hunt in Chinatown after the meeting. *Chinatown.*" He grinned.

"You're such a pig," Tracy muttered.

Dylan wisely ignored her.

The door opened again. This time an out-of-breath Úll jogged into the room, likely having sprinted out in front of Ivan to pull off his announcement.

"Ivan MacAlistah! Laird o' the New England—"

Ivan passed the little redcap and strode into the room. Tracy quickly stowed her phone in her purse. Ivan wasn't alone. Another man trailed in behind him.

"Bleed," Úll finished, and quickly closed the door as he retreated from the room.

Ivan moved around the couches to take his place in the chair facing them. The other man, I didn't recognize him, stood behind him. Ivan opened his mouth to speak, but his eyes fell on Dylan.

Not Dylan. Dylan's chair. Ivan looked toward his chess table then turned to look at me.

So, I took a chair. Big deal. I shrugged at him.

I had no clue who the guy standing behind Ivan was. He wore a suit and looked to be in his late twenties, maybe his early thirties. In lieu of dress shoes, he wore black sneakers. He was unshaven and had dark hair that nearly graced the top of his shoulders. The man looked back at me and gave me a smile, but that smile did not reach his eyes.

Ivan got right to it. "Last night, my sources informed me they saw news footage of three wolves and a Neapolitan mastiff roaming the streets of Watertown. This report came in a couple of nights after a similar news story showed *two* wolves in Watertown."

His eyes fell on me before continuing.

"Now, normally, I may not have jumped to conclusions, but the mastiff? And when I dispatched Walter to Watertown," he didn't even pause before raising his voice, "he told me *two* members of this bleed knew about the presence of werewolves in our territory and *failed* to report it!"

Ivan's hands gripped the arms of his chair, threatening to crush them. His fiery gaze swept across the room and settled on Brian and me.

A dangerous silence settled into the room. I averted my eyes from Ivan.

Ivan leaned back in his chair and relinquished the death grip he had on its arm rests. "We must move quickly. You will divide into groups of two. Any two of you should be more than enough to deal with a werewolf."

Any two of us? I didn't feel great about that. My stomach tightened.

Ivan continued, "Jacques and Dylan, take Brighton. Lisa and Walter, take Cambridge. Tracy and Brian, take Watertown."

Richard was left off the list, likely for his station.

"Find the werewolf and kill it. Report your findings to Marcus." Ivan gestured to the man standing behind him.

Find the werewolf and kill it? My thoughts went to Coyotita.

Marcus moved to each of us and handed out business cards. The cards were blank except for a single phone number. We all took them quietly, trying to evade Ivan's attention. All except for Richard, who scowled at Marcus and snatched the card from his hand.

What the hell was that all about?

"Marcus is my new damphyr, and he'll be my liaison to you while you hunt. If you need a body disposed of, contact Richard," said Ivan.

"Ivan," I began slowly. He glared at me. "There is a person helping us. Not a werewolf, exactly. She's a coywolf. Didn't Walter tell you? Then there is the damphyr that—"

"I'm not interested in the damphyr. The werewolf is my priority. And I do not care if it's a coywolf, coyote, or someone's German shepherd. If it shifts to a human shape, we kill it." Ivan locked eyes with me.

I didn't want to see Coyotita hurt over this, but there was no way Ivan was going to budge. All I could do is hope that Brian could get to her first.

"Now go. Put an end to this," Ivan ordered. We all rose out of our seats.

"Lisa, stay behind," he amended. I sat back down.

The rest of the bleed made their way out the door. Brian lingered as if expecting to be held after too. Tracy grabbed his arm and led him out of the room.

Marcus lingered behind Ivan's chair looking smug.

Who the hell was this guy?

The door shut and the room was basked in silence again. Ivan took a moment to cradle his face in his hand before speaking.

"Siobhan, we cannot tolerate a werewolf in our territory. You *know* this."

Ivan was a contained powder keg, speaking in measured tones. As much as I wanted to interrupt him about Coyotita, I held my tongue.

He seemed to sense my distress, and his voice adopted a pleading cadence. "What if she bites another coywolf? Would a new lycanthrope's temperament be as neutral toward our kind? We can't risk werewolves roaming free within New England. They *must* be destroyed. If we allow one in, it'll spread its disease to countless others within so many years."

I could only nod. I made a quick plan to call Brian and tell him to warn Coyotita.

Ivan leaned forward and clasped his hands together. "I know you've had a rough couple of nights."

I looked at him. *How did he know?*

"You called me. Left me a voicemail," he reminded me. "I'm sorry about your friend, the dogsitter. I called my connections at the hospital and your alibi is set up. That'll keep your detective off your back."

I gave a small nod. "Thank you."

He nodded thoughtfully, and his expression softened. "Siobhan, I need to impress on you the dangers of attachment. We've had this conversation over and over and through the decades for over a century. But befriending a werewolf? This isn't just a lack of judgement, this... this troubles me. Please, tell me this isn't anything I need to worry about."

His tone was caring, but behind that façade was a deadly warning.

Marcus continued to loom behind him, unmoving.

It unnerved the hell out of me.

Ivan continued, "For the lives we lead, sometimes the people we care about are put in danger. I'd hate to think a similar lack of judgement on your part was what led to Amy Wagner's death."

I shot up out of my chair, glaring daggers. That was a low blow.

Ivan met my gaze, challenging me.

We locked eyes a moment. I wanted so badly to tell him to go fuck himself.

I held my tongue. I was fully aware I was already treading on dangerous ground.

Ivan leaned back in his chair again. Marcus folded his arms.

"I'll be careful," I said at last. "If there's nothing else, I need to catch up with Walter and go hunt."

Ivan simply swept his hand at the door. I stalked out of the room.

Ivan was wrong about Amy. I was always careful with her. Suggesting I was somehow responsible for her death was the kind of accusation I'd expect from Richard, not Ivan. It made my blood boil.

I couldn't help Amy, but I could help Coyotita.

If Brian couldn't find her and warn her, my bleed was going to kill her.

Episode 27

The Death Sleep

"So, what's the plan?" Walter asked as I strode out of Ivan's brownstone complex.

I barely even registered Walter's question. Ivan's callous suggestion that I had something to do with Amy's death had me seeing red.

"Hey. You in there?" Walter prodded.

"Yea." I snapped out of my consternation. "So... we patrol Cambridge looking for werewolves? It's a stupid plan. I told you about the damphyr who burst into flames and disappeared. Ivan didn't even bring that up. There's more to this than just a werewolf on the loose."

"That information wouldn't change our mission tonight," Walter said. "I told Ivan there was a foreign damphyr around, but he was so worked up about the werewolf, he didn't care. And, for Brian's sake, I didn't push the issue."

"Brian's sake?"

"He blamed Brian for *letting* a werewolf slip into his territory," said Walter.

"Seriously? Jesus."

Walter shrugged. "Regardless, we still need to patrol around. If we see a werewolf, we deal with it. If we some flaming damphyr, we deal with it. The plan doesn't change."

"And Coyotita?"

"Who?"

"The were-coywolf. She's not dangerous," I said.

"It's complicated. She's a lycanthrope. We don't have a lot of leeway here."

"If we can drive her off, maybe?"

"To where? Canada? Theresa owns Vermont and then there's Seamus in the northeast. She needs to be out of the *bleed's* territory, not just Brian's."

I shook my head and gritted my teeth.

"I can't just look the other way or sweep this under a carpet. I'm one of Ivan's enforcers." Walter put a hand on my shoulder as a show of compassion.

I shrugged out of it. If Walter wasn't going to help, then I would deal with it on my own.

Walter and I opted to take two cars to cover more ground. It was a logical plan, but it also gave me the freedom to call Brian in private.

Brian was on board without an issue and made the plan to head directly to Whitney Hill Park to find Coyotita and warn her.

I asked about Chewie. Brian said he was riding with him on his own patrol.

Damn, I missed that dog. But I couldn't begrudge Brian for reconnecting with him.

I swung by my house in Charlestown and grabbed my shillelagh and pistol. Coyotita aside, there was something else out there, and I wasn't about to engage whatever it was without some weapons.

Driving around Cambridge was torturous.

I tried driving down side streets looking for any places that might be ideal for coywolves to avoid detection. I drove behind loading docks and into backlots. I couldn't find a thing.

I couldn't stay out of my own head. The entire mission revolved around either hurting an innocent being or engaging an enemy we didn't understand.

Coyotita was in danger. This... person, who had been a wild animal, now had human intelligence, and she was mourning the death of her mate.

The more I worried, the more other unpleasant matters resurfaced. They compounded together and weighed on me like an anvil crushing my spirit. Amy was dead. Chewie may never live with me again. And I may have blown it with Neil for good.

The loss of a potential thrall was one thing, but who was I kidding? I'd lost a lot more than that.

The more I drove, the more frustrated I became.

Fuck this.

I needed to call Brian, confirm Coyotita was safe, and go home. This was a waste of my time.

Before I could call him, my dash lit up with an incoming call.

Who the hell is Larry Doone?

"Hello?"

"Lisa, it's Tracy. You still in Cambridge?"

"Yea." My chest tightened. Tracy never called to be social. Something was wrong.

Tracy made a sound like she was in pain.

"Tracy, is everything okay?"

"No, it's not fucking okay. Why do you think I'm calling you? Your boyfriend thought he'd be smart and slip into the woods to warn his coyote friend."

Boyfriend?

"Brian and I aren't—"

"Who the fuck cares? I followed him to this little strip of woods, and we both got jumped by the damphyr."

Two vampires against a damphyr should have been no trouble.

"Where's Brian?" My stomach was in my throat.

"I... I don't know. He went down. I had to run. He was fast. Strong. I turned into a bat. Had to take some guy's phone."

I had more questions, but Tracy let out another wail of pain.

"Where are you?" I asked.

"Hiding behind some trees. There's a building here. Says Bright Horizons on it."

"Near the CVS?"

"How the fuck should I know?"

"Just stay put. I'm on my way."

"No. You need to get to those woods. Come heavy. See what you can do for Brian. I need to fly off and feed. I'm pretty fucked up."

"Was Chewie with—"

She'd hung up.

"Shit!" I slammed my car's steering wheel.

This entire operation was doomed from the get-go because Ivan didn't want to deal with the details. And now Brian was hurt. Or worse.

I called Walter and explained what Tracy had told me. We both agreed we should lead-foot it to Watertown and hit the park. Walter called for backup, but I impressed upon him that I wasn't waiting if Brian was still out there.

He begrudgingly agreed to go with me, and the backup, if we needed it, would have to come later. I wasn't going to wait.

I banged a U-turn and sped toward Whitney Hill Park.

About five minutes into my swerving, gas-burning suburban drag race, my phone lit up. Detective Pierce was calling me. The same asshole who was inclined to think I killed Amy Wagner.

I let it go to voicemail.

Whitney Hill didn't have great parking. There were some spaces close to its adjacent football field, but that was the far end of the actual woods.

I parked on the side of Marion Road, hopeful no busy-body would care that I left my car parked in front of someone's house.

I fought every instinct to charge into the woods alone.

Walter had a point about backup, and I decided to wait a little while for him to show up.

Thankfully, his SUV pulled in behind my car about five minutes later.

"You waited for me." He seemed surprised.

"Let's go." I started walking toward the woods.

"Hold up."

I stopped and whirled on him. Impatience screwed up my face.

"This thing, whatever it is. It's more than a damphyr. It can disappear in flames and bested two vampires. Or maybe we run into the werewolf. We try to find Brian, but if we get into an altercation with anything, we have to run. If Tracy and Brian couldn't take this thing, you and I won't do any better."

"Fine," I said. I marched into the woods. Walter was right, of course. We couldn't take whatever bested Brian and Tracy. But I wasn't going to think about that. I had to find Brian.

The small strip of woods didn't offer a lot of places to search. I was optimistic about finding Brian quickly. We realized at once that we were alone in the woods. The upper and lower paths were clear. If there was someone here, he was either gone or hiding.

Walter walked beside me as I forged down the lower path first. It ran parallel to the football field and emptied out into someone's yard.

It was clear.

We doubled back and headed up the upper path. Walter and I walked in silence. The path flanked a row of houses and sported the iconic signpost that told the direction and distance of faraway cities with a series of wooden arrow-shaped signs.

We were very close to Coyotita's den. I hoped she'd gotten out, but I didn't want to check on her while I had Walter in tow.

The upper path spilled out into a street. We were alone, but I smelled blood.

Walter picked up on it too. "That could be anyone's. There's no one here."

Growling.

A low, rolling growl permeated the darkness. Walter shifted his stance and stood back-to-back with me.

Then silence.

The smells mingled together. Blood. Dog. Fire.

Then the smell of dog was gone, replaced by something else.

Coyotita, naked, strode from behind the trees. "Lisa."

Walter shifted his weight again. I moved in front of him with lightning speed. "Don't you dare. She's been helping us."

Walter relaxed, and I turned to Coyotita. Even in her human shape, she had bloody wounds and bruises. They were healing, but they were fresh.

"Brian's missing," I said.

"No," Coyotita said. "Follow me."

She led us down the slope to her den. The small hole was still obscured by brush and other flora.

Before I could ask any questions, Chewie wriggled out of the opening.

"Chewie!" The poor barghest was a little beaten up and walked to me with a limp. He pushed his head into my stomach, and I scratched behind his ears.

"Brian is also inside. He fell and did not wake. I pulled him inside my den," Coyotita explained.

Walter appraised Chewie and looked at Coyotita. "How big is your den?"

"My mate and I dug it large to house all our forms," she explained.

"He may have fallen into the death sleep," I said. "Can we get him out?"

My phone rang again. I didn't even bother checking to see who it was and hit the button to ignore.

Coyotita eyed my phone, looking perplexed a moment. She looked back to me. "Yes. Let me get him. There are still many hours of darkness if you want to let him rest somewhere else. These woods are not safe."

"But you stayed," I said.

"I did not want to leave Brian," Coyotita said, plainly.

I shot Walter a look to reinforce my position on Coyotita.

"Let's just get him out of here and back to his house. Then we can figure out the hunt when everyone else has arrived," Walter quipped.

"Tell them to wait outside the woods until you and I return," I said.

"We don't both need to take Brian. Someone needs to stay here."

"I don't want to leave you alone with Coyotita." I frowned.

Walter huffed. "I won't touch her. She saved one of ours. Between you and me, we never found her. But Coyoteeya—"

"Coyotita," she corrected.

"Coyotita. You should go. When the rest of the bleed gets here, it won't be safe for you."

Chewie bumped into Coyotita's legs. She stooped down and nuzzled into him. "I will do as you say."

She crawled into her den. The sound of scraping dirt soon followed. The smell of freshly overturned soil hit my nostrils. Coyotita emerged a moment after, bare ass first. I looked away from the R-rated spectacle and smacked Walter on the arm so he'd pay her the same courtesy.

Brian was produced from the den in short order.

He was unmoving. Bloodied. Broken.

Vampires don't need to breathe as mortals do. We still take air in and out as part of a reanimated respiratory system, but oxygen isn't required to sustain us. It just helps us imitate life.

But in the *death sleep*, Brian's chest did not rise and fall. He looked dead. Truly dead.

My heart sank. Chewie whined and sniffed at him.

I crouched down and put my hand on the large mastiff. "He's okay. We got to get him back home and into his basement. Then we'll get him blood."

"He can have some of mine," Coyotita offered.

"Like hell he can!" Walter spat.

"Take it easy," I said to Walter. I turned to Coyotita. "We can't drink lycanthrope blood. Bad things happen."

"I did not know," she said.

"It's okay. And he needs a lot, so none of us here can give him what he needs. We'll have to work something out after. Maybe tomorrow night."

Chewie whined again.

I pet him. "He'll be okay, buddy. I promise."

My phone rang again. This time, it pissed me off.

I answered. "*What?*"

"Lisa? It's Sophie. From the coven."

It was more than unusual for the coven to call me. "What is it?"

"I... we've detected something terrible. Evil. We need your help."

I looked around the woods. "An evil? Where?"

"It's in a park. In Watertown."

"Whitney Hill Park?"

"Yes. How did you—"

"I'm here now."

"Lisa, you need to get out. You need to get out now!"

Episode 28

Evil In The Woods

If the Peabody Coven was telling me to get out of the woods, I wasn't about to argue or hesitate. The coterie of seven women was heavily steeped in divination and had a knack for knowing when the shit was about to hit the fan.

Walter hustled behind me as I carried Brian to my car. Chewie loped beside me, letting out mournful whines.

"What's going on? What did your coven say?" Walter asked.

"They're not *my* coven. Can you get the door?"

Walter opened my car's back door for me while I hefted Brian. I gingerly laid my friend down across the seats.

"They sensed something evil in the woods and urged us to get out. No surprise considering it took down Tracy and Brian. But if the coven is warning me, I'm not taking it lightly."

"So now what?" Walter asked.

"Wait outside the park. And I mean that. Stay out on the street if you have to."

"I'll call the others."

"No, not yet. I need to get Brian safely tucked away at his house and then head up to meet the coven to discuss whatever it was they sensed."

"You can't do that part over the phone?" Walter asked.

"Apparently not."

I was about to explain more, but Coyotita came out of the woods. She was still naked. "I should go?"

"Yes, and head north," I said. "It's not safe here with whatever that thing is and it's going to get worse when the rest of my bleed shows up to hunt it."

"I will go," she said. She looked behind her toward the woods. For a moment, she was quiet. "My mate is gone."

It was a heart sinking moment, but we were also standing at the end of Marion Street talking to a naked woman.

Before I could urge her to be on her way, Coyotita walked off. "Goodbye, Lisa."

As she entered the brush, Coyotita fell to all fours and fluidly shifted into a coywolf. Padding into the woods, she disappeared from sight.

"Damn, she can change forms fast," Walter said.

"Come on. We gotta get moving."

I opened the passenger side door, and Chewie hopped in. "Stay here and don't call the troops in yet."

"I thought I was the enforcer here," Walter frowned.

"There's stuff going on here we don't understand. Until I call with more information, we shouldn't take any action."

"I should call this in to Ivan." Walter made it sound like it was a bad thing. Like tattling.

I shrugged. "Knock yourself out."

Driving was hard with Chewie trying to rest his head on my lap. The poor dog was absolutely forlorn over Brian.

"We're going to get him home and safe. Don't you worry."

I hoped my words comforted him more than they did me. Getting Brian to rouse from his death sleep was going to take a lot of blood.

I shifted my attention back to the other colossal problem this evening – whatever we were dealing with in the park.

I called Sophie back.

"Hello?"

"Hey, it's Lisa. I'm out of the park."

"Good. Can you get here? To Andrea's?"

"Yes, but I need to drop off a friend. Can you tell me what we're dealing with?"

"There's a... demon loose."

"What? Hold on. A demon? I'm already dealing with a werewolf and a damphyr. And the damphyr is way more powerful than he should be."

"It's not three beings. It's one."

"How?"

"We can explain when you get here. I need to help Alice do another reading. When can you be here?"

"I don't know." I sighed in exasperation. "Two hours?"

"Hurry."

Brian was the priority, but I also needed whatever information the coven had discovered. I pressed on the gas pedal.

Brian didn't live far from the woods, and I pulled into his driveway a few minutes later. Here is where I got creative.

I let Chewie out of the car and went around the back and pulled Brian out. I slung one of his arms over my shoulder and carried him while his feet dangled on the ground.

From afar, it would look like I was helping an inebriated friend.

If anyone came closer, my *Weekend At Bernie's* gambit would have been blown.

When I got to his front door, I propped Brian's weight onto one arm. With my free hand, I shoved the front door forward.

The deadbolt smashed through his door frame cleanly but left the door intact. A clean break.

It wasn't my first time.

Chewie padded inside behind me as I made a beeline to the basement door.

The last time I was in Brian's basement, I almost got fried by his ultraviolet light boobytrap. This time, I pulled off one of Brian's shoes and tossed it down the stairs.

Nothing triggered.

Beside me, Chewie woofed.

"Coast is clear, buddy."

Brian's basement was unfinished. The side to the left had his UV boobytrap and some storage boxes. It also opened to a bulkhead leading outside.

I found his saferoom on the right. Like mine, it was a room built within the basement itself.

I set Brain down and tested the door. This was a door I didn't want to smash down, even if I could. If built right, his safe room should have been able to withstand anything I could dish out.

The door was unlocked, which made sense. Like mine, the door to Brian's saferoom locked from the inside.

Chewie whined at Brian's side.

"He's going to be okay. He just needs to drink. Tomorrow night, we'll bring him something."

Or *someone*, more likely. I'd have to be careful no one lost their life over it.

As always, Chewie seemed to understand every word I said. He padded over to me and pushed his block head into my stomach. I scratched him behind his ears.

"Let me get him inside."

Chewie backed off a little and I picked Brian back up and went into his saferoom. It was a lot like mine, with a bed, a nightstand, and a small chest of drawers.

I laid him on the bed and kissed the top of his forehead.

He looked paler than normal; his body having taken whatever blood-stores it had to heal what it could. His body had become stiff like a corpse.

It wasn't easy seeing Brian like this. I wiped my eyes with the back of my hand.

Chewie hopped up on the bed and curled up next to him.

"Chewie, I can't lock this door. I can close it and he'll be safe from the sun, but I can't lock it. You need to guard him, okay?"

Chewie replied with a sonorous woof.

It felt awful to leave Brian in that state and abandon Chewie when he was so upset, but I had to get to Peabody.

An hour later, I was at Andrea's house.

Pungent chemicals assaulted my nose when I was shown into Andrea's den, the small room that served as the coven's meeting place.

A wet spot on the carpet near the coffee table betrayed the origin of the scent. Some sort of cleaning product did its best to mask the smell of vomit.

Alice's divination runes were strewn on the table's surface, but Alice was nowhere to be seen.

"It's bad," said Sophie, signing as she talked.

Sophie looked like she had a massive invisible weight on her shoulders. The usually peppy druid hipster looked strung out and forlorn.

The entire room was somber. Shaken. I glanced back at the recently cleansed splatter on the carpet.

"Where's Alice?" I was able to sign without speaking. I simply signed *where* and then each letter of her name. I forgot how to make an *e*, but Andrea got it.

"In her divination, she connected to the demon. She saw what she needed to, but it made her sick just by sensing it." Andrea signed. I wasn't fluent in ASL, so it was Jennifer who interpreted, the coven's only resident witch.

"She threw up," Marisol said, as if it wasn't obvious. "She's still in the bathroom."

"She's been in there a while. I'll go check on her," said Su-Hyun, scurrying out of the room.

I'd been around over a century and a half. I'd encountered lycanthropes, fae, seirenes, and a pukwudgie. I know the old gods exist; the Norse, the Olympians, the Tuatha de Danann. I've heard of demons, sure. But I'd never met one.

"We weren't aware it was a demon. We weren't sure what it was. We thought it might be a damphyr, but it was able to burst into flames and disappear," I said.

"Fireshifting," Jennifer said. She spoke as she signed for Andrea's benefit and my own. "It's like a teleport."

I nodded a little. "So, what do we do?"

A few eyes fell on Sophie.

Sophie brought up her hands to reply but took a deep breath before speaking. Her signs were shaky and stunted as she spoke. "I need to build a ritual circle while the coven boosts my power. It'll be dangerous. The demon will need to be in the circle."

"How do we get him into the circle?" I asked.

All eyes shifted from Sophie to me.

Well, fuck.

Marisol broke the uneasy silence. "You. We need muscle to wrangle the thing and force it into the circle."

"Once it's inside, it'll be trapped. The ritual will banish it back to wherever it came from," Brenda added.

Sophie bobbed her head along with what her compatriots explained.

"We'll need more than me. The creature already took out two of my bleed." The whole thought of tussling with this thing made me uneasy.

"You don't need to kill it or even subdue it. You just need to push it into the circle," Andrea offered. Jennifer continued to interpret for my benefit.

Just. Yea, sure.

We'd all be lucky to get out of this alive.

Episode 29

Showdown With A Demon

I FOLLOWED THE PEABODY Coven to Whitney Hill in my car. All seven women had piled into Brenda's minivan. Alice was back on her feet, looking a little pale, but no worse for the wear.

A couple of the women brought supplies with them. Sophie brought a big canister of salt, and Su-Hyun carried a plastic grocery bag filled with what looked like strips of yellow paper.

Both cars were parked at the Victory Field lot, and we trekked across the football field to the entrance of the woods. The football field was ringed by a racing track and a low fence separated the wooded conservation area from the field.

The women were an assortment of abilities for getting over the fence. Andrea and Jennifer, the eldest women of the coven, bemoaned the effort on first sight of the obstacle and struggled climbing up enough to get a leg over. Sophie, Brenda, and Marisol fared better and were sure footed as they hit the other side. Alice and Su-Hyun, young women in the twenties, were nimble and scaled the fence with ease.

I simply jumped over the damn thing.

"Show off," Marisol muttered.

What was I going to do, put on some act of me needing to climb over? They knew what I was. But I couldn't help grinning at her.

Walter crossed the open area toward us, putting the women on guard.

"He's with me. I told you we needed more muscle," I explained.

"Is he a...?" Sophie didn't finish her question.

"Yes," I answered.

Walter looked over the assembled group. "This is them?"

"No, this is the Harlem Globe Trotters." I put my hands on my hips.

"Funny. You know you kept me waiting over two hours?"

My expression softened. "Sorry about that. But I needed to see them. They can help us get rid of this thing."

Walter gave a slow nod, looking wary himself. He kept looking at Sophie, who was signing everything that was said.

"First things first. Walter, this is the Peabody Coven. Ladies, this is Walter."

"You gave them my name?" Walter frowned.

I rolled my eyes. "We're going into the woods to banish a demon. I think we're all good secret keepers here."

"A demon?" Walter frowned.

Andrea made some signs. Sophie interpreted, "Go ahead, Alice."

Alice let out a breath. "This demon can wear the shape of the ones it has killed and taken power from. We know of at least two forms; a damphyr and a werewolf."

"Sort of a coywerewolf. Or Werecoywolf," I said.

"Huh?" asked Alice.

"Nothing. Go on."

"The demon siphons power from the things it kills, so either form is more powerful than both its victims were in life. It seems to linger around the area because it's tethered to the place it came from. I think its plan is to break free once it steals enough power and go where it pleases."

"The place where it came from?" asked Walter.

Sophie shifted uncomfortably.

"Hell or maybe one of the other dark planes. It was... summoned here by a dark wizard," said Alice.

Sophie made face at Alice but signed her response.

"You're lying," said Walter.

"First of all, stop zoning in on her heartbeat," I said. "And second, drop it. The point is there is a demon on the loose and we need to deal with it."

"I'm not dropping it. She's lying to me. Someone *summoned* a demon here." Walter took a step closer to Alice.

"It was me," Sophie said.

Walter bristled.

"Sophie!" scolded Alice.

"No, it's okay." Sophie looked at Walter. "It was the book. The necromantic book we got from Lisa. I destroyed it, but its dark energies ripped a wound in the earth in these woods. A demon must have crawled out after. I never knew."

"Relax, Walter. They're on our side," I said.

He eased up but flashed a look at me.

His look told me he was not okay with this. I was going to have to do damage control before he went tattling to Ivan. Ivan knew about the coven, but if he thought they were dangerous, he'd order them killed.

An uneasy silence settled between us all.

Su-Hyun's hand slowly slipped into her bag.

Walter was in front of her in a blur. "What do you have there? You gonna pull something on me?"

Su-Hyun's eyes went wide in terror. She back-peddled away from him.

I was on Walter a second later. I grabbed his collar and pulled him backwards. "What the hell is wrong with you? She's probably reaching for something defensive. You're scaring everyone."

"What if she was reaching for a wand or something?"

"A *wand*? Are you serious?"

"I don't know! They summoned a demon! That thing almost killed Brian and Tracy."

Andrea stepped forward to Walter. Walter's lips curled into a snarl.

"Andrea..." I realized she couldn't see my lips move or anyone's signs. She'd locked eyes with Walter.

She signed as Sophie spoke. "Before you think about spinning some story about us being dangerous and unchecked, I'll remind you that we've been allies to your bleed through Lisa for a long time. We were the ones that destroyed the book that had spells to ensnare and control vampires. A spell you yourself fell victim to, if I'm not mistaken. And we were the ones that discerned the nature of the threat in these woods, and we are the ones you need to vanquish it."

"A threat you caused." Walter matched her gaze evenly.

Andrea didn't back down.

"Enough." I put a hand on Walter's chest. "Walter, if you sell them out to Ivan, then you're an idiot and an asshole. Andrea also helped me find the werewolf that was causing us trouble a few years back. The one that killed Allen."

"I thought your seiren friend found the werewolf," said Walter.

"Lucy saw the werewolf in a vision and warned me. Andrea's coven helped us find him."

Walter looked thoughtful a moment.

"Any bleed would be lucky to have magical allies. I need you to think about the big picture here," I said.

Walter remained in thought, staring the women down.

"Walter," I scolded.

"Fine. I'll let it slide. This time," Walter warned.

Walter shoved his phone back into his pocket. "Alright. Jacques and Dylan are on their way. I told them to be cool with the witches."

Technically, Jennifer was the only witch among them, but I let it go. "Thank you."

Sophie kicked forest debris away from a small circular area to expose the bare ground underneath. "Jen, you should have brought your besom again."

Jennifer nodded to whatever that meant.

Sophie poured salt from her canister in a circle but stopped short of completing it. "When we finally get this thing and push it into the circle, I'll salt off the rest and it'll be trapped inside. Then we can do the banishment ritual."

"How are we going to lure the demon here?" I asked.

"This area of the woods is his tether. He can only go so far from it in any direction in a radius. It means he's likely to pass through here eventually," said Sophie.

I frowned. "How far out are Jacques and Dylan?"

"Forty minutes, give or take," said Walter.

"Then we should leave the area until the extra help arrives."

Sophie finished laying down her salt. "Good idea. I'm all set with this."

"Good. Let's head back to the football field to wait," I suggested.

"Wait." Walter put a hand on my shoulder. "You smell that?"

I took a deep sniff. The same odd scent hit me. Clothes with no human-like smells. The last time I smelled something like this, I wondered if it had been a pile of clothes. It wound up being the damphyr.

Walter didn't wait for me to confirm it. "He's here."

Andrea signed at Walter and I, while Sophie whispered. "Didn't you say he took out two of your number already? Should we retreat until backup arrives?"

The demon in a damphyr skin lumbered toward us.

"Too late. It's seen us," I said.

The shifting started as it strode toward us. It didn't shapeshift like anything I'd ever seen before. Lycanthropes and vampires stretch or compact. Our body parts elongate or sprout new features in a literal transformation from one form to another. It doesn't take a tremendous amount of time like the movies, but we can't walk and transform at the same time. Our legs would give out.

But this thing? It *rippled* into its new form. In a matter of seconds, an otherwise human body mutated into a seven-foot-tall beast. The coywolf's features stretched and bent upright into a monstrous aberration.

Its jeans and flannel shirt hung off the beast in rags, unable to contain the creature's massive frame.

Its lips turned to a snarl, exposing long, deadly teeth. Its ears pressed flat against its head. Wicked claws curled in anticipation of rending flesh.

The women of the coven stood between us and the beast. The thing wearing Coyotita's mate's skin stalked toward them.

I gave a nod to Walter. He inclined his chin back at me.

We leaped over the gathered ensemble of women and landed in front of the monster.

"Back off! Stay behind us!" I called to them.

I pulled the gun from my holster. I was loathe to use it with houses so close, but I really didn't have a lot of options.

The impact of each round sent the creature stumbling backwards. The shots echoed through the park. It bled from several holes in its chest.

The beast opened its jaws and let loose with a deafening cry. Like a coyote's yipping whine turned up to eleven. Its shrill wailing sent shivers up my spine.

Walter huffed. "Oh good. You pissed it off. Are those even silver?"

"No. But it's not really a lycanthrope. It's a demon. What takes out a demon?"

"No idea." Walter scowled.

It charged us, claws leading the charge, with jaws wide.

Walter met the demon head on and slammed into him. The monster bit into his shoulder and raked claws across his back.

Walter cried out.

I circled behind the beast and slammed into it from behind. We had to get it into the circle.

"Walter, pull it to the circle!" I backed off again, preparing another shove from behind.

Walter hollered in pain. He was getting the brunt of it.

I slammed into the creature again, causing it to stagger toward the circle. Walter had his arms around its waist, trying to pull it and doing his best to endure the bloody thrashing the demon was delivering.

Inch by inch, we edged the bastard closer to the circle.

The thing whirled on me, spinning within Walter's grasp. Walter kept pulling. I leaped back to avoid a swing of claws.

I really didn't want to attack this thing head on, but Walter was now pulling from behind.

I slammed into his front. It was like hitting a wall. I bounced back and fell on my ass, narrowly escaping another clawed barrage over my head.

The demon turned back on Walter. I backed off like a crab and got to my feet.

One of the women pleaded, "We need to help them!"

"No!" I shouted, putting my hand up like a traffic cop. "Stay back!"

The beast bit down on Walter's shoulder again. Walter cried out once more. The creature shook him in his massive maw. Walter was like a chew toy.

It released Walter, and he slammed into a tree. The creature stalked toward him. I grabbed its arm and pulled.

It lifted me off the ground like I weighed nothing. A quick snap of his arm and I went sailing through the air, slamming into the ground some twenty feet away.

Walter was back on his feet, bloody and broken. One of his eyes was swollen shut. His right arm hung limp at his side.

The demon swept his claws across Walter's throat.

Precious blood ran from Walter's neck like a faucet. He clutched at his throat with his one good hand. He fell to his knees and his eyes found mine.

"Run."

Walter crumpled, bleeding into the ground.

The beast turned to me, baring bloody fangs.

I got to my feet.

I looked at the coven. They were rooted to the ground in fear.

I cried to them, "Run!"

I charged the monster.

The Demon And The Dark Spiral

I RAN HEADLONG AT the beast with the visceral realization that I could meet my final death.

If I retreated, the creature would kill all the women in the coven. I was their only hope of surviving.

All I had to do was buy them some time.

Wicked claws slashed over my head as I ducked and brought my fist into the demon's gut. In its werecoywolf form, it was much taller than I, so my strategy was to stay low and pick low targets.

I circled around to his flank and kicked at one of his legs. I may as well have kicked a wall.

The creature spun on me.

I kept moving.

The women of the coven were not running. To my horror, they were gathering around the monster.

"What are you doing?" I shouted at them. "Run!"

"He's almost in the circle. Look!" Sophie pointed at the salt circle she'd drawn out. The demon had one foot inside.

I just had to push him in, and Sophie could seal off the circle, trapping him inside.

Sure. Piece of cake.

It meant I needed to push or pull him into the circle and that meant grappling. It meant I was going to get claws and teeth for my effort.

I slammed into him, wrapping my arms around his waist. I pushed him with all my might. My feet slipped on the ground as I tried to gain purchase and move him those last few inches.

His bite came down on me. The monster's fangs ripped through my jacket and shirt and pierced into my flesh. I cried out, and my hold on him faltered. My knees buckled. Pain radiated through my shoulder and down my spine. Every muscle along my back was on fire.

My feet came off the ground as the beast lifted me up in his maw. He shook me back and forth like a chew toy and then released his jaws, letting me sail through the air and slam into a nearby tree.

Then he marched on me.

At least he was still focused on me. The circle trap was a bust. I called out to the coven again. "You have to run! I can't push him in!"

I struggled to get to my feet, bracing myself against the tree for support. I found I couldn't move my left arm. My shoulder was bleeding bad.

I had to hand it to Walter. He lasted a lot longer than I was going to.

Movement from the left. A blur of fur and claws.

A second beast slammed into my attacker, raking claws and gnashing teeth. The new combatant was unmistakably another werecoywolf in her hybrid form.

Coyotita?

The two tussled on the ground clawing and biting. It was impossible for me to tell who was who.

"What's happening?" Brenda shouted.

"I told you to run! The second one is on our side, but I don't know if she'll be enough," I called back.

My shoulder throbbed in pulses of searing pain.

The women weren't budging. Sophie was repairing the scuffed-up areas of her salt circle.

God damn it.

"Coyotita?" I called at the two wrestling monsters.

One of them raised her head briefly to swivel her ears at me. Her neck was bleeding. I took that as an acknowledgement.

"Help me drag him!"

I was one-handed, but I grabbed onto the forearm of the demon. Coyotita clamped her jaws on his other arm and together we pulled.

She was doing most of the work, but I did what I could to keep the demon from swiping at her with his other hand.

Together, we pulled him into the circle.

"If we let him go, he'll just run out," I said.

Sophie was way too close to us for my comfort, but she worked to seal off the circle with more salt. "Just hold him until I'm done, then you can let go. This will only trap him, not you," she said.

Salt poured into the remaining inches of the circumference. The hair rose on the back of my neck and the distinct smell of cinnamon hit my nose.

Magic is weird.

"Let go. Get out!" Sophie shouted.

She didn't have to tell me twice. I let go and jumped back.

Coyotita and the demon continued to maul at each other. I moved in to pull her off him.

"Stop!" Sophie called. "You can't try to enter the circle once you've left. You'll disrupt it. She needs to let go and get out now!"

Exasperated, I shook my head. My good hand cradled my aching shoulder.

"Coyotita, you need to get out! Let him go! He's trapped and we're going to send him back to where he came from. Coyotita!"

"If she doesn't let go, he could pull her through with him," Sophie urged.

"Coyotita! Let him go!" I shouted.

Either she wasn't listening, or she just wanted vengeance on the monster that killed her mate so badly that she didn't care.

I assumed it was the latter, so I switched tactics.

"Your mate wouldn't want this. He wouldn't want you to die. Coyotita, he wouldn't want this for you."

Her ears swiveled back at me, even as she had the demon's abdomen clamped in her jaws. She was bleeding from her back and stomach.

"Let him go. Don't let him drag you to where he's going."

"Get her out now!" Sophie yelled.

Her ears swiveled to Sophie and Coyotita released her jaws. She barked at Sophie as if to rebuke her, but she leaped off the demon and out of the circle.

Her massive lycanthrope form was hunched and bleeding, and she whined that same mournful whine she cried when she'd found the body of her mate.

The demon got to his feet and took a step towards me. He hit an invisible wall. He looked this way and that and tried to exit another way but found unseen barriers all around him.

He howled and let his shape melt down into the damphyr again. He tried to breach the circle again but was still unable.

A plume of flames erupted, consuming his body. But when the flames died down, he remained. Trapped.

He cried out, screaming with a human voice.

Sophie chanted. Her coven sisters surrounded her with their hands clasped.

The earth around the demon's feet shimmered. It became hazy and blurry, like heat rising off a desert road.

I don't know what I expected, perhaps the ground cracking open and swallowing him whole. Instead, the blurry haze settled into the area of the circle like a fog.

Slowly, despite his hollering and futile pounding on his invisible prison, the creature sank into dirt. No matter where he ran within the circle, he continued to sink. Trapped in a hazy elevator to hell. Soon he was knee deep in the effect, then hips, then shoulders, and at last, his head went under. Like drowning in solid ground.

The haze dissipated, and I saw the earth shimmer again.

"It's done," said Sophie.

"Finally," moaned Walter. He'd propped himself against a tree, bloodied and broken. In all the fuss with the ritual, I never saw him rouse.

"Walter, you're okay!" I breathed.

"That's relative. But yea... I'll make it." He chuckled a little. "Ow!" He clutched his stomach. "Hurts to laugh."

Coyotita melted to her human shape. She didn't look much better than Walter. I wanted to hug her.

"I could not leave until the creature that killed my mate was destroyed. Or... " She pointed at the ground where he had stood. "Whatever that was."

We heard police sirens in the distance.

That tracked. I'd fired a gun a few times and we'd spent the remainder of the evening yelling and screaming with neighboring houses just a stone's throw away.

"Shit," said Marisol. "Now what?"

Before I could answer Coyotita melted into her coywolf shape. With a swish of her tail, she sprinted away.

I never thanked her.

"Lisa," said Walter. "You need to charm them."

"Police investigating a noise complaint and possible gunshots? Not likely. They'll be too on guard."

"I can't do it looking like this," said Walter.

"I'm not much better." I gestured to my shoulder. My left arm was still too painful to move.

"We aren't getting out of here before they get here. You may need to dig deep on this one."

I frowned. Walter was talking about tapping into my curse to draw enough power to overwhelm them and confound their minds. Anyone can be charmed with enough power. For a cost.

"Fine. But you need to call Dylan and Jacques and tell them we're all set. Tell them the police are here and we can't have them showing up in the middle of all this."

Walter wasn't paying attention. His gaze lingered on the women.

I suddenly became aware of how much blood he'd lost.

"Are you alright?" Alice asked, stepping forward. Her eyes were locked on Walter's.

"Hey." I stepped in front of Walter's line of sight and snapped my fingers a few times at him. "Get a hold of yourself. You can hunt later."

Walter looked away and let out a sigh. "Yea. Yea, sorry."

Alice halted in her tracks and quickly melted back into her coven.

"Call Dylan and Jacques." I urged Walter again.

"Right." Walter fished for his phone, letting out a string of "Ow. Ow. Ow." as he did.

The sirens got louder, and soon the woods was bathed in blue and red pulsating lights.

"Wait here," I said to Walter.

He nodded at me as he chatted on his phone.

Headlights lit up the park as the police car turned onto Marion Drive. Two officers got out, leaving the flashing lights and headlights on. A man and a woman.

My left shoulder was still savagely wounded and bloody.

I had to charm two police officers, who would already be guarded, while covered in blood.

My stomach roiled at how much I'd need to tap into my curse to pull this off.

Everything I'd held on to, everything I'd fought to keep for over one hundred and fifty years, was all going to be lost in a matter of moments once I pushed them into submission with my gaze.

The dark spiral loomed like a yawning abyss, as if black tendrils wrapped around my heart to pull me down. My curse knew when I was weak or desperate. But this time, I'd let it take me.

I reached into myself, beckoning the well of power that laid dormant inside. It answered like a desperate, scorned lover, resentful, but willing.

The rush of power was warm and intoxicating. But I still needed more.

How pale would I get? Would my skin rot? My heart sank as I forced myself to dig deeper.

Deeper into darkness.

Episode 31

Bleeding

MY STOMACH COILED IN upon itself as I left the woods and made my way across the small clearing that transitioned to the dead end of Marion Drive. The officers were already out of the car and making their way into the clearing.

Their flashlights nearly blinded me.

"Jesus, are you okay?" the woman asked.

Her partner inclined his head to the walkie talkie affixed to his shoulder. If he called this in, if more police came, or if an ambulance showed up, there would be a lot more people to deal with. Two people were bad enough.

It was now or never.

Like a snake, my curse slithered up from the depths of its confinement. The rush consumed me. It was exhilarating, liberating, and terrifying.

My eyes focused on them both. "Look at me. Pay close attention."

The woman's flashlight drooped slightly. The man tilted his head from his radio.

"But you're... bleeding," the man said dumbly.

A hand fell on my shoulder. I'd been so focused on channeling power; I hadn't heard the women walk up behind me. I nearly jumped.

"Stop," said Sophie. "Lisa, stop."

I turned my head to see Andrea, clasping my shoulder. She held Sophie's hand and Sophie held Alice's hand.

"Let us help you," she added.

Andrea gave a mischievous smile and inclined her head.

Well... damn.

A new burst of energy filled me. Warm and bright. I let out a gasp as I reeled from the power.

The two officers shook their heads, snapping out of a charm I'd never completed.

"Everyone step away from the wounded woman," the woman said.

A voice crackled over the man's radio. "Do you read me? What's your situation?"

The man leaned to his walkie talkie once more.

"Stop," I said. "Look at me."

The well of power in me was not in balance. The curse fought against the new surge of magic and tried to gain real estate within my heart. I didn't need it anymore, but it fought me as I struggled to push it back down. Tingles of pleasure and promises of power rippled over my skin.

Andrea's power was different. It was soothing. It was warmer. The snake promised power in exchange for my soul. Andrea was a friend lifting me up. It was compassion. It was palpable. The chain of power through Andrea was rocket fuel in a cozy blanket.

Whatever power my curse promised, it couldn't hold a candle to it. The snake quickly lost its purchase on my heart, and I banished it back to the depths where it belonged. As it retreated, an angry promise lashed across my consciousness. A threat from my curse that it would hold my heart again and pull me into that dark spiral.

But not tonight.

Without so much false hope and darkness filling my soul, a vast font of benevolent energy filled me from toes to crown.

My eyes fixated on the two officers.

"My injury is not as grievous as it looks," I began. "I'll drive home and bandage it up."

"You should go to urgent care," the female officer suggested. Her expression was vacant.

"Yes. Thank you. And we will all be leaving the park now, as it is after hours," I offered.

"The neighbors heard gunshots," the male officer said. His eyes were glassy, and his flashlight hung at his side.

More pleas came from his radio. "What is your status? Please confirm."

"They were mistaken. There are no guns here," I spoke in a calm, measured tone. "There were no gunshots."

Warmth pulsed through me. Euphoric tingles danced all over my skin. I would have said I felt drunk if my senses weren't so sharp.

"Well... alright. But you should leave now," the man said.

"Yes. We will. Go back into your car and drive away. Radio in that you asked some people to leave the park. Tell them you found no trouble."

"Try to be more careful. And get that looked at," the woman said, shining her flashlight toward my bloody arm.

"I will. Thank you."

Both officers turned off their flashlights and got back in their car.

One three-point turn later, and they were driving away and out of site.

Andrea released her hand from my shoulder.

The warmth dissipated slowly, leaving only tingles behind.

"Wow." I turned to Andrea and beamed at her. I signed, "thank you."

Andrea signed her reply.

"She says you're welcome and that it was the least we could do for your help," Sophie supplied.

I wondered if Andrea knew how much she just saved my ass. I was literally a breath away from a plummet into the dark spiral. I wanted to hug her, but I didn't want to bleed all over her.

All I could do was beam at her, like a drowning swimmer to the hero who pulled her from the water as she was about to go under.

Alice broke me out of my gushing. "We really need to get out of here before the cops snap out of it and come back."

The next night was about rousing Brian out of his death sleep.

I parked my car on the street behind two other cars in front of Brian's house. I didn't have any thrall to send, but I wanted to check on him, nonetheless.

Walter stood in the yard.

"Lisa. You're looking better," Walter said.

"Same for you," I replied.

"Bled all over my upholstery. I was lucky I didn't fall into the death sleep myself. It was hard hunting in that condition."

Walter looked paler than normal. He must have pulled on his curse to charm people. The sight of him bleeding all over himself, would have been terrifying.

"You're just standing out in the yard?" I asked.

"It's my job to direct the thralls on where to park and to coordinate them into the house. I don't want this to turn into a clusterfuck for the neighbors to see." He folded his arms.

I smirked at that. "Is Brian awake?"

"No. Tomorrow night. He still has injuries to mend. Plus, he'll still be down a pint or two. Ivan sent a couple of his thralls. Richard too. Tracy brought Tomás. Did you bring anyone?" He looked behind me as if to see if someone would pop out of my car.

"No. No one to bring."

"What about Eric?"

"Eric? I set him free three years ago, so he could get married. Remember?"

Walter shook his head. "I'll never figure you out, Lisa. So, is everything done?"

"As done as it can be. The coven is all set and very thankful. I trust you won't spout anything about them to Ivan."

Walter nodded. "Between that Coyoteeya and your witch friends, you have me keeping a lot of secrets from Ivan but... yea, don't worry. Greater good and all that."

"Coyotita. And thank you." I gave him a wan smile. "I called Marcus to report it in. Ivan's new damphyr. What's your bead on that guy?"

Walter shrugged. "Dunno. He's new. Don't really know him."

I didn't push the question with Walter. I didn't know enough about Marcus to start poking around. I didn't know why I needed to call him instead of dealing directly with Ivan. I didn't like it. I didn't trust it.

"Anyway, there isn't much to see. Brian's still in the sleep. Tracy's inside with the dog, if you want to go in," said Walter.

I looked toward Brian's house. I didn't want to go in.

This was the vampire equivalent of seeing a loved one in the hospital. Sure, you wanted to see them because you cared about them. But you dreaded the idea of seeing them sick or broken.

I deflated with each step as I trudged toward the house.

Tracy was there, sitting on Brian's couch. She looked up from her phone, saw it was me, and looked back down at her screen. "Still no thralls?"

I ignored her and made my way down Brian's basement steps.

"Not going wake him up with thoughts and prayers," Tracy muttered. I heard her just fine.

The others must have came and went. I stood alone outside the door to his saferoom. Chewie emerged from the cement bunker and drove his head into my thigh.

"How are you holding up, sweetie?"

I stooped down and touched my head against his. "Yea. Me too."

Chewie's presence bolstered my courage. We were two kindred spirits pained over the condition of a dear friend. We stepped into the saferoom together.

A little of Brian's color and some of the red in his hair had returned. He looked more asleep than truly dead.

My chest untightened at that.

Trails of blood ran from the corners of his mouth and down his chin. He'd been feeding on instinct as bloody wrists had been dangled into his open mouth.

I retreated from the room looking for something to clean him up. It wasn't like a vampire would have tissues on their bedside table. I found a roll of paper towels left on top of his water heater.

I went back and sat on Brian's bed. I used the paper towels to wipe the trails of blood off his face. His mouth moved slightly as stray drops of blood trickled through his lips.

He was still in the same bloody clothes I brought him home in last night. I drew the line at undressing him.

Chewie's ears perked up and he let out a chuff.

"What?" Nothing was in the room with us. I couldn't hear anything except the bleeping of Tracy's game upstairs.

Chewie nipped at the hem of my jeans and pulled at my leg.

"Hey, what are you... okay, I'm up. I'm up."

He padded out of the safe room, looking behind him to see if I was following.

"What's going on?" I followed him, and he started off again.

Chewie went up the stairs and through the living room.

Tracy didn't have any snarky words for me and didn't acknowledge us walking through the room.

Chewie stopped and pawed at the front door.

Oh. He needs a potty break?

I opened the door for him. Chewie trotted outside but then stopped and looked back at me.

"What? You don't need my help with that."

Walter, in the front yard, looked at me like I had a screw loose.

Chewie let out another chuff. This one was a little more insistent.

I laughed. I missed my little adventures with Chewie, and I felt like I hadn't laughed in nights. I followed him out the door.

Across the street, red taillights dimmed from Neil's car. He'd just gotten home.

There I was in Brian's front yard as he got out of his car. I looked down at Chewie. "You little meddler."

Chewie responded by butting his head into the small of my back and pushing me forward.

"Hey, wait. Chewie!" I tried to whisper-yell at him, but it was no good.

I tried to sidestep, but Chewie was no ordinary dog. He matched my evasion and continued to push me further along. Before I knew it, I was corralled into the middle of the street.

A car door slammed shut and there was Neil, taking in the entire escapade.

Chewie broke the silence with a woof.

I wasn't exactly in a space where I was up for this, but I couldn't exactly walk back to the house like nothing happened. I found myself walking the rest of the distance to Neil on my own, succumbing to my fate.

Neil's surprise melted into a smile. There were those dimples again.

"Hi," he said.

"Hi."

Episode 32

The Awakening

Neil broke into laughter.

It was infectious, and a chuckle burst out of me. The absurdity overpowered the awkwardness, and I found myself laughing with him.

He stooped down and gave Chewie long scratches across his back. "What are you up to, Chewie? Dragging ladies to my door?"

"He must have heard you come home or something. We were inside." I smiled apologetically.

"Smart dog. Magic dog." He grinned as he stood up.

I'd almost forgotten I'd told Neil that Chewie was a *magic dog* after he saw Chewie vanish in a plume of black smoke.

All I could do was grin back like an idiot.

"So, um... how've you been?" he asked.

"Good. I got all that stuff sorted out. Things are good."

We'd already had this conversation. My small talk game needed work.

"You still out of danger?"

"Yea, I had that sorted out. I'm sorry you got pulled into all that."

Neil rubbed the back of his neck. "Actually, *I'm* sorry. I bailed on you that night. I didn't like how we left things."

"Well, things got pretty intense."

"Yea... but still. Someone tried to kill you, Lisa. I shouldn't have left you."

"Well, I wasn't mad at you for leaving."

"Yea, well..." Neil looked over my shoulder and beyond me. I turned around. Walter was standing in Brian's yard frowning at us.

"Who's that guy?" asked Neil.

"Oh, that's just Walter."

"What's his problem? He's glaring at us."

"He's just overprotective. Don't worry about him." I waved my hand.

"Is he your," Neil mulled over the word. "boyfriend?"

"Walter? No." I grinned.

Chewie let out a woof and wagged his tail like a windshield wiper on high.

Neil rubbed the back of his neck again as an awkward silence settled between us.

I searched my mind for a new topic to bring up. Anything supernatural was off the table. The weather? The New England Patriots?

"It shouldn't be this awkward, should it?" Neil shattered the silence.

"What?"

"This. Us. I felt like we were heading somewhere. We'd made this connection, and then all that shit happened."

"We never did get that game of pool in," I agreed.

"Right? I was really looking forward to that."

"Me too." I found myself smiling.

"Yea, well, we should do it."

"Really?"

"Yea. We should." Neil adopted a more confident smirk. He knew he was right.

He owed me that game, dammit.

"Then you better call me." I smirked back at him.

A single butterfly alighted within my stomach. Did I just reverse-ask-out Neil?

"I will."

"Okay then."

"Okay."

We both laughed. "Well, I should get back to Walter before he has a conniption."

Neil settled into a mild smile, and his eyes sparkled at me. He wanted to kiss me. I could see it in every aspect of him. His posture, his expression, and how he had taken a step toward me.

But no. Not now. Not here.

I turned away. "Call me."

I smiled over my shoulder at him as I walked back across the street. Chewie padded along beside me, tail wagging in victory.

"Who was that?" Walter frowned.

I watched Neil go into his house before looking back to Walter. "Brian's neighbor, Neil. I met him a while back. I was just saying hi."

"Looked like more than hi."

"What are you, my mother?"

"He's a human, and we're here to do a job," Walter said.

"No. He's a friend, and we're here to help a friend recover from his serious injuries."

"He's not your friend, Lisa. We don't make friends with humans."

"Speak for yourself." I was bristling. Tension settled into my stomach.

Walter shook his head. "I'm not trying to be an asshole. We can't be friends with humans for what we are. You form too many attachments, Lisa." Walter looked toward Neil's house and then turned back to me. "It's dangerous."

I must be out of my mind.

Last night I made plans to go on a date with a man whom I was grooming to be my thrall. I found myself pacing in my living room, strung out over the entire quandary.

There was a reason Ivan had an apartment building full of thralls. It takes close to two months for a person who's lost a pint of blood to replenish their red blood cells. It's dangerous to them to take more, and it's the reason most old and powerful vampires have dozens of thralls at their disposal.

Me? I had zilch.

I could never keep them. I always hated the idea. It was great to hunt less, but I never wanted to know the people behind my sustenance. It made it personal, and that made what I had to do more horrific.

Over the decades, I'd acquired and released several thralls. I just couldn't feed from people I cared about.

And I cared about Neil.

The more I fretted, the more my gait quickened across my living room as I continued to pace back and forth.

Maybe Walter was right. I get too attached. And this wasn't just the fact that I genuinely had feelings for Neil. I cared for the others too. Even as platonic as things were, each and every one of them mattered to me.

Ivan would often scold me for the same thing. He'd say I'd get too involved, that I let people get too close. Perhaps he was right, but I'd rather be someone who still held onto their compassion than someone so detached from humanity that their collective population of thralls was nothing more than cattle.

This pattern of thinking inevitably led me to William. My creator had always admonished me over the topic as well. But William took things too far.

I halted in my tracks as my stomach tightened. No, I wouldn't think of that.

I needed to solve the problem with Neil.

How do I bring someone into my life if they are anything but my thrall? I can't expose what I am otherwise. He'd have to be enthralled to me.

Or did I care about Neil so much that I had to let him go?

Black smoke wafted from the kitchen.

I bristled.

Woof!

"Chewie?"

The massive half-Neapolitan mastiff, half-barghest padded into the living room, tail wagging in rapid fire.

"What are you... is Brian awake?"

Chewie let out another excited bark, hopping off his front paws to accentuate his enthusiasm.

I thew my arms around him.

In that moment, Chewie was a life raft in the churning sea of my self-doubt and anxiety. I let out a breath and focused on the positive. Brian was awake. Brian was okay.

And Neil? I'd figure that out. But dammit, we were going to go on that pool date.

A knock came to my door.

"Looks like I'm miss popular tonight, huh Chewie?"

Chewie chuffed in response.

I crossed the room and peered out the door's sidelight to see who it was.

Michelle. I was surprised to see her. She was alone.

I opened the door to greet her.

Her face was sullen. Her body was rigid.

"Michelle?"

She looked up at me, her eyes were bloodshot and filled with anguish.

Her open hand flew at my face. "You monster!"

A Deadly Coincidence

I caught Michelle's wrist before she could slap me.

"What are you doing?" I was more concerned than upset.

Tears streamed from her eyes, she pulled on her hand, and I let her go. She looked terrified.

Michelle stood rooted to my front step. Her heart raced in quick beats. The color was washed away from her face.

I didn't know Michelle well. I'd met her a few times before I'd released her then fiancé, Eric, from under my sway. I wanted him to live a normal life, and he couldn't do that as my thrall.

That was three years ago.

"Michelle," I prompted.

"He's dead. Eric. Did you...?"

"Dead?" My stomach turned sour. I couldn't believe what I was hearing, but what was equally shocking was she thought I did it. "God, no. Michelle, I wanted him to live a life away from all this."

I didn't want to have this discussion with her standing on my front step. "Come inside. Tell me what happened."

Michelle's entire posture slumped. She stared down at her feet.

A moment passed in silence.

"Michelle. I cared for Eric, and I won't hurt you. Please come inside." I stepped aside. Michelle gave a small nod and stepped through the door.

Upon seeing Chewie, Michelle startled.

"He's okay. That's Chewie. He's a big baby."

Michelle relaxed somewhat, but she eyed the big mastiff warily.

I gestured at the couch, and she took a seat. Michelle was an attractive young woman in her early thirties with dirty blond hair and deep brown eyes. I remembered Eric telling me how beautiful she was.

I took a seat beside her and faced her. Chewie curled up on the floor on the other side of me and away from Michelle. "Tell me what happened."

"Someone shot him," she murmured. She turned to face me. "Someone shot him."

My heart skipped a beat. He'd been murdered?

"When?"

"A week ago. He went out to Stop and Shop to get a few things for me. I was baking and needed condensed milk." She put her head in her hands. "It's my fault."

"It's not your fault." I put my hand on her shoulder, and she flinched and pulled back. I retreated my hand away.

She looked up at me as if to apologize, but her eyes still held fear.

"Sorry. Go on," I said.

"He was shot in the parking lot while he was getting into his car." Her breathing was ragged as she struggled not to break down.

"I'm so sorry."

"You didn't do it?"

"Of course not," I said gently. "Why would I?"

"To keep your secret. I know what you are."

I let out a breath. "I let Eric go to protect him. I wanted him safe from this life. And that included me."

Michelle's eyes fell to her lap. She looked thoughtful.

"I'd offer you something to drink, but I don't keep much of anything here. Water?"

She shook her head. "No. Thank you."

"Do the police have any leads?"

She shook her head again. "No."

A week ago. My mind went to Amy Wagner, my dog walker who was strangled in her apartment. Both murders took place within a few nights of each other.

Both were people I knew.

"I'm sorry, I shouldn't have come," Michelle said.

"I'm not offended by your accusation. And I'm sorry for your loss. Eric was... he was a great guy."

"He loved you, you know. He never admitted it, but I could always tell. The way he talked about you."

My lips tightened as I gave an awkward nod. She wasn't wrong. I'd always known how Eric felt. But what does one say to that?

"I should go." Michelle stood.

"You don't have to."

"I should. I'm still dealing with the funeral home and all of the—" she put a hand over her face.

I wanted to put my arms around her and comfort her, but I knew she was still afraid of me. I gave her a moment.

The silence put me back inside my own head. First Amy and now Eric. I don't believe in coincidences.

At last, Michelle turned to me and nodded a few times. She opened her mouth and then closed it again. She looked so lost.

I got to my feet. "If you need anything. Anything at all, just let me know."

"Okay," she said in a small voice. "Thank you. I'm sorry I—"

"Don't be. I know what it's like to lose a loved one."

She seemed surprised by that, but she turned, wordlessly, and made her way to the door.

She paused a moment. "There's a wake Saturday night. If you want to go. RJ Ross in Wrentham."

"RJ Ross." I repeated the name of the funeral home to help commit it to memory. "Thank you. I'll be there."

With that, she saw herself out and into the night.

I plopped back down on the couch. My heart was heavy over Michelle's loss.

But a chilling awareness ran down my spine. This wasn't a random murder.

Chewie's snout nestled into my lap, pulling me out of my turmoil.

I scratched his head.

His positive influence fell over me again. It wasn't anything magic or supernatural. It was just... him.

I elected to seize those positive vibes. Brian was awake, after all.

"You want to go see Brian?"

Chewie's tail came to life in a back-and-forth swishing frenzy.

Whatever sinister connection existed between Amy's and Eric's murders would have to wait.

I needed a night of good cheer. Or at least a distraction.

Brian still looked like hell.

Streaks of gray peppered his ginger hair. Blue ghosts of veins were visible along his pale flesh. His curse had pulled him back from the precipice of death, and his body had paid the toll.

"How are you feeling?"

"Better than I look, actually." He smirked at me.

We sat in his living room facing each other. Me on the couch, him on the love seat. Chewie curled up at his feet, the bulk of the giant dog coming up to Brian's knees.

"What are you going to do about um..." I just waved my hand in his general direction.

"What, you don't think it's a good look for me? I was thinking I should try out for an extra on one of those crime dramas. I can be *guy in morgue*."

I laughed. "Brian."

He laughed too. "I'm kidding. No, I'm going to stave off things for a while. Take it easy. Abstain from pulling on my curse, like you taught me."

"How will you hunt with no charming gaze?"

"I'll manage. Might work something out with Tracy or Richard. I really should get thralls of my own."

I bobbed my head in agreement. I was still a little distracted from earlier.

"So, what's wrong?" asked Brian.

"Huh? What do you mean?"

"I can tell when something's upsetting you, Lisa. I've known you a long time."

"Fifty some odd years," I agreed.

"So, spill it."

I let out a breath. "Eric's dead."

"What? No."

"He was shot. Murdered. A week ago."

"God, Lisa, I'm so sorry."

I closed my eyes and resolved to share everything with him. "I'm worried it's deeper than that. Amy Wagner was murdered a few nights after Eric."

"Amy?"

"I hired her to take Chewie out during the day."

"He used to just poof outside when he needed to."

I waved that off, a little frustrated that Brian was missing the point. "I didn't know Chewie could do that when I hired Amy. The point is, two people who knew me personally were murdered within a week of each other."

"You think they're connected?"

"I don't know. Maybe. It's too much of a coincidence."

A silence fell between us. Brian looked at his hands. Blue veins ran across his pale hands like roadmaps. He looked up at me. "If this was connected to you, then why? To what purpose? And who could be behind it?"

"Those are the questions, right?"

But I'd already suspected the answer to one of them. Because this had happened to me before. I made a pained expression.

"What?" Brian asked.

"I don't like talking about it. I never told you about William, did I?"

"William? He left the bleed when I was still a páiste. I knew you two had a falling out. I knew he made some deal with the New York bleed." Brian shrugged. "You never opened up about it. I never pushed it."

I mulled it over. Memories flooded my mind. After so many years, they still crushed my heart under their weight. I tightened my jaw and prepared to walk myself down that road again.

"Lisa, you don't have to—"

"No. I need someone I can trust who knows what happened."

I took a breath. "William had always scolded me for making friends among mortals. But in truth, he started first with my family. My family had moved to Boston in 1850. The potato famine pushed a lot of us out in those days. It was me, my mother and father, and my younger brother, Bradon."

Chewie got to his feet. The click-clack of his nails on the hardwood floor came toward me as he moved from Brian to me. He curled up at my feet.

I smiled down at him.

"My little sister, Moira, was born a few years later. Then my youngest sister, Fiona, was born a few years after that. William turned me in 1860."

I shook my head. I really didn't want to get into the whole story, so I cut to the chase. "He'd warned me to break off ties with my family. Said it was a risk to the bleed. But I didn't listen. I didn't want them to think I'd abandoned them. I didn't want them to worry."

"Oh, God," Brian said.

I nodded and wiped my eyes with the back of my hand. "He killed them. All of them. He blamed this... faction of people. Nationalists who hated the Irish. They called themselves the Know Nothings." I shook my head.

"It wasn't them, but I believed it was. A few of them had roughed up my father and brother just prior."

"But, you didn't find out until years later?"

"Decades later. Fifty years ago?" I tried to remember. "He'd let slip something in conversation that only someone who had been inside my parents' home would have known. I confronted him about it, and he confessed. Said it was for my own good. He said he liberated me.

"Fiona was only seven. When I found her body, she held the poker from the fireplace tight in her hand. I think she tried to fight him with it while he..." I closed my eyes and shook my head.

One hundred and fifty years ago, and I could still see it like it was last night.

Brian reached across the table and took my hand. His icy flesh roused me from my thoughts like a cold shower. I put my other hand over his and gave it a pat.

"Why would William be doing this now? And to what end? Amy was in your employ, and you'd cut ties with Eric years ago. There's no danger to the bleed. And William isn't even in our bleed."

He had a point.

Was I just seeing ghosts?

Date Night

Was I making a terrible mistake?

Heels? No. Heels would be too dressy.

I was playing a very dangerous game. Everything could fall apart if I didn't handle this well.

Boots. Boots might look cute. Where are my black boots?

In the last couple of months, I'd fought a necromancer, been attacked by redcaps, swashbuckled with a vampire lord, and battled a goddamn demon.

Why deny myself? Don't I deserve a little cheer in my life?

Boots on, I appraised my outfit in my full-length mirror.

Is this skirt too short?

I smirked at my reflection. *No.*

Last night, Neil called me as I was driving home from Brian's house.

I had a date.

A chill ran up my spine. My curse slithered its way into my psyche. It latched on to my conflict and anxiety. I wrestled with the idea that I was dipping my toe into a romantic scenario with someone whom I should have only been seeing as a potential thrall. And my curse knew it.

It wanted me to enrapture him. It tempted me with how easy it would be to ensnare him in my gaze and make him into whatever I wanted. Thrall. Servant. Lover.

My curse wrapped itself around my heart and squeezed, feeding off my emotion and looking for any weaknesses in my resolve.

I closed my eyes and let out a long breath. I was not weak. And Neil mattered to me.

I pushed away the temptation. As I did, my curse slunk away, snarling in resentment, back into the dark recesses of an abyss I would never dare to tread.

Another shiver ran up my spine. I needed to be on my guard tonight. This wouldn't be the last time the curse would try to pull me into darkness.

It helped when I focused on the positive. The power the curse offered was a lot more attractive if I was sad, angry, or wounded. I kept that in mind when I left my bedroom into an empty living room.

With Chewie at Brian's, the house felt vacant. Quiet. Hollow.

I thought he might have come with me when I left Brian's last night. I could almost sense his conflict. He wanted to come, but he didn't want to leave Brian. Brian was still recovering, and in his weakened state he was susceptible to his curse.

Right now, Brian needed Chewie more than I did, and I think Chewie knew it.

Chewie would come back.

When he was ready.

Neil and I agreed to resurrect our plans to meet up at Allston Billiards on Cambridge Street. Allston wasn't a town as much as it was a small region of western Boston, and it was equidistance between me in Charlestown and Neil in Watertown.

I parked and looked around the lot. I spotted Neil's car, but he wasn't inside.

I made my way to the front door where a white awning bore the words *Allston Billiards* and an image depicting two pool cues crossed in an X. It reminded me of a skull and crossbones. The picture even had an eight ball where the skull would have been. The sign was illuminated in a dull fluorescent glow.

I immediately knew that I was going to be overdressed.

I walked through the door into a chorus of clacking pool balls. Despite being filled with several people, the pool hall was otherwise quiet. Every couple of seconds a new crack or two would break the silence.

Neil was waiting for me near the door. He'd shaved and put on a gray button-down shirt. He wore jeans and sneakers to top it off.

Yup. Definitely overdressed.

When was the last time I'd been on a date? Seventy years? God, help me.

Neil's eyes were popping out of his head, and his gaze lingered mostly on my legs.

"You look... wow. Hi," he said.

I suppressed a laugh and smiled instead. "Hi."

"Sorry, I just saw you and all the adjectives leaked out of my head. You look stunning."

Stunning? I'd take stunning.

"You clean up pretty nice yourself, but I think I'm way overdressed."

I surveyed the room. People were in jeans, tee shirts, and yoga pants. There was someone who, I was pretty sure, was wearing plaid sleep bottoms. The last time I'd been in a pool hall, the men were wearing suits.

This was one of those moments where I had dropped the ball on my necessity to keep up with the times.

"Who cares? You look amazing."

I drew some eyes as Neil and I walked into the room and chose our pool table. This was followed by annoyed female companions slapping their dates on the arm or cuffing them in the chest. I overheard one woman mutter, "You want to put your eyes back in your head?"

Neil didn't seem to notice, and he handed me a pool cue. "You should know; I really suck at pool."

As far as I knew, so did I. I hadn't played pool in decades. "Me too."

Neil racked them and offered me the break.

I accepted and rounded the table to line up my shot. Had I ever broke before? I couldn't remember. I must have.

How hard could it be? Just whack the cue ball into the others.

I oscillated the cue stick back and forth within my hold to get my angle right. Satisfied, I pulled it back and let it rip.

A sonorous cacophony of clacking erupted from our table as colored balls went flying. A few stayed on the table and ricocheted from bumper to bumper trying to exhaust their kinetic energy. Several others sailed off the table and into the air.

"Heads up!" Neil shouted.

A few balls hit the floor and rolled in scattered directions. A couple more landed on the tables of other players. One of them slammed into the wall.

Everyone in the hall looked at me bewildered or aghast.

I was mortified.

Sure, I knew my own strength, but that was for the mundane things I did every day like opening doors, operating the pedals of a car, or typing on a keyboard. But breaking? Where you're supposed to give a little strength to get a good ball dispersion? I hadn't gauged it well at all.

I could feel my cheeks getting hot. I was sure I was blushing. Neil was immediately running interference and making apologies to the other players.

"Our bad."

"Must've gotten an odd angle there."

"Is this your 4-ball or mine?"

"Big Papi over here with the cue stick, am I right?"

Soon, Neil had people smiling and laughing, and he returned to our table with an armful of balls.

"Sorry about that," I said, sheepishly.

"No, no, I'm impressed. You're like the Happy Gilmore of pool."

I laughed. I actually got that reference.

"So... I'm no rules lawyer, but I think this means we need to rack them again and start over. Do you mind if I...?"

He didn't have to say the word *break*. "Oh, God. Please. Yes."

Neil broke in a very human, non-explosive kind of way, leaving him as stripes and me as solids. He maneuvered around the table as he eyed the 11-ball.

"So, how do you want to do this? You're supposed to call your shots, but honestly, I'm not that good and we'll be here all night. Typically, what I do is I shoot and I if get something of mine in, I go again."

"I think I play sort of the same way." I recalled. "But I played it so you had to call the ball and not the pocket. If you got the ball you called in *any* pocket, you could go again. If you missed or got some other ball in, your turn was over."

Neil bobbed his head. "Alright. Let's do your way. I like it."

Neil hit the cue into the 11 and the ball bounced around harmlessly. "Told you I suck. You're up, Happy. Just give it a little tap-tap-taperoo."

A laughed. "Shush, you."

I leaned over to take my shot. The 6-ball was tantalizingly close to the side pocket. I took a moment to consider my strength and took my shot. The cue ball made contact, and the 6 bounced off the corner of the pocket's bumper and whirled away to the center of the table.

I stood up and leaned on my stick. "This is going to be a long night." I grinned.

"No complaints." Neil flashed that dashing smile of his as he circled around the table to hunt down that elusive 11-ball again.

Butterflies invaded my stomach in a delightful tickle that made my cheeks flush and warmed my heart. I wanted to giggle.

A moment later, he was looking at me with a thoughtful expression.

"What?" I asked.

"You're an adventure," he said.

"Huh?"

He stood up from his shot. "Before I met you, I'd go to work. Come home. Maybe watch some TV or play video games. And that's it. Sometimes I'd go out with friends, but nothing crazy. Until you."

"Crazy?" I grinned, raising my brows at him.

"I don't mean *crazy* crazy. We rescued Chewie. We did our New Hampshire adventure. Driving around all New England on some quest."

Quest?

"Hell, even playing pool with you is adventure," he waved his hand around to mimic the flight of balls from the table through the air.

"Very funny." I was still grinning.

"I'm trying to say it's been kind of like a romantic adventure. Like *Romancing the Stone.*"

"*Romancing the Stone*? You realize that would make you Kathleen Turner."

Neil adopted a thoughtful countenance. He leaned back down to line up his shot. "You could do a lot worse than Kathleen Turner, Lisa Cooper."

I laughed again.

Neil missed his shot. I got my next shot in and missed my follow up. And so it went; two horrible pool players trying to sink balls with nothing more than tenacity and delusion.

The hours slipped away, yet our games moved at a snail's pace. My next attempt to break wasn't so explosive.

It didn't matter how bad we were. For the first time in a long, long time, I felt normal. I felt like a woman out on a date with a man. I felt human.

And that's when my curse slithered its way out of the depths.

Charming Neil now would be child's play. He was already enamored with me. With my charming gaze, he'd be eating out of my hand. I could feed from him. I could have him for whatever kind of relationship I desired. It would be easy.

"No."

"No? No what?" Neil was rubbing a chalk cube on the tip of his cue stick.

"I..."

"Are you okay? You just went pale."

"I look pale?" Panic seized me.

Neil shook his head as he peered at me. "No, your color's returning. It was like something came over you suddenly."

I let out a breath. My curse tried to turn my happy feelings into greed, tempting me to take more. It failed, and I felt its influence slough off.

"You alright?"

I gave a quick nod and a wan smile. "Sorry, yes."

Neil looked dubious and genuinely concerned. He set his stick against the table and came to me. "Let me check."

"Check?"

Neil placed the back of his fingers gingerly against my cheek. "You're warm, but not hot."

"Neil, I'm fine."

"Lisa, you just went pale as a ghost. You're not hypoglycemic or anything, are you?"

"I don't even know what that is."

"Aren't you a nurse?"

"Um..."

Neil put his palm against my cheek. "Well, you're not clammy or anything like that."

His hand was warm. Gentle. I leaned into it, slightly. I couldn't help myself.

He smiled at me.

He slid his hand across my face and let his fingertips dip into my hair.

My heart began to race.

"Well, if you're—"

My phone rang.

Neil pulled his hand from me.

Son of a bitch.

"Sorry." I went to the stool where I'd placed my purse and fished out my phone.

I checked the caller ID.

Detective Martin Pierce.

Son. Of. A. Bitch.

Episode 35

The Interrogation

Detective Pierce's calling wasn't going to ruin my night. I knew I could take any questions he had about Eric's murder in stride. Things were going great with Neil, and I wasn't about to let Pierce get under my skin.

"Hello?"

"Ms. Cooper. So nice of you to take my call. As always, you're a hard woman to get in touch with."

Smarmy prick.

I didn't take the bait. He and I had gone over why I was so hard to get in touch with, what with my being a nurse and all.

"How can I help you, detective?"

"You know, I wasn't going to call you about Eric Perry's murder," he said.

He paused there and let the statement linger. It was always an interrogation with this guy. I didn't respond.

Neil must have seen the dismay on my face. He looked at me with concern as he leaned against the pool table. I tried to play it down by rolling my eyes.

Pierce continued, "But then, last night, I got word that Lee Kingsley had been murdered."

If I needed to breathe, that would have sucked the air out of my lungs. I couldn't hide my reaction, and Neil stood up straight, eyes wide with concern.

He didn't wait for me to answer. "That's three murders in less than two weeks and all three victims knew you. I find that very interesting, Ms. Cooper."

I composed myself. "I hadn't heard. I haven't seen or spoken to Lee in two years."

"But you did date."

I cringed at that. Lee and I dating was sort of our cover story. I was grooming him to be my thrall after I let Eric go. Lee was more than interested. A little too interested.

Lee's roommate had gotten nosy. He wondered if Lee and I were *hooking up*, so the easiest thing to tell him was, yes, we were dating.

"We did. But we broke up. Like I said, I haven't seen or heard from him in two years."

"You don't seem broken up over the news," the detective said.

"I'm more annoyed at your implications, detective. I knew Lee less than six months; we saw each other for a while, then I ended things with him."

Poor Neil was only hearing one half of the conversation and trying to play the supportive date. He looked concerned and lost.

"Where were you this past Tuesday evening around seven p.m.?" he asked at last.

Fighting a demon.

"I was out at a friend's house. Walter Garvin.." It wasn't entirely a lie.

At Walter's name, Neil gave me a perplexed look. Neil knew Walter. Sort of. He saw Walter giving us disapproving looks from across the street the other night.

But the truth was Walter was a good alibi. I was actually with him that night, and Walter would cover for me in a pinch.

"That sounds nice. What were you doing?" Pierce asked.

"He'd been trying to get me to watch *Planet of the Apes* with him for ages, and I finally caved."

I can think quick on my feet when I need to.

Pierce didn't miss a beat. "Charlton Heston, Mark Wahlberg, or James Franco?"

"Franco. The newest one. Walter wants us to watch the whole series together."

"What was your favorite part?" His questions were rapid-fire.

I didn't just volunteer *Planet of the Apes* lightly. I love those movies. They're classics.

"All the scenes with the Orangutan, honestly. Especially the scene where he's doing sign language with Caesar."

Pierce grunted at that.

"Alright, Ms. Cooper. Do me a favor, and don't leave the city, hm?"

"I have no plans to. Is there anything else, detective?"

"No. That'll do for now. If you think of anything else, you can reach me on this number."

"Thank you." I hung up.

Neil was instantly at my side. "You alright? Was that the police?"

"Yes. An old friend was killed. He was asking me some questions."

"Jesus. I'm so sorry," said Neil.

"It's fine. I need to make a quick call. Can you give me a few?"

"Sure."

Poor Neil was looking at me with concern, but I couldn't let him in on this. Not yet.

I went to my purse and fished out my burner phone. I dialed up Walter and took a walk out to the parking lot.

"Yea," Walter answered with his usual phone etiquette.

I brought Walter up to speed on the impending phone call from detective Pierce. Turns out, he'd never seen any of the *Planet of the Apes* movies, so that was a complication.

"Just tell them you've only watched the first one and you wanted to watch the rest with me," I said.

"Fine. I'll let you know what he says. If he gets too close, we may need to—"

"Just answer his questions and be helpful. Stick to the story I gave you," I said.

"Suit yourself. Oh, I have someone trying to call me. That might be him."

"Alright. Talk later."

I needed a moment before going back in. The news of Lee's murder had me reeling.

Amy Wagner, Eric Perry, and Lee Kingsley had all been murdered within a two-week period. It was a coincidence I could not ignore. But why? In the case of Eric and Lee, I hadn't spoken to them in years. What was the connection?

Neil came out the door, pulling me out of my thoughts.

"Hey, are you okay?"

I wasn't.

Tonight was supposed to be my one night. One night away from all the fucking bullshit. No necromancers, power-hungry vampire lords, werewolves, or demons. Just one night for me. And Neil.

In that one moment, Neil's genuine question of concern brought everything to the surface. I wasn't okay. I was sick of it. I was sick of all of it.

I moved to him, up against him. And Neil did what every proper date should in moments like these. He took me into his arms.

And for the first time in a long time, I felt safe. I felt the world melt away.

If I thought about it too much, I knew Neil couldn't protect me from the horrors that had pushed me to my wit's end, but I didn't care.

He held me close, and I lost myself in his embrace.

Time stood still, and, for a few, fleeting seconds, I was simply a woman on a date with a man.

"Lisa," he said in a gentle voice.

I ignored him. I closed my eyes and rested my head against his shoulder. His arms tightened around me.

"It's okay," he said.

I pulled back a bit. "We were having such a good time and then I got the news that someone I knew died and then the detective was asking me where I was, and..."

"He was insensitive. And tonight was amazing. You want to call it a night? It's okay if you do. Next time, we can do something else we're horrible at; like darts or... curling."

Curling got a chuckle out of me. I pictured Neil running across the ice with a little broom.

He smiled at me.

"Yea, okay. But yes to the second date." I finally stepped out of his embrace. I was pretty sure I was blushing. "How much do I owe you for the table?"

"What? No, nothing. I already took care of it."

"Fine, but next time, we go Dutch."

Neil grinned. "Only if you wear those wooden shoes."

I thought about that. "I have a pair of cork wedge mules. Do those count?"

His mouth fell open as he considered my proposal. "I don't know what any of those words mean."

I hugged him. "Thank you."

"For what?"

I spoke into his shoulder, letting myself indulge in his arms once more. "Just... everything."

"What are you doing tomorrow night?" Neil asked.

"I have a wake." I pulled out of his arms. The reminder that Eric's wake was tomorrow night was sobering.

"Oh, I'm sorry. For your loss, I mean. Is that the person you found out about tonight?"

"No. Different person."

His eyes widened at that. "So two people? Lisa, that's awful. I'm sorry."

I gave Neil a wan smile. "He was an old friend. We'd drifted apart, but I still want to pay my respects."

My phone vibrated. Text message.

I glanced at the screen and saw it was from Walter. I'd read it later.

As if prompted by my phone's buzzing, Neil said, "Well, I'll call you. You going to be okay?"

"Yea." Another weak smile.

We hugged again and went separate ways to our cars.

I opened the text message from Walter.

"Detective jammed me up on some of those movie questions. He knows you lied to him."

Well, fuck.

Episode 36

Breaking The Witness

THE LAST TIME I went to a wake was in March of 1932. I still remember it clearly.

I met Danny O'Reilly and his brothers in an Irish pub in Cambridge. The O'Reilly brothers were a musical trio that played at the pub. Danny played the tin whistle.

The brothers' music had reminded me of simpler times, of years long past, living in the Irish North End.

When I was mortal.

Danny O'Reilly was in his eighties when he died. His heart gave out in his sleep. Peaceful. He'd led a long, good life.

The same was not true for Eric Perry. Eric was young. He was murdered and robbed of whatever future he had.

The entire room was somber and quiet. This was no Irish wake.

Mourners sat around wearing drab clothes, murmuring condolences to one another. There was no music. There were no toasts. No one stood before the room to regale the bereaved with stories of Eric's life.

I stared into the casket as I knelt and signed the cross.

The body didn't look like Eric. He was plastered in make-up. His features were sunken, and his mouth was clamped tight from the stitching. It almost felt like some sick joke where Eric would suddenly round the corner and laugh at us for falling for what was clearly a dummy in a coffin.

But that didn't happen.

I rose to my feet and made my way to the reception line where Eric's widow and family lined up. How they had the strength to put on such a social front, I didn't know.

Michelle's eyes widened at the sight of me. I could still see tinges of fear, even though she'd invited me. Perhaps she was surprised I showed up.

I refrained from hugging her for how anxious she looked.

"I'm so sorry, Michelle."

"Thank you. Your coming would have meant a lot to him. And thank you for the flowers." She gestured to the arrangement I'd sent to the funeral home. A wreath of lilies, carnations, and other flowers hung on a metal tripod amongst a phalanx of other bouquets and collections.

Michelle hugged me. It nearly caught me off guard. She didn't say anything, she just held on to me.

I whispered, "If you need anything, you know where to find me."

She nodded once into my shoulder and pulled back. She wiped her eyes with the heel of her hand. "Thank you, Lisa."

The only other two people in line were Eric's parents.

I'd never met them before. I gave my condolences and neglected to tell them who I was or how I knew their son.

There wasn't much more for me there. I'd paid my respects and gave my condolences to Michelle. It was the proper thing to do.

I turned my attention to the door. There was no reason for me to linger. I didn't know any of the other mourners, and I wasn't there to make new friends.

My heart seized when I spotted Richard.

What the hell was he doing here?

He was dressed in a black suit. A black vest and tie completed his look. He was looking over a posterboard standing on a tripod. The posterboard had dozens of photos of Eric displayed in a collage.

I marched over to him.

"What are you doing here?" I whispered.

Richard dragged his eyes from the pictures and over to me. He looked surprised. "Lisa. My condolences."

"What are you doing here?" I repeated.

"Paying my respects." He smiled.

I frowned. This was an absolutely tasteless theater for his games. "You didn't even know Eric."

He shrugged. "I don't see why that's a factor. He was very dear to you, Lisa. I'm not callous."

"How did you even know—"

"Come now, if you think I don't keep tabs on you, you haven't been paying attention."

"Well, I'm leaving. So, have fun driving back to Worcester. Great prank, Richard."

I brushed past him.

He grabbed my arm.

"Let me go," I whispered.

"Always cutting to the chase, aren't you? You're no fun. You want to talk? Let's talk."

He pulled me into another room.

"I really have nothing to say to you, Richard."

He didn't respond. I wondered if I should be worried.

There were other mourners sitting in ornate cushy chairs in the second room. The room also had a couple of collages on tripods.

Richard's eyes took on a hue of red. It was his *fear gaze*.

"Leave us," he said to the bereaved.

They swept out of the room, blanching at the sight of terror in Richard's eyes. One of them had the will enough to mutter how rude he was being, but he hastened out of the room with the others.

I hadn't used a fear gaze in years. It brings the darkness of our curse to the surface for everyone to see. It's dangerous, and it gives the curse a foothold in our thinking, affecting our actions. I could have used it a couple of nights on those two police officers, but I was fairly certain it would have backfired spectacularly. Fear may have compelled them to shoot me rather than run away.

"That was unnecessary. These people are grieving," I scolded.

Richard frowned at me, apathetic. "You want to know why I'm here?"

"Let me guess. Ivan never approved of my cutting ties with Eric, so you're here to spy for him. On me."

"I'm not the spy." He grinned.

Richard took a step closer and lowered his voice. "You are about to assemble the pieces of a puzzle that have lain dormant in your mind; collecting dust for the past one hundred and fifty years."

"What are you talking about? What puzzle?"

Richard reached out and stroked my face. I stepped back from his unwelcome touch. "I wanted to kill you so badly. All those years ago," he said.

He was talking about the year 1863. The year we killed his creator, the then Lord of the New England bleed. In one night, Richard had lost his station, his power, and nearly his life.

"I'm aware of our rivalry, Richard. What are you talking about? Why drive all the way down here to pose me with riddles?"

He smirked at me. A smug curl of his lips that made me want to smack it off his face.

"What do you know?" I urged.

"I should leave. I have that long drive to Worcester and all."

"Richard, people are being murdered. Three people have died so far. Tell me what you know."

I was foolish to try to appeal to any sense of humanity he had left.

Richard smiled playfully at me. "Tut tut, Lisa. Play the game. I drove down to keep things interesting. To let you know you're up at bat. A sports metaphor, yes? Don't strike out."

With that, he stepped around me, and strode for the door.

"Richard," I called after him, but it was a whisper.

The funeral home was still deathly silent, after all.

I followed Richard out the door and into the horseshoe shaped driveway outside. Before I could catch up with him and pull him aside, I was intercepted.

Detective Pierce stepped in front of me, tiny notebook in hand.

"Ms. Cooper."

What the hell? Did everyone know I was going to be here tonight?

"Yes?" I answered in an exasperated tone. I watched as Richard waved at me and disappeared behind the building and into the main parking lot.

"Had a few follow-up questions, if you don't mind," said Pierce.

"You know, coming here is in extremely poor taste."

"I know it's not ideal, but you continue to be a tough person to pin down, Ms. Cooper. I came here on a hunch, to be honest."

"I was just leaving, actually."

"This will only take a moment. Now, you and Walter Garvin saw a movie together, but he didn't seem to recall the details all that well."

I shrugged. "He may not have been paying attention."

"Was he distracted?"

"I don't know. I was watching the movie," I said.

"Didn't you say he watched it before and wanted you to watch it?"

"No, I only said he wanted us to watch it together. I never said he'd seen it before."

Pierce smirked. "And was this movie on Blu-ray or DVD?"

"It was his copy. Blu-ray, I think."

This was a typical *break the witness* tactic. Pierce would try to trip me up. He'd see if I could repeat the details I gave him accurately. Then he would throw false information at me to see if I'd take the bait.

This wasn't my first time.

"What was Mr. Garvin wearing?"

Dammit.

"I don't remember."

"What were you wearing?"

"I had on my black capris and a blue top."

"He said you were wearing jeans," said the detective.

And there it was. Either Pierce had asked Walter what I was wearing and Walter said *jeans*, or this was some bullshit the detective was making up on the fly to see if I'd adjust my story.

If Walter had said jeans, then Pierce already knew I was lying. My only move here was to double down on the capris and hope he was trying to throw me.

I frowned at him. "I don't know what he was talking about. I had on capris."

The detective scribbled a few things into his tiny notebook.

I let myself get annoyed. People who are telling the truth have nowhere to go but pissed off once they've provided the correct information. That was the role I was playing.

"Is there anything else, detective?"

He looked at me, thoughtfully. He held my gaze for a moment and then tapped his pen on the little pad.

"We're pulling camera footage from some of the traffic stops in and around Mr. Kingsley's street where apparently you *weren't* on the night of his murder."

It was all I could do not to smile. Him playing this gambit meant he still suspected me, but he didn't have a thing on me.

I made my frown go deeper and I shook my head, mustering up the most insulted look I could. "Go ahead and pull them, detective. I wasn't there."

He bobbed his head at me. "Alright, Ms. Cooper. Alright."

That's when I saw him. Parked across the street from the funeral home was a black Honda CRV. The driver's side window was rolled down. From within the shadowed confines of the car was Marcus, Ivan's new damphyr. He was taking pictures of me.

Pierce was talking again, and I'd let Marcus' spying distract me. I was a lot less concerned with Pierce and more interested in what Marcus was playing at.

"Are we done here, detective?" This time, my haughty tone wasn't staged.

Marcus put his camera down and turned his attention to the steering wheel. His window rolled up as the car pulled into the road and drove out of sight.

Pierce looked behind him and to the CRV speeding away. "You seem distracted by that."

"Are we done here?" It was a question, but my tone was insistent.

Pierce tapped his notes again. "Have a good night, Ms. Cooper."

The detective turned and walked off, heading to an unmarked Ford parked on the street.

I meandered into the back parking lot. Seething.

I didn't have time to worry about Pierce. I had bigger problems.

Ivan was spying on me.

Episode 37

Otherworld

"Are you kidding me!" I'd lost all pretense of decorum. I'd spent the entire ride home from Eric's wake seething, and it was all I could do not to call Ivan from the car.

"Siobhan, I will not engage with you while you carry that tone," Ivan said.

I paced around my living room, phone in one hand and my free hand gesticulating wildly. "You had your damphyr *spying* on me! At a wake!"

"Are you so surprised? This isn't about you. It's about the bleed. Marcus got sloppy. I will speak to him about it."

"So, you're more concerned that he got caught?"

"One of my tasks as Bleed Lord is to take measures to ensure our safety. I do what must be done to keep our secrets. These invasions of privacy are not limited to you. Tracy can be reckless. Dylan can be irresponsible. And you can be... sentimental."

"I've been careful." It came out more defensive than I meant it.

"Have you? Siobhan, you went to a wake. People must have been asking questions about how you knew the deceased. It was careless of you. I admire your compassion, I truly do. It's a testament to your strength that you have kept it for so long. But it is also a weakness."

"We've had this conversation, Ivan."

"And we will have it again!" The Lord of New England erupted. After a moment, he continued calmly, "When you let them in, the door works both ways. You are in their life. They are in yours. We enthrall mortals to keep them by our side, to do what must be done, and guard ourselves from their curiosities."

"It was a wake, Ivan."

"I'm sorry for your loss. I remember Eric. But those he left behind are better not knowing you exist. You must understand that. They'll ask how you knew him and force you into lie after lie. Trust me, the lies pile up and it's easy to forget which lie you told to whom."

I shook my head. In the silence, Ivan spoke again.

"I was worried you might have gone to the wake. I sent Marcus to check. I planned on calling you to console you on your loss, but also to guide you."

"I'm not a páiste," I bit back.

"No. No, you are not. Forgive an old man for forgetting sometimes. You are among the last of us that were there, all those years ago. You are very dear to me, Siobhan. Perhaps I do get overzealous. I know I've said this before, but I love you like you were my own scion."

I huffed; my heartstrings pulled. "I know. It's just—"

"I know. I should have more faith in you. I suppose there is a place in the middle where things ought to be. You, more guarded about the mortals. Me, perhaps less controlling."

"*Perhaps*?" I grinned at that. "How did you even know where the wake was?"

"The newspaper. When I heard Eric had passed, I wanted to see where the wake was because I was worried you would show up."

Fair enough.

"Alright. I'll be a bit more guarded, but you keep Marcus on a shorter leash. If I catch that douche bag peeping on me again, I'm going to bounce his head off his SUV."

Ivan paused before answering. "Very well. Consider the... *douche bag* restrained."

Now there's a sentence I never expected to hear from Ivan.

I withdrew my fangs from Evan. It had been a literal pain in the neck feeding on him from the passenger seat of his car, but the empty parking lot offered us ideal privacy.

I was lucky to have found him. Hunting was always tough on Sunday nights. I should have hunted last night, after my call with Ivan, but I was so annoyed that I ended up spending the evening stewing in my house.

"So, do you need a ride back to—"

My phone rang. I took a glance at the display. I smiled when I saw Neil's name. "Hold that thought. Stare into my eyes."

I pulled away from Evan and held his gaze.

I licked the blood from my lips before I answered the phone. "Hi, Neil."

"Hey. Wanted to see what you were up to."

"Oh, just out running errands." Evan's eyes became droopy, and I gently nudged his chin so he'd stay locked onto me. "Actually, can I call you right back? I'm just checking out."

"Sure, no problem. Talk to you later." There was a smile in his voice.

"Thanks. Talk soon."

I hung up.

"Evan, thank you for a wonderful night dancing."

He lolled his head into a sort of nod.

"I'm going to leave now. If you start to feel dizzy when you're driving home, pull over and get some rest."

"Yea... okay... can I have your number?"

I smiled at him and patted his cheek. Then I got out of his car.

My own car was still parked at the club. I rang up Neil as I walked.

"Hey, that was quick," answered Neil. "Buy anything nice?"

"Just... um... detergent. Brillo pads. Things like that."

"Exciting." He laughed. "So, hey, I wanted to see what you were doing tomorrow night. You want to go out for a bite?"

I had to laugh at that.

"What?"

"Nothing. Um...," I sputtered and drew a blank.

A dinner date would not be ideal. Vampires *can* eat food. We can chew it up and swallow it, no problem. It's what comes after that's the issue. We can't process it. Our digestive system is dead. Eventually, we throw it up. Whole chunks of food. It's awful and disgusting.

Eating in front of mortals is a great way to keep up appearances, but I avoid it like the plague.

"Hello?" Neil snapped me out of my wandering mind.

"Sorry, it's just that I had such a great time with you playing pool. I want to do another thing like that. Maybe we'll have another adventure."

"Like you launching pool balls everywhere?"

"Yes." He was being cheeky, but the tickling butterflies returned to my stomach.

"Ever been to Sacco's?" He asked.

"What's that?"

"Candlepin bowling. Little balls."

"You just want to see me destroy something with a bowling ball, don't you?"

"That's why I suggested candlepin. The balls are smaller."

I chuckled. "Very funny. Okay, it's a date. Where is this place?

"Somerville. If you want, I can...," Neil trailed off.

"You can...? What?"

"Sorry, some dude parked outside my house, and he's got out and is heading toward my front door. What the hell?"

A sinking feeling came over me. "What's his car look like?"

"It's a black SUV."

My heart dropped into the pit of my stomach.

"Neil... you need get away from the window and barricade yourself into one of your rooms." My voice was shaking.

"What?"

"You need to hunker down and call 9-1-1. That man is there to hurt you." I tried to control the desperation in my voice, but I didn't have time to explain everything to him.

"What are you talking about?" His tone was frustrated.

"Neil! Please, get off the phone with me and call 9-1-1. Barricade yourself up in a room somewhere. I'll be there as fast as I can."

"Lisa, I don't—"

"I'm hanging up now! I'm calling 9-1-1 too. Just promise me you'll do as I ask. Do *not* answer the door."

"Okay, okay."

I reluctantly disconnected. One of us needed to call 9-1-1.

My hands shook as I dialed the three digits.

He was killing everyone close to me. And Neil was next.

The conversation with the emergency operator was a blur. I gave Neil's situation and address, and they told me they were dispatching an officer. My mind was a haze, and I scarcely registered her questions as I answered them.

My mind reeled. Driving to Neil's could take thirty minutes or longer. The fastest way there was as a bat; just one, swift bee-line from here to his house. I'd be naked when I got there, but I'd worry about that later.

I ducked down an alley and fumbled around for my dress' zipper. There was no time to overthink this.

A cloud of black smoke erupted next to a dumpster.

Chewie materialized from the darkness.

"Chewie." Tears welled in my eyes. He knew. He must have.

He let out a sonorous bark.

"I know. It's Neil. I have to get there."

Chewie rushed me. It wasn't affectionate, it was aggressive.

"Chewie! What are—"

He bit down on my calf. His teeth ripped through my boot and sank into my flesh.

I cried out. "Chewie!"

Black smoke engulfed me. Everything went upside down. I was floating. I was dizzy. I felt nauseous. All I could see was Chewie's obsidian fog.

A bright light stung my eyes. When I opened them, the smoke was clearing.

I was lying down. Chewie had released me, but his bite still stung. Grass lay beneath my body. Everything was bright.

Too bright.

I rolled over and gazed upon a blue sky speckled with white, fluffy clouds.

Panic seized me. Wherever we were, it was daytime. I rolled into a ball to shield myself.

Yet I felt nothing.

I wasn't burning.

Chewie woofed at me.

I raised my head from my arms. The large dog was on his feet, swaying his head for me to follow him.

"How? Where are we? How am I not burning?"

He barked at me. This time, it sounded more impatient than before.

I got to my feet and took in my surroundings.

A rocky, green field surrounded me. In the distance, a monolithic stone structure rose from the grass. It reminded me a bit of Stonehenge, with its giant standing stones and circular pattern. In another direction, the field gave way into a forest.

I looked into the sky, shielding my eyes against the brightness. I looked this way and that, but I could find no sun.

"This isn't.... Earth."

Chewie walked in front of me and bumped into me, trying to herd me to follow him.

Once my racing mind settled, I turned to him. "This is *Otherworld*. You took me here to help Neil?"

Chewie woofed. I could swear it was his way of saying *no shit*.

He took off at a run and I followed.

It was tough keeping up with him, but I didn't want to take the time to strip down and change into my wolf form. I hoped we didn't have to run far.

It hurt to run. My bite wound was taking its sweet time healing.

The more I thought about it, the more I realized why he bit me. Vampire blood can allow fae to remain on Earth longer. It gives them the power to slough off the pull back to Otherworld. It's how vampires keep so many redcap retainers on hand.

Perhaps Chewie needed my blood to bring me here.

Too bad I couldn't ask him.

After around five minutes, Chewie halted and sniffed the ground. A couple of hummingbirds sped past us. They stopped, turned around, and inspected us a moment.

They weren't hummingbirds. They were tiny people with wings like butterflies beating in a colorful blur. They frowned at me and spewed vulgarities in Irish. Then they sped off again.

Chewie woofed and gently put his jaws around my calf again.

"Oh. Right. The return trip. Do what you gotta do."

His teeth sank into me. I winced in pain and gritted my teeth.

The black smoke billowed out and encompassed us.

My world turned upside down once more.

Episode 38

The Truth Comes Out

THE BLACK SMOKE DISSIPATED, and I was laying on grass once more. It was nighttime.

I was in Brian's yard. Neil's house was just across the street. A black Honda CRV was parked outside.

"Chewie..." I turned to find Chewie laying on his stomach, head down. He was panting like he'd just run ten miles. "Chewie?"

He whimpered. It was an apology. The two jumps to and from Otherworld must have sapped his strength.

"It's okay, sweetie. I got this."

Or so I thought. When I made a move to run across the street, my legs almost buckled. The wounds where Chewie bit me hurt like hell, and neither of them had begun to heal.

I made it across the street as fast as I could, limping as I went.

My gut twisted into itself as I made it to the door. I dreaded the thought of what I would see inside.

The door was busted open. Neil, thankfully, hadn't answered it. I made my way inside. For a moment, I thought the house might be empty.

Soft footsteps. Marcus appeared from the kitchen, gun in hand.

A startled look flashed on Marcus' face that dissolved into a frown.

"Don't make this more complicated, Lisa," He snarled and pointed his gun at me. A silencer was neatly fastened to its muzzle.

"Where is he?" I gritted my teeth.

"Must have run off. Thanks to you, I suppose." He scowled at me like I'd inconvenienced him.

"You're a dead man." I took a step toward him. My bloody calf protested, shooting jolts of pain through my leg.

He waggled the barrel of his gun at me. "I'm Ivan's damphyr. You can't touch me."

"I'll make my apologies."

I charged him.

I made a move to dodge his shot based on where I gauged he was aiming. I'm not faster than bullets, but I'm quicker on the draw than a mortal with a gun. The tactic usually works.

If it weren't for my damn bite wounds.

My leg gave out, and I stumbled. Marcus adjusted his aim and fired. The shot went off in a muted *pffft*.

The slug hit my shoulder. It was like a sledgehammer. It twisted me back. I lost my footing and fell on my ass.

Marcus stepped up and trained his gun on me.

My shoulder was on fire. Blistering agony radiated down my arm. I grunted through gritted teeth as I tried to bite back the pain.

"One shot to the head won't kill you. But it'll get you off my ass long enough to get out of here. Once I tell Ivan—"

He'd stepped too close. I kicked his shin with my good leg. Marcus cried out and shot again. Pressure and heat followed the *pffft* of Marcus's silencer. The bullet slammed harmlessly into the floor beside my head. I leaped on him as he staggered backwards.

We both tumbled to the floor. My shoulder screamed in protest. With my good arm, I punched his nose, breaking it. Then I held his wrists against the floor. He struggled beneath me in vain.

Until now, it had been all a rush of adrenaline, but Marcus's words finally sunk in.

Once I tell Ivan.

Ivan did this.

Ivan.

My curse surged to the surface, asking to take the reins. Marcus had to die, and my curse promised sweet retribution.

For Amy. Eric. Lee.

Neil.

My fangs elongated as I pinned Marcus to the floor. Gun still gripped; it lay useless in his hand while I held him.

"You can't! I'm under the protection of the Lord of New England!" he pleaded.

"I don't care." It was the curse talking. Its will, my voice.

I sank my fangs into him. His blood was richer than a mortal's. The coppery taste was masked by the subtle sweetness of Ivan's blood.

He struggled in futility. I kept drinking.

"Lisa!"

My head pulled back from Marcus.

Neil stood, dumbfounded. He looked from me to Marcus and back again. "I... called 9-1-1. They're on their way. Can you hold him?"

"I—" A bead of blood ran down my chin.

Marcus sneered at me. "Look at you. He knows. He *knows*!"

"Shut up!" I made a move to shake him, but as I adjusted my grip on his wrists, Marcus jerked his arms and got leverage underneath him.

He headbutted me. With Ivan's blood in his veins, it was a solid hit. I rocked back. He rolled on top of me and out of my hold.

"You can't beat me," I promised.

"I don't need to."

Marcus swung his gun around and shot Neil.

"No!"

For one heartbeat, time stood still. The pit of my stomach filled with lead. My heart rose into my throat and seized upon itself.

Neil collapsed as Marcus scrambled for the door.

There was no decision to make. I went straight to Neil. He'd been shot in the shoulder. His face was screwed up in pain.

"Neil, oh my God." I put pressure on his wound.

"Lisa, you can't be here," he choked out.

"What?"

"When the police come. Jesus, look at you. Your mouth, you're..." He couldn't finish. Instead, he cried out pain.

"It's my fault. Neil, this is my fault." My tears fell on his face.

Tires squealed. Marcus had made his escape.

Neil took deep breaths as if he was trying to keep from drowning. His face had lost color.

"Stay with me, Neil."

"You're not... a witch," he said.

"Neil." I wanted to keep him conscious. In that moment, it was all that mattered.

"You have fangs," Neil mustered. His words were breathy.

"Stop talking."

"Are you a vampire?"

Every fiber of my being knew I shouldn't have answered that question. "Yes."

He smiled. Through his delirious, bleary eyed, painful haze, he smiled at me.

"I still want to go bowling with you," he said.

I gasped out a laugh and held a hand over my mouth. Tears meandered down my cheeks. Even shot in the shoulder Neil was still... Neil.

Sirens wailed in the distance.

"You need to go. It'll be easier without you here. To explain. I..." Neil winced and grunted in pain again. "It'll just look like a home invasion."

I thought about that. Neil's gunshot wound looked bad, but it wasn't anything vital. I couldn't tell if the bullet went all the way through. There was too much blood.

He'd be fine. I had to convince myself that. I needed to find Marcus and finish this.

"I need your car."

"Keys are in the dish... by the door."

The sirens were getting louder. I kissed Neil's forehead and made my way to the door. The keys were in a green glass bowl along with a couple of pens and some business cards.

"I'll find you in the hospital when this is done."

"Go," Neil insisted. The delirious goofball was still smiling.

I sped all the way to Back Bay. In the state of mind I was in, if an officer had pulled me over, I would have charmed him into next week.

Thankfully, I made it into town without any police trouble.

I did a shit job parallel parking. On my best nights, it's a frustrating ordeal, but tonight? The only reason I didn't simply leave the car in the middle of the road was because it was Neil's. The nose of the car angled slightly into the street. Good enough.

I ran down the sidewalk to Ivan's brownstone. I was making the assumption that Marcus, in Ivan's employ and feeding from him, must have been staying in the same complex along with Ivan's thralls.

The vestibule had rows of buttons to ring each of the tenants. I couldn't very well ask Ivan to buzz me in. The door inside was locked, and for a moment, I debated ripping it off its hinges.

I decided on something more discreet.

I buzzed 210. Roger and Raphael's room. I'd been there once before. Ivan let me feed from Raphael. It didn't go well. I was too hungry, and my curse got the better of me. But they were the only ones I knew in the complex.

"Hello?"

"Roger? It's Lisa. Can you buzz me in?" I tried to keep my tone nonchalant.

"Lisa? Why not buzz Ivan?"

"Ivan doesn't want to be disturbed. He said I could come here for a drink, but I forgot the apartment number he gave me. I have to go inside and get it from Úll."

"What was the name of the person you're supposed to meet?"

"He didn't say. He just gave me the room number. I'm sorry, I should have written it down."

There was a pause. My chest tightened at the prospect that Roger might be calling Ivan to confirm my bullshit story. If that happened, Ivan would surely march down here and put a stop to this whole thing. My only chance of getting at Marcus was if I did so without Ivan's knowledge.

I hit Roger and Raphael's button again.

Roger's voice returned, "Sorry, Lisa. Please give me a moment."

"Okay." I tried not to sound impatient. After all, according to the lie I just fed him, why would I be in a rush?

Another moment passed.

"Sorry, Lisa. I wasn't able to reach Úll," Roger said.

"That's okay." I effected a smile to keep my tone friendly. "I'll find him. Just buzz me in, please?"

"Well... okay. But don't come to us for a feeding. I don't mean any disrespect. It's just after what happened last time, you know?"

"No problem, Roger. I completely understand." I hadn't noticed I was clenching my fists.

The door buzzed.

I nearly tore the door off the hinges as I dashed from the vestibule and into the lobby. The trouble was, I didn't know which apartment Marcus was in. The stupid business cards he handed out only had his phone number.

But I had other ways of finding him.

I was still a vampire after all, and as much as I loathe the term, I am a predator. Ivan's Brownstone was only three floors. Ivan had the third floor all to himself. That left two floors for me to case.

I moved quietly. I listened. I smelled what was around me.

There were many sounds and smells to take in as I moved from apartment to apartment. Someone cooking, a couple arguing, a baby crying.

Dear God, was Ivan feeding off parents of a baby?

Everyone who lived in the brownstone was enthralled to Ivan, but they all had normal lives. Apparently, some had families. I overheard a father helping his son with homework, smelled the distinct aroma of cigars, and from another apartment, whisky.

One apartment had their TV blasted on high, another's resident was snoring in their sleep, and yet another was hosting a small get-together. They were playing cards.

I came up empty.

Unless...

I backtracked to the apartment with the blaring television. It was hard to hear what else was going on above the racket, but I took a deep inhale through my nose. I smelled blood. I smelled a gun.

One quick shove, and I pushed the door's deadbolt through the doorframe. I had to be as quiet as possible. Ivan was still upstairs, and he could hear as well as I could.

A suitcase stood by the door. Marcus came around the corner, gun in hand and phone to his ear. His nose was still bloody from when I hit him.

His jaw dropped.

Over the phone, a woman's faint voice inquired whether he wanted a window or aisle seat. Marcus tossed the phone on his couch and leveled his pistol at me. "Sir?" came the woman's voice over the phone.

I glowered at him. "So, you thought you'd skip town. Turned up the TV so Ivan wouldn't hear you on the phone with the airline."

"Ivan isn't a forgiving man. None of this was supposed to be traced back to him. There's no hope for me."

"No." My curse slithered its way into my psyche and displaced any inclination toward mercy. "There isn't."

Retribution

Marcus was a good ten to twelve feet away with his pistol pointed directly at me. His television was still blaring. Some old sitcom with canned laughter. Between that and the silencer on his gun, there was a good chance Ivan wouldn't hear the gunshot from upstairs.

"What's it gonna be, Lisa? You aren't faster than bullets, and I've seen how you move on that injured leg. I'll pop you in the head and, by the time you wake up, I'll be clear out of town."

He grossly underestimated how quickly I could recover from a gunshot wound. He was right about my injured leg, though. The shot in my shoulder was completely gone. Chewie's bite wounds were still healing at a snail's pace.

"There's nowhere you can go, Marcus. Ivan has a long reach. He'll find you," I said.

"So, I'm supposed to just let you kill me?"

"I don't care what you do. I'm just telling you the facts."

"Fuck this."

Marcus' arm went rigid. That was my cue to move.

He'd tightened his arm to brace for the coming recoil. It's a split-second telegraph many shooters have right before they pull the trigger. For most people, by the time they notice the arm stiffen, it's too late.

But I'm faster than most people.

I put weight on my good leg and ducked down with lightning speed.

He shot. It went over my head. I sprang at him.

He got another shot off, and it grazed my side. It stung like a dagger raked across my ribs. I collided with him and grabbed the pistol by its barrel. We both hit the floor.

His strength was no match for mine. I pinned his pistol hand down while I cocked my fist back. My curse wanted to make him suffer. Cave his jaw in. Snap his ribs. Drink him dry.

Wait.

I couldn't just murder him. How would I deal with a dead body in Ivan's building? I'd let my anger cloud my judgement.

I hesitated during my momentary clarity. Marcus tried punching me with his free hand, but I grabbed his wrist and held him fast.

The hatred I felt for this man was fueled even more by my curse. Like gasoline on a fire. He had to pay for what he did, but I had to be smart about it.

Footsteps. Someone was coming. I'd let myself get too distracted. The door swung open behind me.

"Police! Get up! Ms. Cooper, get up!"

Detective Pierce.

"It's not what it looks like. He killed Amy, Eric, and Lee. I found him. I have him."

"Get up, Ms. Cooper. I'm not going to ask you again."

"We're both dead now." Marcus grinned at me.

I slowly got up. "He has a gun."

"I'm dropping it," Marcus said. He let the pistol fall from his fingers.

"Step away from him, Ms. Cooper. Mr. Jones, put your hands up."

Marcus slowly got to his feet, raising his hands above his head.

"Why the hell wouldn't you call the police? You came here on your own?" Pierce scolded.

I didn't say anything. I was too busy glaring at Marcus.

"Hands behind your back, Mr. Jones." Pierce took a step toward Marcus.

"I can't go to prison," Marcus said.

"Yes, well, you're under arrest. Should have thought about that before you murdered three people," Pierce said.

"I can't go to prison," the damphyr repeated.

With inhuman speed, Marcus dipped down, grabbed the pistol off the floor and whirled on Detective Pierce.

I moved on Marcus. Pierce was a pain in my ass, but I couldn't let him get shot.

Marcus pivoted and shot me twice in the stomach. The blows from the slugs knocked me back and knocked me down. My stomach was on fire, and I was bleeding horribly.

Another shot fired. Marcus reeled back. Another shot. Marcus crumpled to the floor.

Pierce holstered his gun and ran to me. "Jesus. Hold on. I'm calling an ambulance."

The detective pulled a radio from his belt. "Shots fired at 397 Commonwealth. Male suspect down. Female bystander down. Two shots to the stomach. Need an ambulance." His tone was desperate.

"Roger that. Dispatching," came the radio's reply.

"Hold on, Ms. Cooper."

There was a bonfire in my abdomen. Scorching, pulsing waves of pain stabbed through me. I gritted my teeth. I could feel my body working to heal itself, but there was a lot of damage.

"You know.... I'm not a suspect anymore... you can just... call me Lisa."

"Shut up. Don't talk. The paramedics will be here soon."

I was pushing the bullets out, slowly. Everything inside me was knitting itself back together. Pain still coursed through me, but the telltale pull of flesh mending to flesh put relief on the horizon.

Pierce was putting pressure on my wounds. I knew he was trying to control the bleeding, but I wanted him to knock it off. The added pressure just exasperated the entire ordeal.

"The hell?" Pierce pulled his hand back. "Is this a bullet?"

I didn't have a good answer for that. He'd stuck around too long and witnessed my healing process in action. Not that it mattered. Marcus had sat up.

Pierce was too dumbstruck over the bullet that had magically floated to the top of my wound to notice.

Marcus reached for his gun.

"Look out!" I shoved Pierce off me and away.

Marcus's shot fired through the space where Pierce had hovered over me. He and I both scrambled to our feet. He got another shot off. It hit my arm.

It hurt to move. Every inch of my stomach cried in burning pain.

I had to punch Marcus with my left hand, but it did the trick.

Marcus spun across the room and slammed into the wall. His face was awash with blood. His jaw was skewed to one side. He made a feeble attempt to raise his pistol at me again. I batted the gun from his hand and took Marcus by the neck.

I lifted him up and slammed him into the floor.

He was a heap, lying in a pool of his own blood and a few broken teeth. I'd let my curse fuel my rage again. It's hard to think clearly after so many gunshot wounds.

Detective Pierce stared at me, mouth agape. He was still sitting on the floor where I had pushed him.

The last bullet fell from my stomach, pushed out by mended flesh. It landed with a *plink* on the hardwood floor.

Charming gaze was out of the question. He was way too freaked out for that.

"What are you?" His eyes were like saucers.

"It's complicated. But I didn't kill anyone. And I'm not your enemy."

"You saved my life."

I gave a slight nod to that. I tried to look thoughtful. I tried to keep things calm. "You should cuff Marcus. He may heal some of these injuries over time. And I need you tell the ambulance that the woman you reported ran off while Marcus and you tussled one last time."

"I can't say that." He was exasperated now.

"Well, I'm not going to be here. So, you have to tell them something."

"I can't let you leave." Pierce made a move like he was going to unholster his gun, but his fingers fumbled around the handle.

I watched him wrestle with his conflict while his sidearm remained where it was.

"Goodbye, detective."

I strode past him.

"Ms. Cooper," he insisted.

I stopped.

"You have to tell me something. Give me something. An explanation." He got to his feet and produced handcuffs.

I didn't turn around when I answered. "Detective, there are things in this world that are hidden from mortal sight. Monsters exist. And if I were you, I'd book Marcus Jones on three homicides and forget everything else you saw here tonight."

The clink of the handcuffs indicated he'd cuffed Marcus. I wasn't going to linger for anything else.

I still owed Ivan a visit.

I pushed Úll Buachaill aside when he answered the door. The little redcap stumbled and regained his balance.

"What the feck, Lisa!"

"It's alright, Úll." Ivan entered the greeting room from his study. "I was expecting her."

Affronted, Úll brushed the sleeves of his purple surcoat. "Done muffed up me finery."

Ivan made a gesture for me to enter his study.

I was not in the mood for his civility. I had no intention of playing the guest here, but I took his invitation and stalked into the other room.

Ivan closed the door behind us.

"It was you this whole time." I whirled on him. "You know, I thought… I suspected… but no. I never dreamed you could be so monstrous. Murdering people for what? For what!"

"Siobhan, I'm prepared to talk about this calmly."

"I don't care! Do I look calm to you? This ends now. Don't ever come near the people in my life again. And that includes your lackeys."

I was seething, but I had never spoken to Ivan like this. I never had a cause to. Ivan was also the most powerful being I knew. I was scared, but my anger drowned my fear.

Ivan glowered at me. "Or what? You are in no position to make demands of me. I told you I have a responsibility to the bleed. Your anger has made you forget your place."

"Haven't you a *shred* of decency?" I shouted.

"Look what you have done, Siobhan! Gunshots in my home. Police. Paramedics. Witnesses! This is what happens when you let mortals get too close."

"What *I* did? You set this in motion when you killed—"

"It's how you reacted. It's how you took it upon yourself to get involved. Sloppy and careless, putting us all at risk." Ivan's ire was measured but simmered under the gravelly tone of his voice.

"So, I was supposed to just sit back and let Marcus murder Neil? Fuck you."

Ivan sighed. He closed his eyes and took a moment. It was a little sobering, and my fear bristled under the veneer of my anger-fueled courage. Ivan had a curse of his own, after all.

"Neil." He said his name like invoking a plague. "You will enthrall him, yes? I do hope so. It's been months now. He is a risk. And I will do what I must."

My mouth fell open. "You stay away from him."

Ivan shook his head. "Impetuous. You insist that you're not a páiste, but in all your years, you still can't fathom this simple truth. We cannot let the mortals close."

I scowled at him. My curse boiled beneath my skin. I should leap upon him. Sink my fangs into him.

He met my gaze and his visage darkened. Disapproving and challenging. Daring me to make a move. "No," he said. "Not impetuous. Naïve. Foolish. This lesson I am teaching you is one you should have learned when your family was killed all those years ago."

"Don't you bring them into this." I bristled.

"We were short sighted. We thought you would understand after such a grave loss."

My head spun. The walls closed in around me. My stomach dropped. "*We?*"

Ivan straightened, appraising me. He didn't speak.

My curse, having spent most of the evening bubbling over, all but seized my body. There was nothing left in me to push it away. There was no desire and no will to hold it back.

"We!" I shouted.

"Come now, Siobhan. Did you honestly never puzzle this out? After all these years? Never suspected? William and I did what we thought was best. Your family was too close to you. And thereby to us."

I snapped.

Whether it was me or my curse urging for vengeance, I no longer knew nor cared. It was all a blur. And I all I could see was blood.

I bared my fangs and leaped at Ivan.

Episode 40

Consequences

Nothing mattered anymore.

I had abandoned all rational thinking. I was never going to be a match for Ivan, but I didn't care. Blinded by rage, vengeance, and the bloodlust of my curse, I battered the Lord of the New England bleed.

My wild swings weren't picking targets, but Ivan put his arms up to shield his face. He kept his elbows tucked close to his chest to protect his heart.

I forced him backward and up against the wall. I punched at his side. My fist impacted into him, shattering a rib.

I had made peace with the idea that Ivan might kill me this night, but before he did, I would dole out as much pain as I could. If I couldn't kill him before he killed me, I would at least make him suffer.

My flurry of blows continued to pummel him. Ivan remained on the defensive. Even a broken rib didn't prompt him to attack back.

He slammed into the wall, knocking a painting off its mounting. I shouted at him; a verbal barrage laced with expletives and abhorrence.

My fists continued to batter him.

"That's enough," he said at last.

Ivan stepped to the side and out of the trajectory of my attacks. He moved faster than I registered.

He backhanded me. It sent me staggering to the side. I tumbled over a leather armchair and slammed into a wall.

I got to my feet. I picked up the armchair and launched it at him.

It hit him as he swung his arm to deflect the impact. The broken chair flew across the room and crashed into his desk.

"I see you still have much to learn, Siobhan." He charged me.

His fists hit me like Mack trucks. Ivan was the prime specimen of the power for a vampire his age. He was a being who had embraced his curse, instead of forsaking it.

I tried to block as he had, but Ivan shattered the bones in my right arm. Then he undercut me and shattered ribs on my left side. I cried out.

My body had doled out a lot healing already, and I'd lost too much blood to take this kind of punishment.

Fear gripped me. I realized I could wind up in a death sleep if my body used too much blood to heal what Ivan would be dishing out.

Only my rage kept me on my feet.

My parents. My brother. My sisters.

Amy, Eric, and Lee.

I dropped my guard and swung out with my left. I caught Ivan's jaw and felt it shatter. He stumbled backwards.

Ivan bellowed through his misshapen mouth and closed the distance between us in the blink of an eye.

A sinking feeling took me when he seized me by my hair. It was over.

I don't how many times Ivan struck my head into the wall. The drywall gave way. I saw stars. Pincers of pain ran through my scalp as my hair ripped. My temples stabbed at me each time my head pushed through the wall, past insulation, splintering exterior plywood and hitting brick.

My vision grew dark. I was dizzy. I called for him to stop.

He didn't.

There was a pounding. It took a moment to place it. Everything sounded muffled. My ears rang. The pounding was at the door. I caught the word *police* from the other side of it.

I was yanked from the wall. Ivan placed his hands on either side of my face. He snapped my head too far to one side. There was a crack and a sharp pain lanced through my neck.

When I opened my eyes, I was lying on the floor of Ivan's study.

I rolled over and looked up at him. He was standing over me.

My hands were pale. I didn't hurt as much anymore. My blood had gone to mending everything that had been broken.

"This was my final lesson on the subject of your mingling with mortals, Siobhan. I don't *want* to hurt you again. Do not put me in a position where I must choose between you and the safety of our bleed."

"I hate you." My voice was hoarse.

Ivan gave a stiff nod. "In time, you will understand. I thought perhaps one hundred and fifty years had brought you to that place, but I was mistaken. Perhaps William was soft with you. Perhaps so was I. So often, I have thought of you as my own—"

"Don't," I gritted.

I got to my feet.

"The police are gone. I had to charm them." He frowned. "I don't have to tell you that bringing police to my door is something I will not tolerate a second time."

I glared at him, but the raging fire of my curse had dwindled to a small flame. It didn't have the power to compel me after fixing so much that was broken. All I had left was my own hatred, but I also had my common sense.

I couldn't beat Ivan.

"Now, get out of my house. And I want you to think long and hard about what happened here tonight. You can be angry. You can even hate me. But don't you ever bring your mistakes to my home again."

"This isn't over."

"Yes, it is, Siobhan. Get out of my sight."

I wrested my eyes off him and turned away. I had nothing. No power. No leverage. I strode out of the door feeling more empty than angry.

I refused to buy into the notion that my mortal friendships brought on this problem. It was Ivan that created this issue. I knew in my heart that I was careful enough to maintain mortal relationships. I'd done so for decades.

It was something Ivan and William never understood. The curse had made them callous and distant.

I had always refused that path. For over one hundred and fifty years I had staved off the ravages of my curse. It kept me grounded to humanity. It kept my skin warm and allowed me the color of life. It helped me resist the sun. But in doing so, I sacrificed the power due to a vampire my age.

It left me without the strength I needed to protect the people I cared about.

I looked back at Ivan's door. This *wasn't* over.

If it was power I lacked, then that was what I would seek.

But one thing became clear that night: to protect Neil, Ivan MacAlistair had to die.

Also By J.M. Celi

Magic is never easy.

The Peabody Coven does things a little differently. The seven women combine dissimilar magics across their various cultures and methods. This CONVERGENCE allows the coven to create powerful effects wielded to protect and defend the Massachusetts territory.

When the coven's druid discovers a great evil in a nearby park, the coven must come together to combine their magics to vanquish a harmful blight on mother earth.

But what can corrupt the land can also corrupt the mind.

The Wicked Wound of Whitney Hill is a stand-alone short story that ties into the events within "The Unlife of Lisa Cooper".

Buy on Amazon:

https://a.co/d/5wJjkIX

J.M. CELI lives in New England with his wife, son, and a small grumble of pugs.

Web Page: https://www.jmceli.com
Amazon Author Page: https://tinyurl.com/ynyvhnfh
Goodreads:
https://www.goodreads.com/author/show/23410446.J_M_Celi